HEALING GAY SEX AND LOVE

A GROUP EXPERIENCE

DOUGLAS SADOWNICK, PH.D.

PSYCHOLOGY FOR THE PEOPLE BOOKS

Douglas Sadownick

ISBN: 979-8-9987952-2-0

First Digital Edition: September 2025

Disclaimer

This book blends memory, therapy, fiction, research, and philosophy. Events, settings, and dialogues have been reconstructed from memory, creative imagination, and three decades of psychotherapeutic listening, then shaped for dramatic and narrative purposes. The figures encountered are composite creations, drawn from many lives and experiences, and are offered as vessels of truth rather than portraits of any single individual. Any resemblance to actual persons, living or dead, is coincidental.

Although much of the narrative centers on culturally diverse gay-identified cisgender men, its form and content remain deliberately fluid—engaging questions of gender, identity, and desire that include, but are not limited to, fixed categories. At once art and reflection, it offers an opera of voices— wounded, desiring, surviving—open to all readers, gay or straight, and to identities not yet named, who have ever strayed, openly or privately, from strictly heteronormative paths.

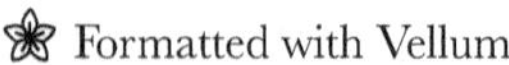 Formatted with Vellum

In memory of Felice Picano (1944–2025),
whose mentorship, humor, and brilliance inform this book.

CONTENTS

NOTE ON FORM

This book is a work of psychological narrative fiction. While it draws on decades of clinical work, teaching, and community life, the group at its center—and the world they begin to imagine together—belongs to the realm of fiction, and at moments, of fantasy.

The form allows for compression, play, and a speculative freedom that social science alone cannot provide. Psychologist James Hillman referred to this mode as *healing fiction*; Henri Corbin described it as *creative imagination*; and C. G. Jung framed it through *active imagination*. With a respectful nod to this lineage, this book gestures toward a utopian vision—not a perfected world, but one shaped through pain, suffering, and hard knocks, where something not yet fully here can nonetheless be imagined into being.

AUTHOR'S NOTE

Why a work of psychological narrative fiction?

Over more than thirty years of work as a therapist, teacher, author, and community-based organizer, I encountered hundreds of gay students and clients who shared the same frustration: gay liberation had given us a seat at the table, but not a menu, a prompt, or a map for where to go next—or how to answer some of the questions that pressed most insistently:

Why all this self-sabotage—with drugs, affairs, provoking fights, and isolation?

Why do I only want to have sex with people I can't love, and love people I don't want to have sex with?

Where do these automatic negative thoughts come from —about cock size, aging, status, inclusion?

If the past is past, why do I still dream of being hunted and humiliated?

Who are we, and why doesn't anyone talk about our ancestors?

Why do I turn cruel when I'm hurt?

What happened to my father?

Is it normal to be this entangled with one's mother?

Why does no one rescue me from my loneliness?

Why does a wall rise up when I try to get anything done?

Is there a god principle in worshipping cock?

Why can't I feel good without waiting for something bad to happen?

Why do I always feel excluded when I watch shows like *Heated Rivalry*?

Why is there so much racism and lookism in the gay community?

My first impulse was to organize the answers and models gay men and students had already begun to derive by looking at their lives through gay eyes—through gay lifespan development—into a guide or social-science monograph.

"Don't use your head at the expense of your turn-on," another voice said.

I WAS ONCE A QUEER, artsy child, born on Shakespeare Avenue in the Bronx, destined to dance and sing, but my lower-middle-class, seemingly loving mother frowned at the flowers backstage, so I got the message—and thank the goddess I was blessed with a more acceptable love of reading and writing.

On the way to a Ph.D. in English, just as the postmodern craze flooded graduate schools, I fell in love with a sexy performance artist—unabashed, excessive, life-changing. At the age of twenty-three, I was on Ground Zero as Larry Kramer wrote "1,112 and Counting" in *The New York Native* in 1983, terrified by friends falling ill. I dropped out of the ivory tower, wrote the "City Boy" column for the *Native*, and eventually helped start a performance art space in Santa Monica, California to help deal with the crisis.

The losses, combined with the psychic wreckage handed down by parents demanding heterosexual conformity, left me unmoored, angry, and raw. Gay-affirmative therapy, discovered in my late twenties, returned me to the depths of my unconscious as a reservoir of gay healing and love. As I engaged in performance art, gay beat journalism, book publishing, and street activism with ACT UP, a new theater opened up to me: dreams, disavowed feelings, active imagination.

In the interior theater of the therapeutic encounter, I learned how to value the voice of an inner authority over the one with which I was raised.

Another recognition followed: much of the pain that drives tragedy in gay life comes from unresolved authoritarianism battering the child self—training people to submit, to split, to police themselves, to mistake obedience for safety. That realization shifted my work toward returning to school for clinical training and a doctorate, eventually leading me to run the first LGBT Specialization in Clinical Psychology in the country. I amassed thousands of pages of notes, clinical material, poems, and unfinished books detailing the questions listed above—and the remarkable answers many gay men had already come up with, but which remained locked away in journals and isolated systems.

～

Okay, now what?

When I entered my sixties, and felt I had given my all to the *daimon* that required me to work in the salt mines of gay trauma and healing, another voice said: *more singing, more dancing—not in a literal sense, silly—but what about your writing?*

The late Felice Picano—editor, mentor, and long-time father figure—helped clarify the path. After reading hundreds of pages, he singled out a small monograph about gay men in group therapy. "Write this," he said. "Start here. I love their voices." When I worried about writing too close to actual clients, he answered simply: "You're a novelist—make them fictional characters."

As I followed Felice's guidance—working to complete the book before he died of cancer in March 2025—I came to understand that fiction allowed for compression without betrayal, intimacy without exposure, and a paradoxical precision born of play. Real encounters—sometimes improbable—could be shaped through the demands of drama into moments that may appear curated but are rooted in my phenomenological study of lived experience, so the reader might think, *Oh, how funny,* and *oh, how sad,* while also encountering a new model for gay self-development.

THE GROUP at the center of the book reflects these origins and contradictions. The men bring distinct histories, desires, defenses, and a capacity for camp into the room. At moments, the work rehearses itself into other forms, moving from novel to play and into contemporary modes of enactment—TikTok, podcasts, film—mirroring the ways gay culture circulates insight through gravitas and grandiosity.

In this sense, the book is less a guide to group technique than a literary study of what happens to desire, shame, authority, and repair when a group of psyches meet in a room —where, as a bittersweet comedy, the stories avert tragedy even as internalized homophobia tempts us toward our culture's appetite for monster stories, and where the sustained effort to heal relationships becomes, in the Shakespearean sense, worthy of a marriage dance.

But comedy, in this tradition, is never apolitical. What unfolds in the room exposes the structures that shape inner life long before they harden into law or custom.

In other words, the same structures that sustain fascist social orders—rigid hierarchy, submission to punitive authority, the policing of difference, the demand for perfection—are installed internally through shame and internalized homophobic domination. Their worst effects are largely hidden.

The most insidious form of heterosexism's internalization employs the voice of so-called "reason" to render gayness as nothing more than a negotiable, transitory category: *you are no different from heterosexuals except for what you do in bed, so don't bother learning about your ancestors, because you have none; once we have acceptance, we won't need the term at all.*

When the dynamic complexities of the gay mind—the vulnerable self, the attacking self, the erotic self, for example—are collapsed into the capitalistic logic of assimilation, whether through heterosexism or postmodern deconstruction for its own sake, the blueprints for cultivating these selves lie dormant, their sprouting seeds denied water and care.

Many of the clients and students over the last three decades whose experiences inform this book recognized a crucial sticking point: without confronting this internal reduction head-on in therapy, gay liberation—as an experience of prolonged healing—cannot evolve. Developing a shared model for inner work thus became not only therapeutic but ethical and, ultimately, activist: a refusal to cooperate with authoritarianism at the level of both action and consciousness.

To honor the work of these clients and students, I give you Harry, John, Andy, Bobby, and Dr. Glitter. The story of how five men come together in therapy and decide to make some trouble for themselves leads them toward refreshing new models and new performances of self and soul—and even the more randy of the Greek classics. This includes tears, high drama, fights, reparation, and yes, disco—yes, singing—yes, dancing, if we all love a dance. Social science just doesn't do "Ring That Bell" the way the men in this book try to.

OVERTURE—FOOLS RUSH IN

The liquid from a French kiss gathered at the front of Andy's palate and, almost with a will of its own, urged him to place his lips an inch from his Grindr hookup's face—just close enough to launch a stinging thread of saliva across the slender man's chapped lips, dying for respite.

Sharing this later in individual therapy, Andy put a finger to the very lips he meant—mum's the word to the guys in the group.

SETTLING INTO MY CHAIR—THE therapist's throne, or so they tease me—I scanned the familiar faces of the weekly Queer Creatives Therapy Support Group in my Hollywood, California office.

A decade ago, we began as a boisterous gathering for writers, artists and actors to process feelings of being mistreated in the movie business while sharing their own creative material before feeding it to the sharks.

Over time, the collectivity evolved into weekly group therapy for lesbian, gay, bisexual and trans people who wanted to heal in a deep and lasting way from the impact of familial and societal homophobia.

During the COVID-19 lockdown, people elected to meet on Zoom.

When the world reopened, the group endured, now in person. With attrition, three gay men remained.

Turning sixty-five, I felt reluctant to add new group members, as an ex-lover from my AIDS-activist days—still family—grew ill and my aging mother began winding down, pulling me back to New York more often.

Meanwhile, the three men had fashioned a small family here, holding one another through their crises. When they began calling each other Dorothy, Blanche, and Rose, it was funny—comforting, even. But home, even in therapy, can start to close in.

THE LIVE WIRE WAS BOBBY—A self-proclaimed Southern belle and renowned film and television art director, able to electrify a room with a single cutting remark, his fake pearls always within reach whenever he caused—or attempted, simultaneously, to avert—a brouhaha.

> Can we please stop yappin' about how hard it is to work in this godforsaken industry, and the state of our lonely, abusive childhoods, and start talkin' about cock, dick, and balls? Pardon my *Francais*. Monogamy, open relationships, top and bottom, cut and uncut, kink and vanilla—and all the freaky in-between. Like—sugar, you tell your partner you might not

be a total pussy bottom after all, and he storms out of the house like a lil bitch. Or what if you're ancient like me and just want to cuddle, not fuck like bunnies, or you'd like your man to change how he kisses you after ten years of swallowing his tongue and gagging for all the wrong reasons?

"Please, Dr. Glitter," Bobby added—a name he'd plucked from a photo of me dancing to disco in the '70s, which he guessed was either *Born to Be Alive* or *Let's Groove*. Now I was Glitter to all the guys and their cohorts, partly to keep me from playing doctor and partly to remind me of our theatrical roots.

"Find us someone hot enough to pop our not-so-figured-out cherry."

He unzipped Clara, named—by Bobby—after a Black neighbor in Clarksdale who had looked after him when no one else quite did, "the only one," he always said, "who gave me love."

The duffel held arts-and-crafts necessities. Out spilled the tools of improvised belief: rolls of tape clouded with lint, half-used paint pens rattling like pills, silk scarves knotted together and warm with old cologne. He grabbed a special collage he had made of a Tom of Finland surrounded by painted faeries, the man bearing a resemblance to a previous Latino lover.

"We're horny for the Truth like she's our long-lost daddy."

"Careful," Andy warned—fluent in Chinese, French, and the gutter. "Oedipus took that looking-for-daddy road—patricide, incest. *Très dangereux.*"

"You want the truth?" John said, bone-dry. "She may show up in a prom dress. Covered in pig's blood."

AROUND THIS TIME, I had been paying attention to a crop of Gen Z and Gen Alpha creators on Instagram and TikTok whose sexual confidence came with an unapologetic middle finger to homophobia—young queer men who had come of age after medication dramatically reduced the risk of HIV and who had, for better or worse, returned to the sexual-liberation ethos of the wild generation before mine.

One of them, with the handle "Brujo Bro," posted short videos urging gay men to respect the discipline of fasting bottoms and to "get the fuck over anonymity" and "racial profiling shit." Funny, sharply produced, with real acting training under the hood, he drew a sizable following. In one TikTok, he peeled off his shirt to reveal a tattooed, worked-for body, shot in his personal car-and-workshop crib. In Spanglish-inflected Gen Alpha cadence, he said, "If yo parents give yah shit for being queer"—then, after a beat, miming hands at an invisible partner's hips—"fuck 'em."

I felt inspired to comment: *Thank you for your activism.*

He replied ASAP—*gracias, y tú también*—and began following my TikToks on the queer hero's journey. He mentioned, in several DMs, anxiety and bad dreams. He had seen posts I'd shared about services at a Queer Youth Clinic I founded. Could I help him get an intake? Could he speak to me?

I gave him my work number. He called instantly.

On the phone, Brujo Bro introduced himself as "Harry," calling me "Doctor" and "Sir." He'd just turned twenty-six; I had to tell him he'd aged out of Colors. I opened my laptop to offer referrals to low-cost clinics. He listened, then brushed them aside, as if it were already understood—by him—that I was his clinician.

Harry—respectful in the way people from good families often are—began opening up: loneliness, sadness, emptiness. By then, he had done a deep dive into ancient performance-art videos and ACT UP demonstrations I made before becoming a community therapist.

Could he come in for a trial session? Did I have student rates?

His father, a leader in the 1968 Chicano Student Walk-outs, had gone on to become a successful business man in the San Gabriel Valley.

"Yeah, my pops got bread now" he said. "But, not gunna lie, no more generous daddy checkios to keep me close, you feel me?"

I already carried several low-fee clients and was concerned I might need to spend more time back East. However kind or self-aware someone seems at first, real care requires time and consistency. One voice said no—to something already complex and perhaps too close for comfort. Another said Harry seemed exactly like the young person who deserved solid gay-affirmative therapy—and, who knows, might one day be right for the group.

He lived in Altadena with his parents and latched onto the fact that I offered Zoom sessions.

He taught yoga and worked, as he put it, as a "sexual brujo"—which he explained as "a skilled masseur who uses plant medicine." Okay. Points for transparency.

My task was not to suppress my reaction but to monitor it —to notice my countertransference without becoming the very moral authority Gay Liberation had fought against.

He never missed a session—always punctual, always Zelling me before we began. Each week, he took copious notes in a battered leather notebook thick with Post-its.

Three months in, I mentioned the existence of the group, that the group had no fixed end, though I might need to leave town on occasion.

He practically jumped out of his Zoom frame.

"Please, Doctor—I need a group like this, with my artist peers, low-key healing energy."

I warned him that these that access to their circle of the remaining gay men, war veterans of trauma and homophobia, might not come without a tussle.

He flashed a smile—lascivious, undeterred—as if ready to make an unholy meal of every one of them, fake pearls and all.

HARRY ARRIVED for his first in-person group—the first time I had seen him live. He came ruddy from the motorcycle ride on the 10 Freeway from Altadena, black-and-gold helmet pressed to his chest, tote bag sagging from one shoulder. Black hair grazed his rounded shoulders; a faint mustache bracketed his goatee. He moved with the shy bravado of someone used to being larger than the rooms he entered, his beauty opening doors—and locking him inside once it did.

Andy leaned toward me. *Bobby will not like this,* he said under his breath, in French.

"Be careful what you ask for," John added, deadpan. "Especially if she's wearing a prom dress soaked in blood."

A silver ring caught light as Harry tried to settle into the room's only uncomfortable seat—a small **G** picked out in diamonds. His left knee kept time as he placed the helmet carefully at his feet, then rummaged for anchors: *The Drama of the Gifted Child,* a collection of poems by Sor Juana Inés de la Cruz, the leather notebook.

Scholarly, Andy noted.

Hot, John thought.

As we were leaving, John gave Harry a quick fist bump.

Bobby clocked it too and raised his eyebrows at me, as if to say: *I couldn't help but wonder… is this how it starts?*

To HELP Harry get up to speed over the next weeks, I explained that we usually began with a ten-minute check-in. Each man had that time to share how the week had gone or what was top of mind. Since we started as a Queer Creatives Support Group, topics could include creative projects, even though it had been a while since we'd done versions of "show and tell," "name that tune," or "perform this scene."

Andy skipped the details of his recent spittle breakthrough and spoke instead of guilt—about not going back to Ohio for his sister's pregnancy, and about the larger drift he was in after Yale when a screenplay he wrote for shit and giggles was picked up too fast by the wrong executive, money that came wrapped in violence and contempt. He'd bought his family a house in Columbus, himself a new body, and none of it felt like he was meeting the current moment.

Bobby kept his entrance safe, describing his ambition to take over the art department from the current director, a man he said had "as much taste as a pageant queen who forgets her gown while her replacement waits in the wings dressed like a cooked turkey in couture." He spared Harry, for now, the long-suffering saga of life with Ezra and their Elizabeth Taylor–Richard Burton feuds where children live and die.

John went last, quietly, about seeing his ex again after years of fracture. Their transition had changed the weather between them; grief had softened into something like friendship. His language loosened as he spoke—less guarded, more street—and both Andy and Bobby clocked the code-switching.

All eyes turned to the new arrival, who—obviously—was not fooling anyone by cosplaying "shy."

Keeping his share "short and sweet," Harry said he was "down to work on his shit" and "show up as an artist." Then, with a crooked grin and a quick salute, he closed: *"Viva la resistencia."*

"Oh, dear young man," Bobby said, "speaking of resistance, you must reveal more—how else will we be able to cook you?"

I spoke over Bobby, reassuring Harry that there was no pressure. Bobby, however, spoke right over me.

"We three have spent several centuries discoursing about when we felt—how to say—different as tiny gay tots," he said. "Perhaps you could enlighten us about your own particular saga in being *diferente*."

"Sᴏʀ Jᴜᴀɴᴀ Iɴᴇ́s ᴅᴇ ʟᴀ Cʀᴜᴢ," Harry said, cautiously. "Poet. Scholar. Colonial Mexico. Wrote love poems to women, no cap. Found her shit in the Church library when I was eight."

Bobby squinted like a queen at court when a foreigner spoke a language she hadn't yet mastered.

"You're the wunderkind, Andy, honey. Ever heard of Sor?"

"How could one not," Andy replied. "The Shakespeare of New Spain—in the tradition of Sappho."

Harry smacked his forehead in mock shock. That gave him permission to read aloud a peculiar stanza:

My divine Lysis: do forgive my daring, if so I address you, unworthy though I am to be known as yours. I cannot think it bold to call you so, well knowing you've ample thunderbolts to shatter any overweening of mine.

The room held still, the words floating like Church incense. John tried hard not to feel struck. Bobby, breaking the silence, leaned forward, plastic purple-and-pink pearls catching the light, his lips curling into a half-smile.

"Careful, Harry, our new novitiate," Bobby said. "Thunderbolts don't just belong to Zeus—or poets—or dead nuns. They belong to whoever dares to throw them. And beauty— well, beauty strikes where it pleases. Once it does, and I speak on behalf of my tender heart, and perhaps not just mine, one is never quite the same."

No one spoke.

John finally exhaled. "Fuck me royal."

Andy crossed his arms. "Language"

Harry looked at them—all of them—then shook his head, half-amused, half-astonished.

"Y'all goofy As Fuck."

ACT I — THE INFERNO

Four men let down their hair—and their defenses—to face their shadows and reopen a long-lost gay thunderbolt.

CANTO 1: FUCK YOU, TOXIC SHAME

In the weeks that followed, no nuclear war—despite Andy's Oracle of Delphi prediction. Things settled down, maybe too much. Harry grew anxious about opening up to the "established gays," men whom he felt had turned rebellion too easily into gay marriage and gay cruises.

The fellows, meanwhile, spoke as if the new recruit weren't there—though each privately found him stunningly mysterioso, and John, who prided himself on composure, found his timing just off.

"How does everyone feel about Harry being part of our group?" I asked.

Bobby rolled his eyes. "We're one group check-in away from a *Golden Girls* reboot. John's Dorothy, I'm Blanche, Andy's Rose—and Harry? He's dessert."

"Dessert," Harry said, with a hint of giving away a big secret, "covered in goddam pig's blood."

"Dr. Glitter!" Bobby said, dropping his knitting needles. "Telling on us!"

Harry snorted, taking his sweet time before fucking with them.

To draw him in, I turned the conversation toward spirituality—territory that usually caught everyone's interest, including Andy, despite his arch cynicism. We were in Los Angeles, after all—the birthplace of both the Mattachine Society and the Radical Faeries.

"What we lacked in pretentious literary *savoir-faire*—and public transportation," Andy would say, "we have more than compensated for with a taste for the cosmic."

WHEN THE ROOM GREW QUIET, I said, "Let's show Harry how we talk about gay identity—how we each came to it."

"I'd like to know if anyone came last night," Andy said. "Silence = Death."

"In church," Bobby said, turning teacher's pet for a change—rather than Andy's. "When I was sucking off the Deacon's son, I made believe I was Jonathan to his David."

John lifted his eyes, almost reverent. "And Jonathan stripped himself of the robe that was on him and gave it to David—"

"Where's my belt?" Andy muttered, fingering his Saint Laurent.

"—and his armor, and even his sword and his bow and his belt," John finished gently, as if reading bedtime scripture.

Bobby leaned back. "And Jesus, of course, doing the hustle with his disciples."

HARRY CLOCKED Andy's eye-roll and jumped in.

"That Jesus shit is delulu."

Bobby recoiled. "Now don't get it twisted. We are *not* dyed-in-the-wool Christians. Lord have mercy. We're camping, card-carrying homosexuals from the world of theaaaatrreee. This began as a support group for artists trying to get back to their craft—before you were born."

"That's why I'm here too," Harry said. "No cap."

Then, unable to resist, Harry added, mimicking, "Jesus, of course, doing the hustle with his disciples," before collapsing into the giggles that had made him TikTok-famous.

"Andy," Bobby said, snapping back into form, "I assume you'll be distributing a glossary for this young man's Vulgar English."

"And one for yours," Harry suggested. "Vulgah Engulish."

Bobby smiled thinly. "Speaking of definitions—could you clarify something? In our five sessions together, you have not once actually come out to us as—"

"A homo," John said.

"Gay, gay, gay," Bobby added.

"Don't really fuck with labels," Harry said. "They box people in."

"Box them in," Bobby echoed.

"So you're DL?" John asked, sweetly.

"We asked for cock," Bobby said to me. "And you brought in vagina."

"Bobby," Andy snapped. "We really going to drive another homie out?"

John leaned toward Andy. "Our Dirty Harry here—more hair on his chest than most."

Harry, just to play along, lifted his T-shirt—revealing a chest that had never known a razor. Bobby and John peered over their progressive lenses.

Andy exhaled. "Are we talking about sex—or Harry's chest hair, or lack thereof? Because I predict John—who likes feminine boys and rough trade—is already halfway there."

"Calling me rough trade or fem?" Harry said lightly. "Why so either/or?"

Andy smirked. "Guess we *are* talking about sex. In our own fucked-up way."

"Gay sex," Bobby insisted.

"Stop it, Mother," Andy said.

Bobby dabbed his eyes with a Kleenex.

"Andy," John explained, "says we're too *Sex and the City* and not enough *X-Men*."

"So does that make Andy Phoenix?" Harry asked. "Or Samantha?"

"Samantha," Andy said, clucking. "How did you know?"

"Obvio, homie," Harry said. "*Que tú eres un pig.*"

"*Pinche pig*," Andy muttered.

"Bro, I be smelling some pheromones."

"You don't say," Andy said.

"Show the fucking world what a dirty slut you really are."

"Not our Andy," Bobby said, mock-horrified.

"Yes, our Andy," John said, watching Andy turn red.

"Bet," Harry said.

"*Bet?*" Bobby recoiled. "What are we betting on?"

Andy flushed. "Despite processing my shame with Dr. G., I still see my mother on Bobby. My aunt on Father John."

"We're moving too fast," I said. "To feel anything—let alone shame."

Everyone turned on me.

"I *love* it when the perfect doctor fumbles," Bobby said. "Thank God he interrupted before we cooked Andy, which would've made Andy cook *me*, which would've—"

Andy's face went red.

"I feel like beating you with a belt."

"The belt!" Bobby gasped. "Again!"

I glanced at Harry. He looked torn—he got Bobby's alarm.

"Harry," I said. "How yah doing?"

"Andy's stuck, Doctor," Harry observed. "I sense the homie is hiding some shit. Ain't that what we talk about in therapy? Naming that shitty feeling—that baddie, *The Shame Kid?*"

The room tightened.

"Will you please shut the hell up about my shame?" Andy burst out. "And that goes for you, Doctor!"

"Ohhh," Harry said, leaning in. "Standing up to the doctor."

"Gonna scream," Andy threatened.

"Wanna borrow my spare earbuds?" Bobby asked Harry.

Harry helped himself.

Andy cupped his hands, but only a whisper came out.

Bobby rolled his eyes. "I've heard church ladies do better at bingo."

Then Andy let go.

The sound ripped through him—high, keening.

Fuck you, Toxic Shame!
Leave Little Weilin alone!

John removed an earbud. So did Harry and Bobby.

"Almost Mariah Carey level," John said.

"Our little Lamb," Bobby added.

Andy blew his nose, cleared his throat, and straightened his crotch. "Anyone got a cigarette?"

Harry offered a vape, then realized it was more a turn of speech.

"Yup," Andy said, regaining his composure. "Harry was right. I was hiding something. So—to finish my story, sans my overbearing mother and father—here goes. This DL Asian bro hit me up on Grindr—wired nipples, Yankees cap, jockstrap. Just as we were about to cum, he opened his mouth. I never did that shit before, but I spat right in his face, then slapped him, and we both came hard as fuck—like the Big Bang, type of shit."

"That's some hard shit," Harry said, giving a sly thumbs up.

Bobby clutched his fake pearls, ice clinking in an iced coffee before it melts in a Mississippi afternoon. "Hard? Shit. *Hard*shit? I don't like the smell of this hard shit one bit."

Harry, under his breath: "You finna learn to love it."

Nobody answered. They knew they were about to face some hard shit—love it or leave it.

CANTO 2: STRANGERS
IN THE NIGHT

I text the guys an hour before session: *running late today. Please wait in the lobby.*

Naturally, Bobby does not.

Thirty minutes early, Bobby posts up at the Natural Foods café, where he can clock everything that matters: which car John is driving. whether Andy has gone to the ICE demonstration downtown, his new *thing*, apparently. And of course, our Southern diva keeps one eye peeled for the masked man on the motorcycle.

Andy jogs in—Eton suit traded for activist wear: jeans, mask, bomber jacket, mustache coiffed, hair pomaded.

John arrives solo—lighter than last week—soft, collarless indigo tunic with kente trim, dark jeans cuffed over polished desert boots, journal and a few books in hand, unusually dapper, perhaps inspired by Harry's Sor *Who?*

Bobby's thrift couture runs black Levi's from the sixties, Daddy's lone fishing-trip tee, Granny's gray sweater, buzz cut growing into reddish-gray curls, silver-horned glasses hiding the bags.

A GMC Sierra Denali noses in. Out steps a tall, clean-cut *prof* type—slicked black hair pulled straight back, faint silver at the temples, long ring flashing, classic brown attaché, gray suit and tie. He makes a beeline—not to the front door.

—but to Bobby.

It's Harry?

"Oh," Bobby says—shocked, then recalibrating—"well, hello, hello."

Harry shakes, not too hard, returning the Southern-belle greeting with a pleasant echo. "Hello, hello."

Trying to free his hand, Bobby says, "Decided to code-switch today? From street to suit-and-tie? Good taste, dare I say."

"Bad taste," John murmurs—referring to Bobby—making sure Maria the barista hears.

"Microaggression," Andy corrects, curt.

"Podcast," Harry interjects, meeting Bobby's appraisal with a sunny shrug. "Popular one. About code-switching, believe it or not."

"I'm a believer," Bobby sings.

Andy raises a finger. "Shhh. Dr. G doesn't love us getting chummy outside the room. He likes the boundaries clean."

Bobby rolls his eyes. The cat's already on the counter, licking itself.

A text from Dr. Glitter: *Didn't see anyone in the waiting room?*

Andy looks up. *Oh merde*, he says in French. "Let's head back to the Medical Building."

Harry—slightly disoriented, having never entered the therapy office through the café—takes a hit from his vape, then hustles ahead to open the heavy metal-and-glass door.

"Finally, a gentleman," Bobby murmurs, waltzing through.

As Bobby and John head down the long corridor, Bobby grabs John's hand, sister-style, and stage-whispers, "Dr. Glitter wouldn't bring in a boy just because he's pretty. He wouldn't do that. Not to us. Not to himself. Right?"

John shrugs, clearing his throat. "Of course not."

HARRY STANDS BACK, offering the others the better seats.

I ask who'd like to begin.

Andy mutters, *"J'suis pas prêt."* Not Andy.

John says, "We did leave with a bang…"

Andy waves him off. "You go. Or the new guy."

Bobby leans toward Harry. "Andrew uses languages like a shield. I can't even ask my housekeeper to slow down—'*María, habla más despacio*'—when what I want to say is, 'God, grant her selective mutism.'"

"Bad taste," John says.

"Microaggression," Andy echoes.

I step in. "Let's honor Andy's boundary. And let's not throw Harry into the fire just yet. Bobby? John?"

Bobby zips his lips. John sets a timer on his Apple Watch.

Harry raises his hand. I nod.

"Fuck it, bro. If you fools won't go, I will. I got shit to say and do."

Bobby gestures like a flight attendant. "One anal explosive here"—nodding at Harry—"and one anal-retentive there"—nodding at Andy.

Harry clocks Andy jotting pieces of his dialogue into his journal.

"The doctor brought me," Harry starts, making sure the scribe gets each word, "to provoke y'all outta your trauma codependency bubbles. *Mean Girls* cock-blocking energy."

"*Who's Afraid of Virginia Woolf?* would've been the classier reference," Bobby chirps.

Andy turns to me. "You did not divulge to Harry that we suffer from cock-blocking disorder?"

John: "Pretty sure he's quoting Dr. Glitter—out of context."

Me: "Verbatim."

Bobby grins. "Oh, we'll give you provocation." Then, turning to John, "Ready?"

JOHN: "It's time to put the son to bed."

Bobby: "No. No, we can't."

John: "We must."

Bobby: "I won't let you kill him."

John: "Someday, baby—some night, some lazy, soft night—he'll come home, drag his tired feet up the stairs, into your room. And he'll be dead."

Bobby: "You can't do that."

John: "Yes, I can. We have to, Martha."

Bobby: "No! I love him."

John: "You can't have him. He's mine. Our son is dead."

"WHAT THE HELL?" Harry says. "Quoting a play whose words I can't follow?"

He catches Andy covering his mouth, giggling.

Harry scans the room. *Do I leave?* He remembers the rule—let the vulnerable one speak, then let the sexy one growl. Then pounce.

"Okay," he says, smoothing his notebook. "I'm gonna let

you in on what happened last night. To jolt you homo-normie shawties awake."

The word *shawties* sits in Bobby's mouth like overcooked asparagus.

Harry barrels on. "You bitches are gonna get hard when I tell you—or wet, Bobby, as the case may be."

A deep inhale. Then he keeps going.

I'm a proud Chicano—Aztlán-type shit. I look low-key fly, but the doctor knows—not cappin'—my head spins. I can pull whoever I want, then wake up anxious as hell—this guy, that guy, maybe even a chick. One bottomless pit of empty-as-fuck fuckie.

BOBBY SOFTENS; a Kleenex appears.

"Bobby's a Pisces," Andy says to Harry. "Water, chaos, dissolution—"

"I'm crying because we have a B," Bobby says. "By which I mean, bisexual."

"Leo Sun, Leo Moon, Scorpio Rising. Venus in Virgo," Harry says, attempting to win back some queer brownie points.

"Means you flirt, fight, expand, and spiral like a cosmic Rubik's Cube," Bobby decrees. "Finally someone in this group who studies the mystic arts?"

Harry adds a queer snap.

Bobby isn't so easily seduced. "So, Mr. Well-Rounded—can you tell me whether you're gay or bisexual?"

"Why so either/or?" Harry says, smiling with a hint of pleasure. "How about both/and."

"So now we have Kierkegaard and bisexuality. Lord, give me strength."

"*Sí, sí,*" Harry says.

"*Sí, sí,*" Bobby echoes, clocking the rhythm.

"Back to Harry," Andy cuts in.

"Please," I say.

Harry continues: "So—back to the story":

I've been chillin' with this boo—or bro—Wes. Latino cowboy-model type. Sweet kid. Real name Juan Carlos; stage name Wes. Three months. He says he's never been to a sex-magic thingamajig, and I'm like—what the fuck? I tell him I'll initiate him—respectfully. I know the ropes.

Bobby clasps his wrists.

Harry slaps his thigh. "I'm so fuckin' stupid. Wes roped me in!"

"Why stupid?" Andy asks.

"You finna see," Harry says. "Soon enough."

"All ears," Andy says, folding his ears into Vulcan points.

Harry reclines in his chair, fiddling with his long, flowing hair:

We roll in his Mercedes like Imma supposed to be bowled over. Ha, kid doesn't know shit about cars—he thinks German means grown, like adulting comes with a logo. Mercedes feels low-key sterile: air cold like a morgue, leather so tight it squeaks when you breathe. My pops people came here picking fruit. Now he's got four whips in Altadena—two silver E-Classes, a black S-Class for church Sundays, and a white G-Wagon that's pure delulu flex. I say it's guilt on wheels—for forgetting where he came from. Or maybe the Walkouts forgot him.

"That's why I drive a GMC Sierra Denali," I tell Wes.

Big body. American steel. Smells like pine and burnt rubber. Hums deep at a light. Growls like a good friend we lost to the streets—keeps me grounded. Like I earned the growl.

"Friend?" Bobby asks, eyes flicking to Harry's ring—the initial *G*.

Anyway—we pull up to this house in the hills, pool glowing like sin dressed up as baptism. He's playing chill, but I see the Bad Boy in his eyes. I tell him: low-key, don't do the most —easy on the molly, maybe a rose-petal blunt, keep it cute. I don't touch coke or crystal. Got limits. Boundaries. Self-respect. These are my limits.

Andy glares at Bobby and John to cool the side glances.

Wes parks himself in the steam room next to a Folsom top— Dr. G's vintage, full harness—and starts fiddling like they had business in a past life. I see him snort something—the way he started twerking; maybe X. By midnight, I'm not gonna lie, some guys I did *not* invite to the party had him laid out like an Orozco mural—sweat, struggle, mythic propor- tions. He forgot all about me. About our pact.

"I took him home after," Harry continues.

He was wasted. I was sober. Had to carry him to the car, drive him to my place, throw him in the shower, make matcha. My mother sat by his side praying in Spanish. I told her he spoke Portuguese. She said God needs no translation.

BOBBY AND JOHN CLAP, as if it's a finale.

"I DON'T THINK Harry's finished," Andy says.

"Oh," Bobby replies, stuffing his hands into his black jeans.

Rage blooms hot in Harry's olive skin. *Don't cry. Don't leave. Breathe. Drink water. Stay grounded, papi.*

Bobby softens—but not all the way. "I've learned not to fight shame. Let it sit. Like Dr. Glitter taught us."

"You're missing the point," Andy says. "Harry's not showing off. He's telling us he got left behind. He got dumped."

Andy gestures to the room.

Those pretty boys—Wes—they used him. Exploited his generosity. Wes got high and drunk so fast he forgot Harry existed. And now we're doing the same—forgetting that Harry, *qua* Harry, exists. Right, John—or should I say Mr. Socrates? Papa Joe? And you, Bobby—we call you Mother, but you make Medea look tame.

Bobby bows his head. "What would we do without our Spock?"

"Please don't Spock me," Andy says. "Just because I don't sob like John or emote like Bobby doesn't mean I'm not feeling."

He turns to Harry, steadier now. "This is how we work.

We rupture. We repair. I've never been in a group like this. I'm an alcoholic—we'll get you there. And if I can speak for my Cowardly Lion, Miss Bobby, we don't want you gone. You're what the doctor ordered. Bobby actually likes you. He just shows his thunderbolt in strange ways."

"I GUESS it's my catty way of dealing with someone who has always hurt me," Bobby says. "Beautiful men with stanzas like you. Also, my husband, Ezra—very arrogant. My mother fed me like love was lard. Neighbor kids called me blubber. *Fat Fairy Fuck. Fag Fat Fairy Fuck.* Blobbie stuck. So I'm a sad old queen."

I let Harry—and everyone else—know this is part of the cycle. Bobby needs help with his rage; people walk on eggshells. Andy is the only one who can crack them.

I can do eggs," Harry says. "That's about it."

He then blows Bobby a bro-kiss.

Bobby touches his cheek. Or rather—Blobbie does.

CANTO 3: THE DAIMON AND THE ABSENT MAN

When we next met, Harry was late—unusual.

I began with check-ins. People noticed his absence, murmured concern, then drifted into familiar grooves: the Industry, old trials, shared readings and performances, the comfort of having survived one another before.

Andy leaned forward. "Is that… an enactment? A parallel process?"

Bobby nodded. "I'm glad someone said something about the *sí, sí*," he said, clocking the rhythm.

"CC?" I asked.

"Oh," Bobby said. "What we're calling Harry. When he said *sí, sí*, we inducted him into our secret society of initials."

"Charismatic Chicano?" Andy offered.

"Curious Catalyst," John said.

"Chaotic Charmer," Bobby countered.

"Chief Complication," Andy smirked.

∼

I KNEW THE TRUTH. CC or no CC—Harry wasn't okay.

After the last session, he felt cock-blocked by Bobby and let down by me.

"We didn't even get to process the shit I felt," he said in individual session. "Andy—not you—threw me a lifeline. Yeah, Bobby opened up, but low-key? That took work."

"I can deal with those homo-normies, Doctor," he added. "But you have to let me be myself. Let me try new shit. Maybe then this strange experiment works—if I can be Hottie Harry. You haven't met him, but he's a character."

I'd never heard someone admit to being attractive with so little grandiosity—or confess he might use that attractiveness for something other than himself. His candor touched me. Since gay men loved male beauty—and Harry had no use for his own—I trusted, improbably, that his heart was in the right place.

When he made a heart sign with his hands, it meant he was trying something new.

Could I trust him?

Please?

I nodded. Okay.

INSTEAD OF FOLLOWING my lead to talk about Harry, the group began reminiscing.

"When Andy first came," Bobby said, "he was a lost pup. Jim pulled you out of Booze, Boys, and Baying in the Night for Lost Attachments."

Andy stuck out his tongue, then softened. "When I made real money, got my parents out of renting. Bought my mother Hermès scarves—she loves Li Xiaqing, China's first female aviator. But the money meant nothing. So I threw it away on Booze, Boys, and Baying in the Night for Lost Attachments."

He took a sip of water.

"Then came the sequel," he said. "Same cop, new enemy —ICE, borders, purity. The studio turned it into a revenge fantasy. I fled to Paris, fell off the wagon, asked my Yalie ex for a Jewish therapist who'd read Proust. That's how I landed here—with you clowns."

"And then you left us again," Bobby said.

"We knew your silences meant Hennessy," John added.

"Now we can't get you to shut up," Bobby went on. "Micro-aggressions, handouts, the history of gay-affirmative psychology."

"Have you become an Eve?" Bobby asked, mock-smoking.

"She's one psychoanalytic understudy," John said.

"Exactly," Bobby said. "And Dr. Glitter—our Margo Channing—had better watch his back."

Andy rolled his eyes. "If I'm Eve, it's because no one gave Margo my syllabus."

I opened my arms. "I think it's good we're revisiting how Andy got here. But right now, Harry thinks you've got your lives straightened out—excuse the micro-aggression—and are sitting pretty on success. It's understandable to resist reopening trauma. But we have a new person. He doesn't yet know how to let you in on his."

"Maybe that's why he's not here," Andy said. "*Où est-il ?*"

"Maybe he's not coming back," Bobby said—unsure whether that frightened or relieved him.

John cleared his throat. "I had an idea. It might move us forward—or backward. This year, not working, I returned to my first love: literature. The Greeks. Sophocles, Plato. The family who took me in off the streets of Atlanta paid for college. Law was the price."

He paused.

"The old stories gave suffering a shape. A man falls, and in falling reveals the law he's lived by. Sometimes I think that's what we're doing here—giving form to chaos."

"Harry," Andy said.

"Me too," Bobby said. "I dreamed of a biracial woman in a 1920s Sunday dress, peacock feather in her hat. She beckoned. I ran."

"Clara," John said softly.

"Harry," Andy said again.

CANTO 4: EXPOSE YOUR GRINDR

Harry burst in—as if he'd jogged straight from Runyon Canyon—long hair damp beneath a sun-baked bandana. His MEChA de UCLA Raza T-shirt clung like wet paint; neon-blue gym shorts flashed. A watermelon vape slipped from his gloved hand; he shoved it into his waistband, tossed down a tote, yanked out a frayed notebook, pages spilling. Still catching his breath, eyes darting, he carried himself as if this had been his entrance all along.

"Hope the Runyon Canyon boys sent us a fruit basket," Bobby said. "We were mourning your absence—assuming you had better things to do. Or suck."

"Yo," Harry shot back, sliding into his seat. "I caught all that just now. That CC shit was not cute."

Harry looked at me and made the heart sign with his hands. I inhaled sharply and wished my supervisor and I possessed telepathic powers.

～

John leaned toward the hurt-looking man as Harry lingered by the doorframe, unsure whether to step in or away.

"Were you gathering evidence," John asked, "or just eavesdropping—and for how long?"

Harry shrugged. "I was debating whether this was the right group. Came late, then heard you all team up with Andy's internalized homophobia—talking about scarves for Mom."

"She likes them," Andy said. "It's the least I can do for her —forcing me to play violin in her studio. If she hadn't been so suffocating, I might not have fled Ohio and landed here."

Andy's irony didn't land anywhere near Harry.

"Where's the sex in that?" Harry asked. "The heat? That's not freedom. That's not queer theory. That's gay assimilation."

"It's like the ghosts of Stonewall chose Harry as their rep," Bobby muttered, "and we're the disappointing town hall."

"Is that how you feel about yourself?" Harry asked, half-hurt, flashing another heart at me. "Sounds like you've got a case of—how did Andy put it in the Welcome Packet he created—'internalized homophobia.'"

"Define your terms?" John asked, the lawyer emerging. "What do you mean?"

"I'll tell you what I mean," Harry said. "I think we're still ashamed. And we dress it up real nice. So let's come fucken clean—open the apps, look straight at the dark side."

"Look forward into the dark side," Bobby corrected. *Forward, not straight. Always a distinction.*

"Hold up," I said, softer than intended. "Let me check in with the others. Maybe what you're doing, Harry, is getting your voice back—after feeling shut out last time."

His eyes flicked to mine as he made the heart shape again; I received the communiqué, and he answered with a quick, grateful gesture.

"You're barking up the wrong tree," Bobby drawled. "John and I don't traffic in sex apps. We read poetry and cling to bad partners."

"I'm single now," John said. "Remember?"

Andy straightened. "Once we go there, we're all going there. Harry–Carrie–Pandora."

He pulled out his phone, eyes daring the sky.

"This is therapy, not acting class," I said, measured. "Not even psychodrama. Andy—are you sure this isn't people-pleasing? Peer pressure? We've been practicing containment."

Andy, radiant: "Today I say, fuck *la containment.*"

Harry nearly bounced, girlish, then—with a flourish we hadn't seen—dropped to his knees, phone held like a wafer, a rosary, a hit of poppers.

"Show me your profile," Harry said. "Not all of it. Just enough bullshit to get this sex show moving. No secrets— unless you mention pain, scat, or money."

Bobby sliced the air—a warning to me.

But John, who relished danger, said, "Let the children play. We need some entertainment."

Andy inhaled, steady, and opened the app. Harry, opening his own, searched for an Asian nearby so he could witness Andy's lies.

Grindr Profile: Andy / RiceKing87

Top · 5 9″ · 170 lb · Muscular

Tags: Jock / Kink / Nipples / Art / NoSmoking / Muscle / Geek / WS

About: Into spit, slow kisses, mutual jo, wired nips, dirty talk. Taken—he knows I'm here. No tweakers. No "No Asians." If you have a type, it should include people. 420 & poppers okay. Body by Barry's. Fluent in five languages. Don't be stupid. Faceless or gaping-ass pics = blocked. I don't take money.

Stats: Man · He/Him · Geek/Jock · Asian · Committed

Looking for: Hookups · Meet at: Your place

Health: HIV- · Covid & Monkeypox vaccinated

~

"WATER SPORTS," Bobby said, scandalized.

Andy turned to Harry. "Bro. You were supposed to edit that part. Your turn."

"Our Andy," Bobby sniffled.

"Like you never tried that shit," John said.

Harry hesitated—then returned the favor and shared his profile, though Andy had already found it.

~

GRINDR PROFILE: BrujoBoi99

Top · 6′1″ · 185 lb · Muscular

Tags: Dating / Jock / College / Daddy / Kink / Rough / Goofy / Movies / Romantic / Weightlifting / Emotional Intelligence / Art

About: Brujo dom—rope, breath, pressure points, eye contact, aftercare. Dark dom, sacred kink. All bodies, all races, all ages welcome. Bonus if you're well-read, hung, call me sir. I ghost ghosts, but bless the generous.

Stats: Man · He/Him · Geek/Jock · Latino · Single

Looking for: Dates, hookups · My place / Yours

Health: HIV- · On PrEP · Covid & Monkeypox vaccinated

~

Andy skipped the Twitter porn handle—but did not edit out *generous*.

"At least you don't say 'No Asians,'" he said, trying to joke. "I hope I didn't embarrass you."

"Drink water," Harry muttered, stretching, offering Andy a sip from his gallon jug. "Hydration is a must for your favorite sport, you dirty Model Minority."

Andy drank as if he'd been wandering a desert.

Bobby sighed, shooting John a look.

Part of me panicked; another part wanted exactly this— the exposure of an idea I'd carried for years: a group where gay men could talk about their secret lives.

Harry offered John a sip and, glancing at me and Bobby, said, "I don't know where that mouth's been, but—fuck it— I'm thirsty," and took a swig.

John then accepted Harry's invitation to stretch alongside him. "This bag of bones could use some loosening."

"Careful, Johnnie," Bobby said. "Don't be fooled by Brujo Boy saying he's got a sweet tooth for the white boy. I reckon he likes 'em darker, older—and, lest we forget, generous."

John turned his sweatpants pockets inside out, signaling their poverty.

As they left, Bobby whispered, "Safety first, sir." It wasn't clear whether he meant Harry or John.

Harry looked for Andy's gaze—but Andy had already slipped out, following an outdated map home, for now.

So Harry walked to his car with John.

CANTO 5: HOW HARRY
GOT HIS NAME

Each man now steps into his own history with the group holding the descent, before they rise again together.

~

THE NIGHT after the big Grindr apps reveal, Harry dreamt of a Brujo—dark-eyed, ash-dusted finger, and a scar that looked like a crescent wrench had nicked his cheekbone years ago.

"What is your name?"

Harry opened his mouth but could not speak. The Brujo allowed his palm to meet Harry's cheek—not cruel, simply corrective, not unlike a mechanic tapping a stuck gauge. Harry sat up in bed, sucking air. In the silence, the question didn't fade, but idled.

What is your name?

~

AFTER WASHING HIS FACE, the 26-year-old man smiled at a memory of cars that took him back just a few years—when he felt young.

"What's your name, bro?" he asked when he saw the 16-year-old boy watching him behind his wheel, rolling a blunt.

He laid out his legal name—Enrique Julio Francisco Martínez González the Third. Julio for Saint Julius, Francisco for Saint Francis.

Guillermo heard, "Harry."

HIS PARENTS' engagement with the Chicano Blowouts—the East L.A. Walkouts of 1968—loomed over the family like a celebrity tale. Black-and-white photos on the living-room wall made the house feel watched over: teenagers pouring out of East L.A. high schools with handmade signs; teachers whose faith was practical; his father—Enrique the Second—short, powerful torso, bullhorn in one hand, rolled-up banner in the other, jaw set toward a better morning.

You kept your Spanish. You kept your name. You did not apologize for the length of either.

When Harry got into UCLA—the institutional heir to those walkouts, home of Chicano Studies—the house turned into a kitchen that cooked victory: menudo, steam, laughter; old comrades thumping his father's back—he felt the impact through the floorboards—saying, "It continues."

Harry discovered that catalogue pages could smell like gasoline and eucalyptus. Chicano Studies felt like home—until he noticed that Afro-Latinx students stopped coming; Indigenous classmates kept showing up and quietly left.

LGBTQ Studies opened up and then walled him in with theory diagrams that didn't bleed. He cut back through the stacks to *Sor Juana, Cherríe Moraga, Gil Cuadros*—to poems whose questions arrived like candles in dry wind.

His father presided over dinner like a humble union boss. Harry arrived once in eyeliner so faint you had to love him to see it. His father's joke was the old kind, the kind that covers a bruise.

"You think César Chávez fought for this?"

Harry smiled big and easy. "Pop," he said, "I'm majoring in breathing. Film minor."

"Try engineering," his father—otherwise kind—said. The line landed like a dropped wrench.

The family's faith practiced in practicalities—monthly bills, work boots, mass. His mother's rosary appeared in one hand while she ruled the neighborhood with stories, gossip, and delicacies. He cried with her at midnight.

"You are the only one who made college," she said.

She grabbed his nails, still dirty from jump-starting a broken-down Volvo that afternoon, grease undercutting grace.

"We want you to have dirty nails," she said, "and yet be clean as a whistle."

He played Tiresias in a queer remix of *Oedipus Rex* and earned a standing ovation, but told no one.

Before therapy, he'd drift east on the 134, windows down. At the crest, the San Gabriels' blue ribs lifted his dread—the view reminding him he was smaller than he thought and safer than he feared.

He drove to a liquor-store parking lot where the light made everyone look arrestable or dead. The Mustang waited, hood primed. Guillermo leaned against it—tank top, chain, Backwood ember pulsing to bass from another trunk. New tattoo at the collarbone. Same eyes, reading you like a timetable.

"Enrique," Guillermo said. Then, softer, "Harry."

Days at UCLA, nights in Pico Rivera. At home, Harry underlined histories of the '68 Blowouts and watched grainy footage of teenagers walking out of classrooms, refusing the arithmetic of their invisibility. In class, he ditched Queer Theory and Chicano Studies for singing and dance. Then he would drive east, sit on a curb, and listen to Guillermo talk about engines the way other people talk about the Gospel.

"Loosen the wheel," G said. "Tight grip makes you flip."

At MEChA meetings, he translated without pause— belonging if he drank beer, flirted with the girls, watched the game.

In Queer Studies, he penciled a note beside Judith Butler: *I'm not an argument; I'm a person.* Then scratched it out—it sounded like a boy in a movie just before a crash.

The first time he brought Guillermo to Westwood was a Sunday afternoon. They sat on the steps of a building named for a man who never imagined them. Guillermo pretended to read the bronze plaque; Harry pretended not to read Guillermo. They shared a blunt, the smoke lifting like incense over a shrine neither quite believed in.

"I'm gonna teach you real shit," Guillermo said, rapping Harry's head lightly with his knuckles. "How to make the car fly."

At home, his mother set two extra places at dinner, the

way some miracles arrive without announcement. His father watched like a man watching the weather.

"Ready?" G asked, as if there were any answers but yes.

Harry took the passenger seat, and the smell of vinyl and weed and warmed-up oil reached for him like a bygone friend you aren't done loving.

Sometimes they didn't drive. They just got high, listened to music, and fell asleep together. Harry started bringing his mother's wool blanket, the one she had made during the years of sadness, when she took him to her mother's house and cried for three years.

When they were asleep, it was okay for Harry to hold Guillermo's hand, to let his lips graze Guillermo's neck.

When Harry saw Ricardo, Roberto, Miguel, and Juan pull up in their cars, he shook his friend awake.

"C'mon, you love birds," they'd say. But they knew Harry was fucking Gloria, Guillermo had his girl, and a few others— word was out that they had all the bitches they wanted.

The wheel under Guillermo's hand was loose in exactly the way you trust when you want the car—and your life—to swing without breaking. The road curled out of Pico Rivera like a dare, past shuttered storefronts and into the industrial apron off Slauson, where warehouses squatted behind chain-link and the asphalt still remembered rubber. Harry sat in the driver's seat, knees braced, smoke from the joint curling between them like a third. Guillermo grinned, eyes half-closed, one hand draped over the wheel, the other by Harry's leg, his thigh.

They'd hot-boxed until the windows sweated. The radio was a hiss of bass and old Chicano rap. When the bass dropped, the world outside flattened, and Harry felt the hum crawl into his ribs. Sodium lights buzzed overhead, bleaching the loading docks and oil-stained concrete into something theatrical and exposed.

"Loosen the wheel," Guillermo said again, easing the car into the open lot.

"You already said that."

"Because you don't listen."

Guillermo showed him without lecturing. A tap of gas—not a stomp. The rear end broke loose just enough. Hands light, then lighter—counter-steer and breathe. The car began to write a circle, tires whispering at first, then singing. Guillermo's hand guided Harry's wrist for half a second—release here, catch it there—teaching him how to let the back end swing without panic, how to stay inside the spin instead of fighting it. One clean arc, then another, the donut widening, tightening, the asphalt taking their initials in heat.

Harry noticed that Guillermo's phone would blow up, but he let Maria's calls go to voicemail. He preferred to sleep at Harry's place, where Mrs. González woke to make the men enchiladas or sweet coffee. She brought a cot into Harry's room, but the boys were too tired to make it.

THE NIGHT of the resurrection began like all the others: music, smoke, laughter hard enough to hide Harry's terror. Harry wore Guillermo's hoodie, sleeves long enough to swallow his hands. Cars circled the industrial park, headlights carving halos in the dark.

Someone yelled, "Spin it!" and the Mustang answered.

Guillermo dropped the clutch, tires screaming, the world a

blur of heat and color. Harry shouted without words. The circle tightened—one, two, three perfect rings—then a shriek of sirens cut through the beat. Red and blue washed the asphalt.

"Go!" Harry yelled.

Guillermo grinned. "Already did."

Harry felt the G-force shove his heart against his ribs. Behind them, the cops gave chase; ahead, the freeway opened like a mouth.

"Left!" Harry called.

Guillermo shook his head. "Trust me."

The Mustang leapt the ramp, weaving through late traffic. Sirens swelled, distant then close. Harry looked over— Guillermo calm, jaw set, a small smile that said he was exactly where he wanted to be. Harry reached for the dash to steady himself.

"Don't—" he started, but the sentence never found its end.

Light, noise, weightlessness. The next thing he knew, silence had bit into his teeth, bleeding. Apparently everyone survived that time.

HE WOKE in his own bed hours later, shirt streaked with black dust and traces of dark blood, ears still ringing. His mother, looking like Sophia Loren, stood in the doorway whispering a rosary so fast it sounded like code. His father's voice from the kitchen—angry, frightened, soft.

"The boy's alive." Then, quieter: "Guillermo's not."

Nobody inquired whether Harry was inside the vehicle. No one had to.

He showered until the water ran cold, then traced the small bruise on his cheek that looked like a fingerprint—the

Brujo's slap, returned to sender. He tattooed a single letter—H —on his shoulder the next day.

The house became a shrine to what had not happened. The family even moved, perhaps not because of the death but because, as the father put it, his contracting business blossomed. That's when they no longer took their eyes off Harry. They stopped calling him Junior and spoke to him by his new name—Harry.

Harry slept with his door open because his mother insisted; she said it helped the air move.

His father stopped leaving for work before dawn. He lingered in the kitchen, shirt tucked, car keys unmoving in his palm, pretending to read the newspaper.

"Coffee?" the old man would ask.

A man who once commanded picket lines now waited for his son's nod.

The mother filled the table with offerings—fruit, candles, a bowl of salt to catch bad dreams. When the novena candles guttered, she didn't replace them until Harry said, "Go ahead." Once, he caught her watching him from the hallway, her face blurred by votive glow.

"You pray," she whispered. "You survived."

His father's voice softened too. No more orders—only questions. Are you eating enough? Need the car? Want me to fix that dent? Harry waved him off, but the older man stayed in the doorway, waiting for a different kind of permission.

From then on, Harry noticed how the house obeyed him. The thermostat stayed at his preference. The radio stations shifted to his playlists. Even the cat began sleeping outside his door instead of theirs. His father's voice grew almost tender when he used the name Harry, as if pronouncing a spell. The mother began consulting him before calling relatives, as if he were the family diplomat.

It was guilt, yes—but also awe. They had seen their son

rise from a night that could have ended the life of their favorite of five. Survival looked divine when you didn't understand it. The parents' authority melted not from argument but from worship.

Mrs. González asked her priest. Did they need an exorcism, or was it just grief?

"Watch him," Father José Rodríguez said. "Don't take your eyes off him, ever."

When he left for UCLA that fall, his mother packed a rosary in his bag.

His father added, "Whatever you say, hijo. You're the one who sees clearly."

WHEN HE JOINED the Hollywood Creative Group, the others didn't know about the ghost in the passenger seat. They saw Harry's appeal, strength, mellow tongue. But these men had worked hard to summon the gay soul and so had a clue. Bobby's drawl cut through the first sessions like sunlight through smoke. "That kind of big-family love doesn't come free, sugar."

HE STARTED the garage project because he couldn't stop the hum, and his father got a kick out of designing a separate abode with his son and his friends. Gloria helped draw the plans and execute the design.

Harry and Gloria had grown up on the same street, two undercover queer kids long before they knew the word. Homework at the kitchen table, notes passed in class, Marlboros behind the rec center. When bullies came sniffing, they moved as one—she threw the first punch, he handled the cleanup.

Harry's mother assumed they'd marry someday, and for years neither corrected her; it was safer. They protected each other from their families' moods and the world's confusion, building a private universe where queerness could still breathe.

Gloria called taking at the garage "therapy with tools." They built benches, hung punching bags, painted slogans. After a year they christened the Space. Men came, and so did very butch women and trans men and women. They lifted, sweated, told stories. Every story ended in acceleration— somebody's father, somebody's lover, somebody's ghost. Harry realized people came to him for the same reason he'd once gone to Guillermo: to be seen while doing something dangerous—not in a car, but in a spiritual moment.

The night Wes didn't call back, Harry sat alone in the garage. Weed smoke curled to the rafters, mixing with oil and sage. He remembered Guillermo's laugh, the roar of engines, the blur of freeway lights. He remembered the Brujo's question. This time he answered aloud, voice rough but steady. "My name is Harry."

The Mustang inside him idled, then quieted.

THAT NIGHT he drove without "Blacks and Browns." Streetlights flickered like an old film reel. He passed a mural of the Virgin de Guadalupe tagged with angel wings and thought, *We keep painting what we can't resurrect.*

When he reached the garage, Gloria was there, welding goggles perched on her head, sparks haloing her face.

"You look like shit, bro."

"Progress."

"You tell them?"

"Yeah."

"What'd they do?"

"Acted like nothing happened. Fed me dinner."

"That's family," she said, handing him a beer.

They drank and shared a smoke. Outside, a neighbor's lowrider thumped a bass line that hit Harry's pulse exactly.

"Ever wish we'd left?" he asked.

"Left where? The planet?"

"Yeah. Just drive till the road gives up."

She laughed. "That's not leaving, bro. Leaving means changing."

He watched her light the backwood, the same flip-snap as Guillermo's lighter. Smoke spiraled between them.

"Ever been shot at?" he asked.

"Once," she said. "Didn't like it. Prefer tools."

He grinned.

Gloria tapped ash into a can. "What's up with you and this John person? You mentioned him."

"John?"

"Don't play dumb."

"We shook hands in Group today," Harry said. "We're not supposed to, but we did."

She looked at him—her dearest friend—and that's when she saw him give up the ghost.

CANTO 6: ANDY'S
GAYS OF WINE ROSES

Andy used to call himself a "Gold's Gym Asian—Part-Time, Non-Union, Non-Molly-Permitting," since a single weekend on X could undo months of hypertrophy and meal-prepped virtue. But if a hot guy suggested a bump, Andy bundled himself up in indecision, weighing Apollo against Dionysus as if his entire erotic future hung on the toss.

He wrote in his journal, in a blend of French, Spanish, Mandarin, English, Latin and Greek, a method he learned when living at home in Ohio to make sure no one could "out" him. He still employed the morse code should the paramedics entering his apartment snatch the open journal that the spilled wine had not yet rendered illegible before his untimely death set in.

Let's see if I can have a tryst without a leather hood. I envy people with the ALDH2 deficiency—the Asian Flush—whose bodies force a stop before blacking out.

To attract men at bars in Columbus, Boston, New Haven, Cambridge, or Paris, Andy didn't have to face the racial filtering that plagued him on the apps.

> Building muscle helps our hero erase the memory of arriving at seven, an Asian immigrant *sans fortune*, after his parents— once prosperous from his father's jewelry store—decided they could no longer trust what the Communists might do next. *Méi bànfǎ.* Better to flee than to wait. They landed near the Columbus clan, *pauperes inter pauperes*, poor as dirt, learning quickly that in America muscle travels better than memory. *C'est la loi du corps. Así se sobrevive.*

The Ohio kids with ruddy cheeks and Buckeyes caps had mocked his English, shoved him on the playground, jeered at his bowl cut. But as adolescence hit, his family called him "Jack in the Beanstalks."

> This buck-toothed Asian Wai Lam in slouchy jeans, a Chinese sewn gown—could pull a Buckeyes cap low over his eyes, roll up his Gap sleeves, and become unreadable. Karate? Kickboxing? *Mutatis mutandis.* He could take the belt —*la ceinture, el cinturón*—and teach them not to fuck with Andy Lamb.

Andy had inherited, not from this cruel to scrawny man, a different generation's larger frame.

He had choices: the soft-spoken French beauty, the leather daddy with a private jet—or both.

But nothing lasted.

The musclebound daddy wanted more than Andy could give, so it ended.

The mixed-race rapper with a smile like moonlight recoiled when Andy showed up unexpectedly with flowers.

The minute a guy even faintly reminded me of Madame Chang, I was out. She'd call every day, rapid-fire Cantonese, listing how proud her mahjong crew was of my film—which, let's be honest, they would never watch—then pivot, *sans transition*, into guilt: how I never flew home, didn't call enough, was selfish. *Bù xiào.* My father threatened to cut me off if I didn't stop fucking around—i.e., stop being a homo. Frankenstein's deadbeat dad makes the creature into a monster; I'm no cockroach. *Non sum vermis.* I'd already made a killing on my first movie—*coup net*, clean hit—so I cut them off. *Me fui.* Cut those bitches. I only called back to wire fifty K into their bank account. *Affaire réglée.*

After the success of his *Tommy Gun*, cop action drama, he was about to sign his first big production deal, which included the sequel.

ONE MIDNIGHT, Andy rolled toward Julien to kiss him, rehearsing words of love.

Julien murmured something back—affectionate, yes, but pitched in a French he didn't quite recognize.

Oh.

So it wasn't Julien.

Philipe—a rail-thin Afro-French man with dreadlocks, lavender on his skin—lifting the covers in a studio on *Rue Vieille-du-Temple*, above a falafel shop. One window faced another. The rent came from Hollywood residuals Andy no longer tracked.

Philippe supplied the record: texts, photos, receipts—three weeks of Andy's own hunger, carefully archived. Andy emptied the Chartreuse into the sink, then the pills beside the butter and jam.

When he looked up, Philippe had left, hurt that Andy had no recollection of his marriage proposal.

THE CALL CAME from the Industry executive.

If you do not get back to work, you piece of shit, Asian entitlement momma's boy, you will face a danger worse than losing your job. You will never work in this town again. The things you did during COVID. How you put people at risk. I have informants. GET TO WORK!

A week later, another message arrived.

It's been a year. Maybe two. You are the only man for me. Master, call your slave before I harm myself. I can't live without you.

Andy nearly fainted. Not from the threat—he'd survived those—but from realizing that the voice of love sounded exactly like the voice of hate.

THE BASEMENT of the Fish Bank smelled of metal and old espresso, a ghost of fish still clinging to the walls. Upstairs, the café announced itself—forks, laughter, steam—but down here it was another country. Concrete walls, one bare bulb, the hum of a fridge. Kofi had cleared the space of ornament: no décor, no music. Just rope, leather, a bowl of salted water, and his body moving with authority.

He wasn't big, but he carried himself like *rue de la Goutte d'Or*. His French was clipped, shaped by mosque, kitchen, club.

"*Respire, petit,*" he said. "No drama. You breathe, you stay."

Andy stood half-naked, wrists bound, the hemp scraping his skin. He had answered an ad to be a slave, wanting to learn what the body learned on the other side. Kofi's breath hovered close—soap, sweat.

The strikes came fast, precise—punctuation marks, not exclamations. Kofi didn't hit hard; he hit right. Andy's knees softened, but he held. His mind tried to name it; the body had already taken over.

"The pain will subside," Kofi said. "You will feel free. You have to communicate."

Kofi circled him.

You resist—I strike your fear. You breathe—I touch your freedom.

Andy screamed—not only from pain, but from recognition. When it stopped, his shoulders trembled, not from pain but its absence. Kofi wiped him down, efficient as a medic.

"*C'est bon.*"

"You like freeing people?" Andy asked.

Kofi smiled, one gold tooth. "Mostly I like the moment they stop pretending they are not a child of God." He dipped his hands in the bowl. "Salt remembers."

Andy sat against the wall, rope marks climbing his skin like handwriting he couldn't read. Upstairs, life resumed. Kofi unchained him, lit sage, and lay beside him.

"Stay awake, *mon frère*," he said. "That goes for all of you."

BACK IN THE STATES, Andy attended classes on S&M and BDSM and met a masked submissive who was into being a Pup. The relationship became ongoing, secretive, structured. The red-haired older man rented an apartment solely for their encounters. They drank. Andy received voice instructions from Kofi. They met intermittently over two years. During this time, Andy's career accelerated.

The relationship fractured when the man begged for more encounters and wired Andy money. When Andy drew blood, the man became needy. "If I bleed, I belong to you."Andy blocked him.

~

After Philipe left, Andy called Bloch. He was an old Yale comparative literature major EX turned psychiatrist. "*Je suis paumé*," Andy said, his voice tight but formal, as if French might lend dignity to collapse.

"*Et maintenant?*" Bloch sighed. "*Tu veux de l'aide, ou tu veux briller?*"

"*Quod erat demonstrandum*," Andy said, trying to be clever and failing.

"I'll refer you to someone," Bloch replied.

Bloch texted him the number of Dr. Sammy Greenberg.

Andy also texted the studio head: *I'll do the fucking sequel. It's a horrible fascist piece of drek, but I'll fulfill the terms of the contract.* He debated the word *fascist*, then sent it anyway.

On the flight, Andy pulled out his first Asian-American cop script—a hen-pecked family man by day, CIA spy by night, with a studly white sidekick. People wrongly thought the success came overnight, but Andy had toiled for a year like a man on adrenaline, translating college textbooks, rewriting scripts, writing a novella no one would ever see about Batman and leather. Reading the sequel he'd abandoned during his month-long debauchery, he laughed at the idiotic dialogue and snarled at the right-wing sub themes the mucky-mucks had manipulated him into adding.

Andy came to therapy, he said, "to clean up his act," and then added, "more to the point, to stop acting."

He acknowledged beer, weed, a spot of Tina—only when he wanted to bottom, which he insisted was rare. "I'm funny, sexy, hot, and I have no idea who I really am," he said. "My success was more for my parents, not me. I need peace with them. Bring me some Heinz Kohut."

I thought this sarcastic intellectual a good candidate for the Hollywood Support Creative Group. His rational demeanor could ripen into fuller expression.

He brought order to the meetings. People clamored for his handouts. When COVID forced a decision—disband or Zoom—Andy voted Zoom first. The group followed. "I'd be in a treatment center if it weren't for you guys," he said.

Then he grew thinner. Then he stopped coming.

After consulting my supervisor, I drove to his Larchmont cottage. His car was there. The house was dark. I called his Emergency Contact; his roommate didn't answer. Then I called is mother answered with brittle formality. "Andrew is visiting," she said. "In Ohio. He is fine. Very busy."

I waited around till dusk, when the roommate got home.

"Get the hell out before I call his shrink," the guy barked at me.

When I said I was the shrink, the tweaker let out "UCLA Ronald Reagan Psychiatric Ward" and "we shot that shit up all last month," before shutting the door.

I WASN'T the only one watching.

On Day Ten, the call came for Andy. A blocked number. Calm, and low and disturbingly clear.

"There's a program. Oceanside. Dual diagnosis. A car is waiting."

Andy didn't respond—not because he didn't understand, but because he knew the voice. The studio asshole? The masked masochist? Or both? Two faces of the same terror. Two executioners, same agenda: get Andy back to work. No, keep Andy from killing himself due to not being able to find love.

As THE VAN curved toward Oceanside, Andy caught sight of the Pacific—silver-blue, indifferent. For the first time in a long while, he felt something like being held.

CANTO 7: ANDY'S GETS HIS BELT BACK

Jim came once a week. Always Tuesday, and with a small bag of oranges. He didn't ask questions, nor offer insights, or pretend to be waiting for transformation. He did, however, brighten when he noticed the Big Book on Andy's tastefully anonymous sober-living bedside table, opening the tome and paging through the hallowed text as if it were his personal Bible.

"What do you want from me?" Andy asked one day, irritated by the silence.

"To finish your projects," Jim said. "And make me a lot of money."

"Are you implying I should sacrifice myself to Mammon?"

"I'm saving your life."

"That's what all abusers say."

"You were the abuser, remember?"

"So why do you keep coming?"

Jim's gaze was steady. "I told you, before you ran off, that I would always be there for you."

"I have a doctor I'd like you to meet."

"I tried therapy," Jim said, "but I only felt that the program got me."

Andy considered saying, *I'll only go forward into your version of recovery if we go to therapy together.*

But his love life was already littered with ultimatums that had never done their job. So instead, he decided to weigh Jim's devotion to the Twelve Steps—and to him—against his own impulse to cut men off who didn't conform to his standards.

ANDY LINGERED in the doorway of the Group Therapy Room longer than necessary, unsure whether to announce himself or slip into the empty seat.

Bon. Très bien. Je suis revenu. (Fine. Very well. I'm back.)

John stood first. Then Bobby. Then everyone—limbs, laughter, tears. Someone kissed his forehead; others cried. The doctor hugged tighter than anyone.

Touchez pas trop. (Don't touch too much, I'm still putting myself back together.)

Then Bobby—off-key, earnest, entirely himself—began: *For he's a jolly good fellow...*

John, watching closely, noticed the difference. Andy's edges had softened. The mask of clever disdain dulled—not erased, but loosened. And somehow that made John feel his own fall might be near. So he grabbed Andy with all his might. As Bobby carried the song forward, the group joined in —singing, laughing, swaying, tipping into joy they hadn't known they'd been missing for their beloved Andrew Wai Lam. It was ridiculous, and Andy let them.

THE MORNING after the gala engagement party, Jim and Andy bade farewell to their mostly sober guests and boarded a plane to Paris. They hoped the city's ancient beauty might stage a renewal of a "normal" sexual life, but somewhere between passport control and the wrought-iron staircase of their Marais loft, the current slipped.

In Paris, Andy took Jim to Chez Kofi, an African vegan spot in the 18th. He said he knew the owner. For once, Andy looked like he could breathe.

He slid a plate across the table—plantain brushed with tamarind, cassava-leaf stew over fonio, fritters still steaming.

"Try this," Andy said. "Chef's guilt trip if you don't."

Jim smiled politely, already having put two and two together.

"We were using then," he said, clocking what this excursion was about.

"I brought you here to the man who taught me what I know," Andy said. "He will help us. He is sober."

Kofi emerged from the back—apron stained, dreads tied up, eyes lighting when he saw Andy. A flash of recognition, not innocent.

"*Nanga def,*" he said, grinning.

Andy laughed. "Only trouble, as usual."

Kofi glanced at Jim, then back at Andy, amusement shading into appraisal. "You always bring interesting men."

Andy enjoyed that a little too much.

Jim excused himself. Andy's laughter followed him, louder than necessary. Something metallic rose in Jim's mouth, then the wave hit, and he vomited up the appetizer.

When he returned, pale, he turned to both Andy and Kofi and said, "I'm ready."

"You are not," Kofi said. "Return to your AA". Keep your dream journal."

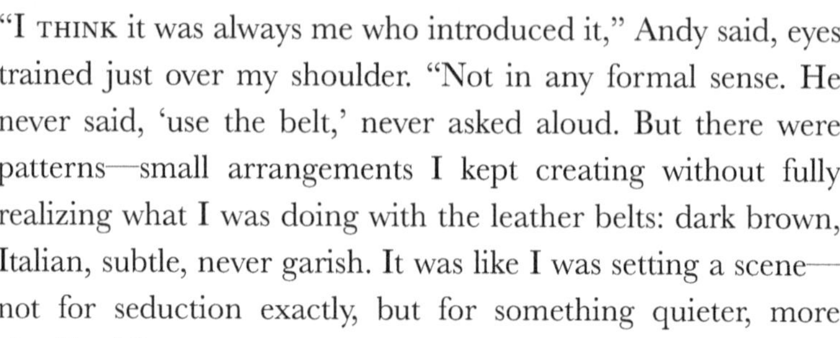

"I THINK it was always me who introduced it," Andy said, eyes trained just over my shoulder. "Not in any formal sense. He never said, 'use the belt,' never asked aloud. But there were patterns—small arrangements I kept creating without fully realizing what I was doing with the leather belts: dark brown, Italian, subtle, never garish. It was like I was setting a scene— not for seduction exactly, but for something quieter, more ritualized."

Andy glanced briefly to register my presence—even though he lay on the couch, as he preferred to do, a true adherent of free association—and continued.

"Jim never questioned it. He never joked, never asked what I was up to. He simply took the cue. I'd pick up the belt, unbuckle it with care, and begin. Not sexually—not in the way one usually means that word. It was always him on the receiving end, always the one undressed. He never got hard, but he called it pleasure."

Andy curled up on the couch.

"When we started living at Jim's house, I felt safe. This powerful man of Hollywood worshipped the ground I walked on. He even loved me when I came out of the shower with my FOBBY hair. In the quiet of his warmth—the nightly conversations over movies, philosophy, poetry, Scrabble—how Jim loved having his friends over for dinner parties, cooking simple food with fine herbs, making space for me to hold forth like a prince among people who truly paid attention. I would never wish to rock that boat."

"I had gone to sleep after one of those evenings—if you can call them that—and woke in the middle of the night from a dream I hadn't had in over a decade. In it, I was a boy, maybe ten, and I was Chinese—not in fantasy, but in that dream-sense of identity that arrives without explanation. I was in a Japanese-run internment camp. Dust everywhere. Men stood in rows, heads down. No one spoke. The silence wasn't peaceful—it was devastating. The punishments weren't shown, only felt."

He paused, breathed.

"When I woke, I reached for Jim. He was there beside me, breathing quietly, turned slightly away. I didn't touch him. I just watched the rise and fall of his shoulders and realized—I don't think he withholds himself sexually to be cruel. I think he withholds it because it's the only way he knows how to remain intact."

He studied his hands, then folded them together.

"It's not that he was unwilling. It's that he was absent, in a very old way. And I think I recognized that absence long before I could name it—because it matched something I carried, too."

Silence—but not the kind that interrupted.

"This isn't about Jim or even our marriage," he said. "This is about you and me, Doctor—and it isn't your fault. What's hidden from our understanding. The lies, the lies, the lies."

"We are lying to each other," he added. "Without realizing it."

I retreated, trying not to look hurt, glad Andy could hurt me.

"I didn't mean to bark," he said. "I'll pay more attention to my dream tonight. I just wish I hadn't arranged the couples session with Jim."

He unbuckled his belt and looked at it intently.

"I'm glad you did."

∼

THE COUPLES THERAPIST, a middle-aged man with soft eyes and a clipboard he seldom consulted, let the silence settle. Andy broke it.

"I guess what I'm saying is," Andy said, leaving off the BDSM past, "it's not that we don't have sex. It's that when we do, I feel alone inside it. Like I'm reaching toward someone who's rehearsing intimacy, not experiencing it."

Jim exhaled quietly but said nothing.

"That sounds painful," the therapist said, then turned to Jim.

"Jim, when did you first learn to dissociate from sexual feelings? Or was that always there?"

Jim blinked once. "Excuse me?"

"I mean, in your childhood," the therapist continued. "Were there messages about sex, about the body, that made it hard to connect desire with safety—with love?"

Jim laughed once, dryly. "I find this line of questioning incredibly tone-deaf."

"If you want to discuss survival strategies," Jim went on, "start by not pathologizing every difference from your ideal of connection. Not every gay couple is about sex, and not every man who isn't interested in sex is broken."

The therapist froze.

"I'm going to stop you there," Jim said, "because you're implying that asexuality is damage rather than something that simply is. I'm part of an online ACE men's group—queer, intergenerational. It's for the asexual community, some are on a spectrum, some are 'gray sexual' and others are 'demisexual.' Some of us are partnered, some not. Some romantic, some aren't. We're not failed gay men who just haven't dealt with our trauma yet."

Jim gestured toward Andy. "Asexuality isn't a lack of love, intimacy, or complexity. I have a real relationship with him. It's real, even if it's different."

Jim, tall and red-haired in Brooks Brothers gray, stood with the clipped elegance of someone who knew his exits.

"This is the most I've ever said about this—and it still feels like I'm being misunderstood."

On his oxblood Oxfords, he turned—one gesture too smooth, too final—and was gone.

Andy's body locked, then pivoted toward the therapist.

"I didn't know he felt like that," Andy said.

"I need to go to him."

JIM SAT IN THE CAR, waiting, the engine idling. Andy opened the door and slid in beside him.

"Hi," he said.

"I didn't mean to—" Jim started, then stopped.

Andy waited. The air hung heavy, broken only by a distant car passing. He shifted, feeling the rough fabric of his jeans against his skin, watching shadows lengthen across the ground.

"I should've told you earlier," Jim said at last. "I've always known. I thought marriage might change something. Or maybe I just wanted to give you what you deserved. But it was built on false ground. That's why I drank. You can divorce me. I won't fight you. You deserve desire, connection—everything."

Andy pulled the engagement ring from his pocket, still wrapped in the handkerchief from Paris. He held it between them, kissed the gold oval, and placed it in Jim's hand.

"Put it on," Andy said. "Now."

Then, softer: "You're the first person I've ever felt safe enough to want forever with. Not because of sex. Because of this. Because you let me see you."

Jim broke—face collapsing, breath tearing loose. Andy leaned in, forehead to Jim's temple.

"This is forever," he whispered. "You are forever. We are forever."

ANDY COULD NOT NAME his offense. When he tried to speak, no voice emerged. His hands were bound. The punishment approached—bleeding and mutilation were promised, but the silence carried a violence of its own.

Then a familiar brown belt appeared, and he screamed.

A voice cut through the terror:

"You've been a bad boy."

"Who the fuck is that?" Andy asked.

"See the face," said Dr. G—less a person than a presence hovering at the edge of the dream.

Andy resisted. The torturer's features began to shift. The officer's outline dissolved, and in his place appeared another visage—his grandfather, Hung Hon Cheung—but no.

Having fought this truth for decades, the word rose through his throat, heavy and clarifying:

"Father."

ANDY CROSSED one leg over the other, the way he grounded himself when with the guys.

"So," he said, "I had this dream. I'm in a camp—a concentration camp. I've done something wrong, though I don't know what. I'm told they're going to torture me."

"I told Dr. G. We began tracing the dissociation back to its origin—a rupture. I left my body in Hong Kong when I was nine. What my father did couldn't be metabolized; it entered not as symbol but as noise—unprocessed, untranslatable. I withdrew, not from weakness, but because the psyche protects itself through absence."

Andy pulled a copy of an article from his folder, edges worn.

> Blum and Pfetzing, in the article, "Assaults to the Self : The Trauma of Growing Up Gay," described this exactly. They wrote, "The gay man as a child is forced to manage, on his own, at a young age, a highly complex and enormously difficult situation that meets all the criteria set out by Freud as traumatic. A dissociation results, with potent ramifications for the gay adolescent and gay man."

"I read that and froze. It wasn't only that I was abused. I had nowhere to put the experience, and no one to help me find a place for it.

"So now, Dr. G and I are not lying to each other," Andy said.

"What are you learning?" Bobby said.

For the first time, Harry and John looked terrified.

In 1970s Hong Kong, Confucian patriarchs were adapting to capital markets with leather in one hand and a savings bond in the other. My father's discipline was statecraft—an empire built on my back. He beat the gay out of me, or anything that would not serve his power. He called the belt "my good friend," and I was expected to thank him for its teachings.

There was no rebellion—only red welts and report cards, only the silence of my mother, who looked away as if shielding her own childhood from memory.

What better preparation for the global marketplace than to beat the individuality out of your son? No wonder I ran to binges in Paris. No wonder I chased men who wouldn't love me and tried to become someone I could never be.

THEN ANDY STOOD, the worn floorboards creaking under his weight. The timbre of his voice, once even, now held a tremor —a subtle break resonating in the otherwise silent room.

He unloosed his belt—this one black, nameless—and laid it gently on the floor.

"I won't tell you what happened," he said, looking not just at Bobby but through him. "I'm going to show you."

He picked up the belt—not with rage, but with precision.

Whack: the jingle of keys—warden's music.

Whack: a scream that never made it out.

Whack: then the buckle, blood, blackout. Once, an ambulance.

Even Harry, unfazed by most theater, clutched his arms and whispered, "bro."

Bobby wiped a tear and, waiting for the energy to settle, said, "Dorothy didn't get into Emerald City without the broomstick, darling."

"Shit," Harry muttered. "Then get that black belt shit back."

DEAR FATHER,

I beg your pardon for this sudden intrusion. Lately, I have been moved by certain feelings, and so I write to ask a small favor. I wonder whether you still have the leather belt you used back in the 1970s—the one you fondly referred to as your good luck belt.

With vintage leather now back in fashion, I can't help but feel a touch of nostalgia. If I could borrow that belt to wear at an upcoming meeting with a producer, it would not only serve the moment but also carry forward a sense of our family's history and inheritance.

If this request causes you any inconvenience, please forgive me. I would be deeply grateful for your understanding and assistance.

With respect,
Your eldest son,
Wai Lam

⁓

THE PACKAGE ARRIVED the following week, delivered by UPS, addressed plainly to my office, with a handwritten card.

A parting gift from a dying father to his beloved first-born—
a son too rarely home, yet never far from thought. The belt
bore not just the weight of trousers, but the unseen burden
of a man's uprightness, the dignity passed from father
to son…

Andy passed around the belt so each of us could hold it.

Bobby began to cry almost instantly—his chest heaving, breath clipped. Harry's jaw tightened, his eyes going dark—not with fear, but fury. John didn't move, his gaze fixed as if staring down a relic from some forgotten war.

Andy stood. Something had shifted in his voice.

He picked up the belt—not with rage, but with precision.

"Yo, my brothers. My name is Andy."

John and Bobby answered, softly but without hesitation: "Hello, Andy."

"I'm an alcoholic."

People snapped fingers.

"And a survivor of severe abuse."

Silence.

"And I'm on Step Four: Made a searching and fearless moral inventory of ourselves."

At that moment, Bobby rummaged through his tote, which he called Clara.

"Don't ask why," he muttered, "but I do happen to have a red pair of patent leather pumps in here."

John blinked. "Why do you have those?"

"Emergency glamour," Bobby said. "You never know when a girl's gotta walk herself home."

He placed them gently in front of Andy.

"To our Dorothy," the guys said.

Andy clicked the heels together once—tentatively, experimentally—and stopped. He looked around the room, at the faces holding him.

"Oh," he said. "I'm already here."

CANTO 8: THE GOSPEL ACCORDING TO BOBBY

"**A**ndy roasted the fuck out of us all," Harry said during the next week's check-in. "I'm scared as heck to go next."

"*Moi aussi*," Andy said.

"It will take a lifetime," John said. "To integrate what we learned with our Dorothy getting her Broom."

"I get the feeling that Dr. Glitter's is saving John to go last," Harry said. "So, it's Bobby or me—or he puts us both in the ring."

Bobby didn't look up. "Oh, so it's *Squid Game* now?"

Harry grinned. "Yeah. Only this time, we gotta save each other."

John gave a low chuckle. "Good luck with that."

Bobby registered this in the way neither men meant: The men of color were going to gang up on him.

Ezra first saw Miss Bobby Blue in a cramped Silver Lake bar, watching a Clarksdale boy who had survived the Delta, the church, the plague years, and a lifetime of shame transform bruised Southern blues into a drag performance, turning armor into beauty. He wanted—needed—to know the soul behind the glitter. But the Diva laughed in his face. "Two fat men got no chance in hell, darlin.'"

When Ezra next saw Bobby Blue five years later in a combination of AA and OA meetings, and felt charmed by how AIDS and Recovery had softened Bobby, Ezra girded his loins and introduced himself again.

"I do declare," Bobby said. "A Jewish man. Never tried Hebrew National myself but I heard it's damn near Kosher."

Ezra realized that Bobby didn't recognize him, for he too had been through years of Recovery.

"Why do I still lose my temper?" Bobby asked.

"Takes time for us wounded gays," I said, "to calm down enough to be able to notice the feelings underneath the Iceberg."

"Recovery, grief, therapy, group, fourth marriage—just what the doctor ordered."

"You now have the ability to know to use your Wise Mind, sometimes after the fact, but at least—"

"Whip out my DBT cards too late—"

"The DBT cards say what Dorothy would do," Dr. Glitter said. "Dorothy Zbornak."

Bobby smiled despite himself. "Yeah," he said. "She never panics. She pauses. Then she kills you clean."

"Why not bring Miss Dorothy to the group?" I asked. "Zbornak."

"You mean how we talk about me:

noticing my defensive reaction, two seconds before reacting;
    breathe;
    connect with the self in the body;
    touch base with underlying hurt;
    and finally
    hold the heart in the heart so it doesn't
    fly headlong into a rage.

"Exactly," I said. "Just because Ezra pushes buttons, doesn't mean you have to prove he's an idiot."

"But he is an idiot."

The doc took off his glasses.

Bobby felt sad, for a moment, as the Tarot cards told him that Doc's ex-lover was sick and dying in New York City, and Bobby feared its implications.

"DIDN'T you say we could bring in authors that are fire?" Harry asked.

I found some poetry that will show you clowns the real me—instead of *he got his parents wrapped around his finger, look at the cars he drives, his always perfectly coiffed beard and hair.* That's just a front to keep the haters intimidated so I can make my way in this racist, homophobic world—and even deal with all you posers, sitting on boatloads of cash, having no freaking idea what to do when you don't get invited to your dinner parties.

"Boy got some class issues," John said.

Bobby felt a prickle of warning he didn't yet understand—something about fathers, nicknames, and food tightening in his chest.

"We used to do show-and-tell," Bobby said. "Share pieces

we'd written or read. Glitter, why don't you bring back more of—dare I say—performing. Prince Harry has no recollection —we used to go to your performance-art space and tell our stories of trauma, before you became a ducccttahhh!"

"Performance?" Harry said, looking interested.

"Oh, darlin'," Bobby said. "Go to Franklin Furnace and you'll see footage of Dr. Glitter onstage when he was your age. Oh, you boys would've made quite the power couple—Jew, Chicano, cut, uncut. Not sure who'd be top or bottom. Maybe verse—though everyone says that."

Then, turning to Harry: "I hear you're quite the performer. I might be tempted to part with my shekels to see if the rumors about what's under that hood are true."

"You can get it for free," Harry said, lifting his shirt just an inch.

Bobby put his hands over his eyes, as if blinded by an eclipse. The others followed suit.

"Read already," Andy said.

"WELL, COOL, I GUESS, THEN," Harry said. "And I think you'll preciate how this poem seriously sums up some shit. It's called *A José, El Gordo, mi hijo* written by Carlos Justino Caballero."

Harry read softly, reverently—in Spanish first, then English:

> *A José, "El Gordo", mi hijo, en un día especial… Perdóname, hijo mío, por los silencios duros y las palabras filosas. Por haber creído que un hombre no llora, y por haberte enseñado a callar cuando dolía.*

He looked up and offered a rough translation.

A father apologizing to his son—his *El Gordo*—on a special day. Forgive me, my son, for the harsh silences and the sharp words, for believing a man must not cry, and for teaching you to stay quiet when it hurts.

"The lines," Harry said. "They capture an intimate, confessional father-to-son apology, kinda bridges masculine pride and tenderness."

"A fat son?" Bobby said—and now the room felt different.

I began to move from the therapist with his hovering attention to the person ready to hold the frame. It had been years since rage broke out and I had to watch out for the group splintering into "who was right" and "who was wrong."

"IT's FOR SURE," Harry said, perhaps starting to catch the drift. "A low-key heavy poem."

"The poet's imagery that cuts through the fat—*hands too rough for tenderness, words too sharp for love*—and he ends with a plea for forgiveness, or blessing: '*Que tu risa, hijo mío, no herede mi rabia.*' In other words: 'May your laughter, my son, not inherit my rage.'"

Bobby's head snapped up. "Inherit my rage?"

"*Not*," Harry said, in response. "Inherit."

"It's wrong to call a child fat."

"Ah," Harry said, sensing some cultural differences. "I gotcha. In my family, nicknames—*El Gordo, La Flaca, El Negro*—aren't insults."

"I think you are insulting *me*."

"What?"

"You chose this poem to call me out," Bobby said. "Fat faggot face!"

"I'm for real lost."

"You know I used to be fat, that I'm in Recovery. You would have thought twice about that poem if you didn't mean to humiliate me."

"I had no idea."

"He all over the Internet," John said.

"Drag shows, interviews—Oprah, three times," Andy filled in.

"Wrote and produced *The AIDS Gospel*." John added. "You can find it on YouTube."

And then it hit Harry. The pig's blood of history. He had stepped in it.

"Bobby," I said. "I wonder if what we have here, is that Harry did not live through the AIDS crisis that everyone here survived, by the skin of our teeth."

Flashback, Bobby Performs "The AIDS Gospel,"

Bobby rises, sequined scarf in hand, wig tossed over his shoulder. He saunters to the center, voice honeyed but unsteady. He is both preacher and penitent, in a corset.

Well, babies… Clarksdale, Mississippi. You can't swing a broom down there without hittin' a preacher or a poet. Daddy was both—a traveling pastor who laid hands on more parishioners than the Bible ever sanctioned. Mama stayed home, alone, turning her heartache into fried catfish and banana pudding. In Clarksdale we didn't have therapy—we had pie, gossip, and prayer that sometimes worked.

He chuckles; the group laughs, then falls silent as his voice lowers.

I was the only boy with three sisters, too soft for football, too shiny for church. Mama called me her 'little angel,' but the boys in town called me worse. First time I fooled around with one—behind the gym, in the Mississippi heat—it got around school by Monday. Teachers whispered. Daddy preached a sermon on Sodom that Sunday, eyes locked on me the whole time. That's when I learned shame burns cleaner than holy water.

He steps out of his shoes, barefoot on concrete.

I ran, honey. Town to town, school to school. Found my people—Black girls with big laughs and sharper tongues. They taught me rhythm, self-defense, and that a good hair flip can disarm a bully faster than a fist. Style saves souls.

He slips on the wig—a cheap pageant blonde—and poses.

Years later, I came to L.A. with a straight man. Lord, what a fool believes. He called me his 'woman' till he hit me like one. I'd serve him dinner and call it love. But drag saved me. Drag and danger. I took the bruises, turned them into glitter. Became 'Miss Bobby Blue.' Did the clubs. Did the marches. Did the funerals.

He removes the wig and holds it like a relic.
"Then the plague came."
The group stills.
"Turn it down, sugar," Bobby whispers. "Just one spot."
A single light remains.

It started like whispers. 1978, 1979—doctors in New York, L.A., San Francisco saw young men dying of rare cancers and pneumonias nobody could explain. They called it gay cancer.

June 5, 1981. CDC report: Pneumocystis pneumonia—Los Angeles. That's the official start of the plague.

Then came GRID—Gay-Related Immune Deficiency. By '82, it was AIDS. By then, the obituaries filled whole pages in *The Advocate*.

He paces.

"We took to the streets. We threw ashes on the White House lawn.

October 11, 1987—the AIDS Quilt covered the National Mall. Two thousand panels. By the next march, five thousand. ACT UP was born. *SILENCE = DEATH.* That pink triangle became our flag."

His voice softens.

"In L.A., Connie Norman—our AIDS Diva—taught us to fight and to laugh. We held candlelight vigils every night outside County–USC. Connie said, 'I'm just a woman with AIDS trying to keep people alive and honest.' She did both."

The spotlight burns his face. He doesn't flinch.

"When the HIV test came out, I took it. Waited two weeks like it was Judgment Day. When it came back positive, I didn't die—I just started waiting to.

There were no meds. No hope. No mercy."

He shakes.

"Reagan never said the word. And honey, by the time he did, half my address book was dust."

He holds the wig to his chest, trembling.

"So I joined ACT UP/LA. Chained myself to the FDA. Got arrested at the Cathedral. Lip-synced 'I Will Survive' while nuns tried to wash me away with holy water. Drag wasn't lipstick—it was armor."

He drops to one knee.

"1996—the cocktail. From dying to surviving overnight. They called it the end. But it wasn't the end.

It was the afterlife."

Bobby rises—older, heavier, glowing.

"Alonzo came then. Ran a Latin HIV nonprofit. Loved me gently. When he got sick, I cared for him at home—flowers, music, friends, morphine. When his mother showed at the funeral to claim his estate, I walked out before I burned the church down."

He exhales.

"After that, I didn't believe in heaven. I believed in paperwork. And somehow, the meds caught up. And I was still here."

A shaky laugh.

"Then came Ezra—my next mistake, or teacher. I thought if I got smaller he'd stay. But changing didn't save me. It only made me visible again.

And then I found y'all."

He pulls out the rainbow glasses.

"The Delta made me. The Blues raised me. ACT UP baptized me. And Dr. Glitter gave me better lighting."

He puts on the glasses.

Blackout.

"I'M SO SORRY," Harry said. "I didn't know."

"Know what?" Bobby snapped. "That I was obese? That I buried my ex from AIDS? Were you not here? Did you not listen?"

Harry wanted to say that Bobby often threw historical elements out as jokes or side-comments.

"I know about AIDS," he said in Spanish, tearing up. "But not enough."

Bobby laughed sharply. "You walk in like a Carlos Castaneda prophet."

"You don't know me," Harry said, jaw tight.

"You're a cock tease," Bobby snapped. "You throw a poem like a net, then vanish when someone bites. Your *orgía revolucionaria mexicana* was an Echo Park fantasy. You are *cosplaying* Harry, sir. Even your fans know this."

I intervened. John looked alarmed. Andy whispered, "Bobby."

But Bobby was gone. *Blobbie* had arrived.

Harry's chest buzzed—memories of being shamed for softness. He wanted Bobby to see him.

"You don't know how good you have it," Bobby said. "Andy's dripping, John's pretending he doesn't crave your holier-than-thou Aztlán-daddy energy, and the Doc's got goo-goo-ga-ga eyes for you. And me? I get jokes. A man at home who loves me—but it took my whole damn life to accept that. And now he won't shut up, and he sure as hell won't lie still on that extraordinarily taut belly. You, you, you have the world as your oyster."

"Bobby," I said. "Is this you, or someone else? Talk to me."

"Someone else," Andy said.

"The house gunna burn down," John said. "We are all in it."

"I never fit in," Harry murmured.

"Bullshit."

"What do I gotta do to reach you?" Harry asked. "Can't you try to see who I really am?"

"Take off your shirt," Bobby said.

"My what?" Harry asked.

"No," I said. "There will be no taking off shirts."

""Please," Bobby said, sounding more like Dorothy. "I need to face my tormentor."

I looked around the room. On the one hand, this felt entirely loaded, and, on the other, I understood the opportunity to shine light on the resentments gay men have related to the Haves and Have-Nots.

Andy and John nodded softly, telling me that we were all in this together. Such bravery.

Harry flashed the heart gesture.

"Only if we call it Empty Chair Work, and we agree that we are acting out our trauma, so we are not re-traumatizing each other."

I received a non-verbal assent from the group.

I TURNED OFF THE LIGHTS, lit a candle, checked Bobby's eyes.

Andy held the singing bowl that belonged to Harry, not knowing quite yet how to play it. John held the sage.

I set up three chairs. One empty, one for Harry, and one facing the two chairs, for Bobby.

HARRY SLIPPED OFF THE HOODIE.

His torso gleamed—thick, sculpted, lived-in, painted, disciplined.

Bobby stared.

"No!" he cried. "This can't be real!"

John murmured, "Be careful what you ask for."

Andy yelled, "Go back to Finland."

But Bobby didn't hear them.

"You mock me for being fat, a sissy, unloved, infected, a slave to others, hurt."

Harry stayed still.

"I sucked your cock after Church every Sunday. I waited on my knees for you to come. When you turned 16, you arrived with your bully friends."

"I hate you!" Bobby seethed, going back and forth from the empty chair to locking eyes with the half-naked Harry.

"Harry Enrique Rodriguez—you piece of entitled, sex-positive, superficial, cosplaying macho superior piece of shit— you are the symbol for the curse of illness I have lived with my entire life. I blame you and charge you."

Andy struck the Singing Bowl.

Bobby's head collapsed in his hands.

Harry stayed open, trembling, the air conditioning giving goose bumps.

Bobby turned away.

Harry gently extended his hands.

Bobby slowly looked in Harry's direction and then they locked eyes.

"Blobbie the Beautiful," Harry said, almost imperceptibly.

CANTO 9: JOHN'S TRAGIC ORDER

By the time it was John's turn in the hot seat, the group had begun working with psychodrama.

John and Andy began arriving early to shape the piece together. Andy would present John's history as tragedy, using classical structure—John's first intellectual language.

For Andy, exhausted by script work, it was a relief to tell a story that mattered.

JOHN WAS BORN in East Point, Georgia, in 1959, an only child whose mother disappeared into a hospital while his father remained, all sermon and storm.

When his father caught the seven-year-old wearing his dead mother's scarf, John was sent to a pastor for what was called "correction." The pastor prayed with one hand and touched him with the other. Soon afterward, John began having dreams of intrusion, violence, and betrayal, and the events followed the dreams. When the pattern became undeniable, his father declared John cursed and sent him away.

His grandmother told him that the Lord moved through certain children differently. After her death, John entered foster care, until Marion appeared, a church accountant and distant cousin who taught him how to survive without drawing attention.

When Marion died, guardianship passed to Martin Young, a public-school principal married to Jillian, a woman who loved John as her own. When John spoke of seeing events before they occurred, Martin identified the experience as Christ speaking.

Martin died in 1994, after John visited him in the hospital and asked whether he had AIDS. John, now a lawyer, arranged the funeral and executed the will.

John advanced through Morehouse College and Howard Law School, teaching at Emory before relocating to Los Angeles, where he founded a preeminent firm.

Love arrived in the form of Carter, a dancer with the Alvin Ailey Company, whose tenderness offered John his first peace.

ANDY (LOWERING THE PAGES):

When John read Plato at Morehouse, he recognized the divinatory voice as what Socrates called the *daimonion*, a presence that warned him of danger and directed his actions with unsettling precision. It was the first time John had a language for what had been speaking to him all along.

When John later entered Hollywood, the daimon shifted from oracle to strategist, advising him when to charm, when to retreat, and when to outmaneuver the white men plotting behind his back. John learned to listen to the voice, but he listened with arrogance rather than humility.

Like Creon, he now stood under order to descend into the underworld in search of Antigone.

ANDY (AS CHORUS, to the room):

In Sophocles' *Antigone*, Antigone defies Creon, placing love and duty to the dead above the laws of men. She becomes the emblem of moral resistance, insisting that she was born for love rather than hatred.

CHORUS (ANDY, Bobby, Harry): Grief teaches the steadiest minds to waver.

ANDY: Like Creon, John built his life around mastery, image, masculine steadiness—believing tightly managed order could postpone the reckoning with grief and love.

CHORUS: The tragedy is not that order fails, but that order denies vulnerability—and with it, truth.

CREON (HARRY READING): The man the city places in authority must be obeyed—in small things and in just.

ANDY (NARRATOR):

Picture a modern, sun-splashed Los Angeles home,

polished surfaces catching the afternoon light, the faint scent of lavender in the air.

BOBBY (AS NARRATOR 2): Enter Josiah—forty. Assistant. Fixer. Bodyguard. Man Friday. Ten years in John's service. Married, two children. Black like John, street-smart yet soft-spoken. He runs the back end of John's life with military-grade precision.

ANDY (AS NARRATOR): Enter Carter Smith—thirty-eight. Part Botticelli angel, part boy-band escapee. Former Alvin Ailey dancer, now a successful choreographer. Married to John for five years, together for ten. Disarmingly femme, sad-eyed, coiffed facial hair. He manages the home, the gossip, the help, the finances, the properties, the parties.

JOHN (AS HIMSELF): Carter dressed elegantly—linen shirts, slim trousers, silver and gold necklaces I bought him. Bergamot always. Always reaching for me—tidying me, kissing me, providing sexual heat when I was, that is, in town.

ANDY (AS NARRATOR): A storm began over the Gulf Coast. Lightning flashed.

Flights to Dallas were canceled. During a layover in Phoenix, John booked a return flight to Los Angeles—two hours. He couldn't reach Josiah. The housekeeper's GPS said she'd left early. Neither Carter nor Josiah answered.

BOBBY (AS NARRATOR): John arrived home exhausted and unannounced.

· · ·

ANDY: The living room looked wrong—cluttered, unfamiliar. Candles burned. A hint of cannabis drifted from the master bedroom.

JOHN: The room tilted. A flash—fourteen years old. My father's boot on the bed. The belt cutting air. Atlanta streetlights. A burrito scavenged behind a gas station. He paused before opening the door.

ANDY: John heard voices from the bedroom. His bedroom.

HARRY (AS CARTER): I shouldn't have done this. I shouldn't have crossed that line. He trusted me. He trusted us.

BOBBY (AS JOSIAH): But I see you as he doesn't. John can't see anything but the next deal.

HARRY (AS CARTER): Don't say his name.

BOBBY (AS JOSIAH): But, baby.

HARRY (AS CARTER): Don't baby me—

· · ·

Bobby (as Josiah): I thought you had given yourself to me. I don't know what that makes us.

Harry (as Carter): It makes you stupid. Hand me that napkin.

Bobby (as Josiah): Let me wipe it off. I put it on.

Harry (as Carter): I need you to leave. No, don't touch me. (Raising his voice). Get the hell out of my house. Do not sully my abode again. And do not—ever—explain my gender to me. You have no standing. Now, go!

Andy: Josiah left but not before knocking over some glassware and what sounded like a wine bottle. This led Carter to scream—

Harry (as Carter): Our bed sheets. I bought those in Italy.

John: I ducked into a side closet so I would not be detected. As I waited, in shock, I heard Carter's cries.

Harry (as Carter): Johnnie, Johnnie. What have we done?

John hid in a side closet, afraid to be seen, afraid to leave, afraid Carter—who had his own sixth sense—would feel him watching. They had rules. Sex out of town was fine. No one entered the house. No one crossed that line. The mystery sickened him. When Carter finally cried himself to sleep, John slipped out into the rain, walked six blocks to a 7-Eleven, battery at five percent, and called an Uber.

JOHN: Waiting in a Chipotle, John typed a note to HR:

> Josiah Washington — employment
> terminated effective immediately.

Andy: In the Uber, John redirected the driver—not home, but Cedars-Sinai. When the driver protested that the app needed updating, John—empty, shaking—said, "If I die in this fucking Uber, I will kill you."

The cardiologist ruled out a full infarction. They called it stress-induced cardiomyopathy—a shock of the heart, not the arteries.

Takotsubo. The broken-heart syndrome.

CANTO 10: THE KING OF THE UNDERWORLD

After the wreck of love, John stood amid the ruins of his empire, undone not by scandal or spectacle but by accumulation, the wealth and status he had gathered since law and business school slipping from his hands like ash, leaving behind a body slowed by illness, days organized around damage control, relationships reduced to history and liability.

I will say unto God, Do not condemn me; show me wherefore thou contendest with me.

It was Carter who washed John's hair, fed John broth, and whispered, "Stay in this world with me, honey," performing the small domestic rituals that dismantled John's fantasy of disappearing without consequence.

"Why am I crying like a woman?" John asked.

"You're crying like a human being, sweetie," Carter replied, "or, if you really need a modifier, like a gay man, and while we're here, boo-boo, your sexism is showing and it does not go with your blouse."

John sat up and drank the broth.

"Remember," Carter said, adjusting the blanket with the practiced intimacy of someone who knows where everything belongs, "we went to see a doctor because we'd become business partners who no longer knew how to mix intimacy with success, or wanted to."

"Yes," John said. "He helped us come to terms with what we could salvage."

"So why did you stop going once the couples counseling ended?" Carter continued, with a tone calm, affectionate, and unyielding. "I kept going, honey, to Dr. Lauren, to find myself—you didn't—and that was the moment I had to decide whether I was simply losing respect for you, or whether I needed to be actively worried about you, or whether, as the saying goes, I needed to 'let you.'"

"And which did you decide?" John asked.

"The jury's still out, silly boy," Carter said, lifting the empty bowl and dotting John's lips with the corner of the bib.

"Now drink your soup before it turns into gruel, because I will not be married to a man who dies of stubbornness and bad timing."

As Carter moved toward the door, John reached out and caught Carter's hand, holding it with a different touch.

"There's something I need to ask you," he said. "A secret I've kept."

Carter turned back, eyebrows lifting just enough to signal concern without panic. "All right, boo."

"Would you be upset if I left the Industry?" John asked.

I hate what I do. The lawyering—deals, actors, agents, all of it. I used to want to be—sounds crazy now—a scholar, or even a professor of the classics, before I sacrificed that to be **a** person who makes money for myself and others. Now my inner voice—what's left of it—keeps telling me to change, to reconnect with who I might have been.

Carter walked over to the window overlooking their garden, relieved and yet suspicious, noting where the rosemary and thyme, once hardy, had begun to brown, before saying, without turning around,

"Look at the herbs. They don't seem to thrive so well here anymore."

Within days, John cast himself upon Dr. G's couch—not to audition for a role but to undo one.

"Can I see you more than once-a-week?" he asked. "Three? Four?"

"That would be psychoanalysis," I said, "which might, in fact, be good for you. I could refer you to a good gay analyst I know in Hollywood, complete with the full apparatus—"

"You have a couch."

"—but if you'd like to continue our work, we can certainly meet more than once a week."

"How could I not have seen all this coming? That I was blind to my affairs?"

His eyes landed on the Sophocles volume on my shelves.

"I always wanted to stage Greek theater," he said.

"I get the impression you might be living it."

"You sound like Carter."

"Carter," I said, with awe and delight.

"I've always had a gift," he clarified, "for hearing a voice of reason that told me things I didn't want to hear—but that led me into enormous success. Why didn't it speak to me about the mistake I was making?"

"Which mistake?"

"That I was an invisible man—not to others, but to myself."

"You're leaving out systemic racism, homophobia, trans-phobia, child abuse."

"You see," John added, "I've been blinded—but unlike Oedipus, I haven't seen my dirty deed yet."

"Because you didn't fuck your mother and murder your father?"

"Yes," he said. "Or am I missing something?"

"The dream you told me about," I said. "Turning your back on a Black homeless person—and instead getting on your knees to suck a white man's cock?"

It's funny with dreams," John said. "It's only when you hear them laid out—by someone who isn't you—that the obvious but hidden symbolism pokes your eyes out."

"Or gives them back."

JOHN RETIRED from the company quietly. His partners thanked him with catered sandwiches, folded napkins, young associates calling him "sir," as though he were already gone.

The weight came off through an inability to stomach food, and a renewed interest in running—the only practice that quieted his mind. Agents and actors he'd known for three decades passed him on the Santa Monica Promenade.

"I am invisible," he said, "not because I am unseen, but because people refuse to see me."

"How do you mean?"

"They can see through the lies—that I am a failure, and that whatever I touched turned to shit."

"That voice," I said, "doesn't sound like you."

"It is," he replied. "Who else could it be?"

"Tell me about your father."

He paused, then smiled faintly. "Before I do," he said, "I hear you run a group for gay men."

"Are you interested?"

"I need a place to be with my peers."

Two years later, Harry would say the same thing.

I WAITED until anyone who had dealings with John had left the group. Bobby and Andy, who had never met him, expected a sharp suit, a pocket square, a bow tie—a touch of Old South rigor wrapped around Hollywood power.

Instead, John walked in tall, thin, greying, looking every bit his sixty-five years, wearing one of Carter's forgotten hoodies, sunglasses pulled low like curtains in a house of mourning.

"Well look at God," Bobby murmured, fanning himself with the folder in his lap. "If this isn't the ghost of a great man returning from the wars."

"We have heard about you, darlin'," he continued. "Ezra Pound—my husband, by the way—called you, well, being a Christian woman, I shan't."

John lowered his sunglasses just enough to reveal one fiercely unimpressed eye.

"Well now," John said. "I heard about you too, darlin'."

Bobby's fan froze mid-air. "Oh?"

"That you think you're Bette Davis when you're really Debbie Reynolds."

And so began a match—or, as Ezra would later put it, a *shiddoch*—made in heaven.

The group helped John speak about Carter, and one trans member shared experiences that loosened something he had never let himself name. Andy nicknamed him Jobbie John.

When medication came up, John straightened slightly.

"Before we try drugs," he said, "let's give this journey toward Dagobah a chance."

"Amen, Master Yoda," Bobby said.

"The Yoda," Andy added, "who teaches Luke how to lift a whole ship with his mind."

"Which doesn't mean," Bobby said, "you can't come in here and just cry."

A YEAR after the heart attack, Harry arrived. Everyone noticed the change.

"The man practically sat up like someone had poured Pentecostal fire down his spine," Bobby noted.

John played down the teasing in group, yes, but—

"He's the person I wish I could have been," John said, holding his forehead as if the confession itself were a migraine. "I've been in agony over this… this 'Harry crush.'"

"He's the child of your hard work," I said. "The being who came alive because you lived as Dante."

"I didn't do anything, Virgil."

"Oh, you did more than you imagine."

"I have a secret."

"Yes."

"I'm kind of hung up on him."

"Really?"

"The same way I used to be with Carter. And that turned out to be a tragedy."

"Why tragedy?"

"I could have salvaged my marriage."

John broke down. "Maybe I'm cursed. Maybe I'm not built for comedy. Maybe I'm a tragedy man."

The man who once enforced the law was learning how to suffer it.

"I'm not trying to yank you out of this depression," I said, "because I think it's cooking you into a new kind of person. But I also think Carter's giving you signals that—"

"I need to let her go," John said. "And until I met Harry, I didn't know."

"About Harry?"

"I know it's just transference, nothing to really write home about."

Acknowledging what John had said threw me.

Treating the attraction as just "transference" meant either John was working psychologically or he was saying the right thing.

"He may not know this," John said, "but he's given me back my will to live."

"He turned on the 'healing' switch inside of you."

"He mustn't know this."

"You speak like it's a crime."

"I can see more clearly now. The rain is gone."

"Ah," I said. "The camp John returns."

"It's not necessary I act out these romantic feelings," John said. "That's not what I want. I do not need another relationship to mess up. Once you get in that shit, it's hard to get out. I need to grieve the one that worked when it did and stopped working when it didn't, and find myself."

JOHN COOKED braised salmon in butter and basil sauce—and set the table with wine and candles, and a cheap Target linen cloth Carter had ordered.

As Carter entered the door and saw the scene, he took a quick inhale. Having spoken honestly about some things, such as business, better than others, such as what they really wanted, Carter took their seat at the table.

After the meal, and the chit-chat that could not cut through the tension, Carter cut to the chase.

"When did we stop being husband and wife?" Carter

asked, as the two often referred to each other with mixed genders.

"When I did not want children," John answered. "I noticed you withdrew your affection."

"Perceptive man."

"It's one of many things I said and did without taking you into account."

"There are others?"

"I want to ask you a question I've been meaning to ask you for the last year, because I've had some dreams."

"When you dream, world, watch out—the Oracle has spoken."

"In my dream, you and Josiah—you had, I think, um—"

"An affair?" Carter said, clearing their throat.

"The daimon saw a version of you that I had blinded my eyes to."

"The Oracle should have told you he was a lying sack of shit who was stealing business from you—excuse my French, my boo."

"You tried to warn me."

"He took some liberties when you were in Dallas. Don't look so surprised. Right before your heart attack. I chased him out of the house."

"Liberties taken for the sake of liberty."

Carter stood up quickly, as if wracked by a terrible omen, or the fear of a big change.

"What happened to our linen tablecloth?" John asked.

"They got stained—out with the old, in with the new."

"I didn't listen," John said. "I didn't support the transition."

"No, you didn't. But you are now."

"I could never have anything with anyone else," John said.

"Never say never," Carter said, drying bleary eyes. "We

were never meant to be each other's final form, but each other's bridge."

"This divorce will be a bitch. We are in each other's asses financially."

"Fear not, Papa," Carter said. "I've consulted the best lawyer in town. Almost better than you."

John looked at the wine, then at the cheap linen.

"Of course you did."

He poured, spilling a little on the tablecloth.

And they clinked glasses.

IN THE FOLLOWING WEEKS, John posed this question to me: "What would the monks have done with my Harry problem?"

"How do you mean?"

"When you lust after a person but know it's wrong to pursue those feelings. You don't want to push those feelings down, but neither do you want to announce to the world something that will destroy everyone."

"Wow," I said, aware that this was the question of a new eon.

"I can't be the only person with this conundrum," John said. "I'm sure some philosopher—actually, I recollect Socrates in Plato—didn't he talk about this?"

"Do you dream?" I asked.

"I think I do," he said, "but I rarely remember."

"Keep your phone nearby and use the Voice Memo."

"Doctor, I barely use my phone now. It disgusts me."

"Buy a journal," I said. "And first thing upon waking, either record the dream or scribble it down in the dark."

"I bought one yesterday—how about that?"

"Start with an invitation. Ask a dream to come. Pose a question before sleep. And when you wake—don't go back to sleep. Turn on the light. The unconscious will answer your question about Harry."

JOHN DREAMED of abandoned buildings in the American South—weather-beaten shacks, paint peeling like skin, roofs sagging under time.

Then a meadow opened—lush, suspended. A rabbit darted, a deer met his gaze with incomprehensible patience. Then a lamb—soft, white, pure.

Carter's face flickered. Martin's voice echoed. His mother's song faded. His father, never a fisherman, threw a line. Harry appeared as a wounded, limping figure emerged—a former king from the savannah, seated on a fallen throne, robes torn, eyes weary.

"It seems like the King Dream isn't just personal to me," John said.

He read Jung. We talked about archetypes—images that shock a person, inborn patterns of meaning and behavior millions of years old—and complexes, the stories that form around archetypes: the Mother complex, the Gay Hero, the Gay Trickster, the Gay Shadow.

"So he's a King with a capital 'K,'" John mused. "Or maybe a capital 'G,' as in Gangster—or as in Gay. Now that's a queer kind of King."

Not knowing who put these words in my mouth, I said, "A GQ King."

"So what do I do with this archetype of the collective unconscious?" John asked.

"Ask him," I said.

"Huh?"

"It's a technique Jung developed. He actually called it the 'new dispensation'—a post-religion theory of change." I mentioned books he could go to: *Jung's Memories, Dreams, Reflections*, and Robert Johnson's *Inner Work*.

That night, John bought the books. The next nights, he read them. Then, one evening, he lit a candle. He took out his journal and conducted a dialogue.

"Who are you, friend or foe?"

"What do you think?"

"Friend?"

"Who else holds you during the night?"

"What do you want?"

"What do you want?"

"Love."

"I am your other half. I want the same thing as you."

"Why do you sometimes turn away?"

"Why do you sometimes turn away?"

"Why did you take so long to come to me?"

"Let's not keep playing this game."

"How long have you been here?"

"Since before He said 'Let there be light.'"

"Are you Jesus?"

"Don't talk down to me."

"Are you spirit or are you flesh?"

"Why either/or? Why not both/and."

CANTO 11: CRACKING EGGS

These private dialogues—often unfolding during private devotions, with Twitter as an unlikely accomplice—returned John to the spiritual vocation that had stalked him his entire life, the one he'd kept at bay until his heart attack opened him to the place in the heart where Lust and Love—quite literally—come together.

He had discovered in his dialogues a series of men who represented his Mr. Right, and when he spoke to them about his needs, they spoke back—first in a mean way, like the Pastor, but eventually like a Special Beloved, ancient in origin, who was there in bed and in even more banal places.

"I like a theology that multitasks," he said. "Killing two birds with one JO session."

"Killing—or living?"

He smirked. "Depends who's writing the doctrine."

"Who is writing the doctrine?"

"A figure did emerge who brought all the hotness together. He said he was King of the Underworld. I knighted him Malik, after my middle name."

Then, more sharply: "Why hasn't anyone written about this?"

"You could."

He shook his head. "The lawyer in me doesn't want proof."

"Proof of what?"

"The Active Imagination woo-woo you got me started with," John said.

"Woo-woo?"

"Got me to look at reality."

"Oh."

"It's not Harry I'm in love with," John said, "whatever love means."

"Oh."

"Has nothing to do with him."

"Really."

"I'm angry," he said.

"At whom?"

"Oh, not you. And not so much me—but yes, me. I'm angry at all of us, John and Andy and the gay community."

"For what?"

"For what we are doing to Harry."

"We are eggheads."

THE NEXT DAY, the eggs were cracked—but so carefully that what got scrambled had nary a hint of shell.

At check-in, John said he'd had a breakthrough in his inner work, having to do with what he called "the problem of falling in love with men simply because they are exquisitely beautiful—warm, inviting, and devastatingly sexy. And how unfair that is to them."

"You mean Harry," Bobby said, pulling out his knitting.

"He seems to have worked better for your Dantesque wallowing in hellfire than Prozac, doll."

"Since Harry arrived," Andy agreed, "John is, as they say in France, *il a fait sa mue*."

Harry watched, skeptical but curious. John did look more solid, less hollow. His molting body had filled out from regular exercise, the El Greco gauntness giving way to a healthier placidity.

"Be that as it may," John said, faintly irritated by the amateur diagnostics. "What I'm saying is that we all need to stop turning Harry into an idol."

Andy worried his hoodie strings; Bobby slouched further into leisure; Harry remained unreadable, lashes lowered.

"I'm not ready to let go," Andy whined.

"What's wrong with a little crush?" Bobby asked. "I've had enduring crushes on all of you. Never needed Active Imagination for it—the matter felt divinely tidy."

John told them that in his dreams and active imagination he'd been engaging a figure—strong, erotic, fierce.

Harry kept his eyes on his notepad, pretending to write.

"What my psyche produced," John said evenly, "predates Harry."

John's speech gathered steam.

"Making wounded gay men into idols is a sickness. It's not fair to them or to us. It makes us vampires. Lonely. I'm sick of it. My descent gave me a new perspective. Without a psychology—without active imagination—gay boys have no option but to keep chasing Harry look-alikes on Grindr, handing over the keys to the Kingdom without realizing they're projecting their own inner gay King. The Greeks called this homo-love—being struck by a god. The god Eros."

Bobby's needles froze mid-loop; Andy cried tears of loss.

Harry looked up, eyes briefly unguarded. "Don't cry. I'm not dead yet."

"It's not funny," Bobby said, trying to be funny.

Harry exhaled. "Look—I flex and clown. I know I'm Mr. Hot Shit. But Doctor John's not wrong."

He shifted in his seat. "I'm not gonna lie—I feel trapped a lot. I crave attention, then it's always the wrong kind. The boys want me to dominate them, turn them into bitch bottoms —car bros especially, after meets, drunk and reckless. I dealt with the endless 'here's some candy, little boy' Snapchats by treating it all as bullshit. No cap, I've kind of given up on sex. I can't come anymore when I'm with someone."

"You don't come with anyone?" Bobby asked.

"Did we just hear this right?" John asked.

"For how long?" Andy asked.

"That's a big revelation," Dr. Glitter said gently.

"I can only when I'm by myself," Harry said, sad boy.

"That's why Gloria and I built *el Garaje de la Ascensión*," Harry went on. "I use the idol thing to get people in the door, help the clowns, then give them an experience."

"Because I've given up on my needs, I've dedicated my lame ass to helping others with their bullshit."

Harry stretched, his gold G ring catching the light, still unable, after all this time, to flex.

"So I guess I'm relieved John's not after my fat ass. Where's my fuckin' shot glass? Let's drink to that. Oh—sorry, Andy. Sorry, Bobby."

Bobby snapped open his fan.

"Enough Dante, enough shadow work. We are gay men— sorry, Harry—Gay, Gay, Gay! You tried to bait me with Bi, Bi, Bi, but I've never once heard you mention a member of the Second Sex. I rest my queeny case."

He looked around.

"Remember why we started: to make art. Going through Hell should make us better artists, not lonely monks praying to a King instead of—well—kissing Harry's cock—I mean, ring."

"Language," Andy said.

"Platonically speaking," John added, "I see no problem in kissing Harry's ring—preferably the one on his finger—if it helps us get in touch with our own inner beloved."

At that moment, Harry extended his ring finger.

"All this Plato shit is moot if I don't get my ring," he said. "Not on my cock, homie—but on my pretty little CC ring finger. Ringie, ringie ring."

Everyone laughed, including Harry—

until he stopped.

PROGRESS NOTES FOR INFERNO

Following the session in which John spoke openly about projection, idealization, and restraint, the group began to confront the question of what could contain the work going forward.

My impending absence from Los Angeles to address chosen and biological family illnesses required us to name what had already been quietly shifting: the group was pressing against the limits of a traditional therapeutic frame.

"And we also know that you are probably leaving Los Angeles for a few months," Bobby said. "How's Peninah?" he asked, referring to my mother.

Harry looked sad.

"But you're not going to abandon us?" Andy asked.

I reassured them that individual work would continue, even at the same frequency, and that Zoom—while imperfect —would allow for continuity. Still, it was quickly agreed that the shared presence of the group room could not be replicated onscreen.

Rather than interpret this moment as a loss, we reminded

ourselves of why the group had begun in the first place: as a place for queer men to think, feel, and make art about being gay that the Industry would not touch—an impulse that had been dormant, not extinguished.

There would be a few weeks, here and there, when I would have to travel, so the group would not meet for about a month in December, during the holidays.

"I wonder," John said, "if that would be a time for us to get together and return to our roots—as a group of Hollywood creatives who need an outlet that's not Hollywood in which to create."

I liked the idea, but I also felt nervous. Yes, we had been through a lot over the last year, and people had grown enormously, but the intensity between Harry and John—and some unresolved tension between Bobby and Andy—gave me pause.

"Maybe if you had a focus," I said. "In the old days, we'd read together."

What emerged over the next weeks was John and Andy's proposal to engage collectively with literature—not as public performance and not as therapy disguised as theater, but as a structured, time-limited inquiry into love, desire, power, and projection.

"I'd love for us to start with the Greeks," John said.

"Plato shit," Harry added. "Boring. Euro-centric."

"The Symposium," John said. "It's actually written about you."

"Alcibiades!" Andy said.

"Abcil—who the fuck?"

"Stop playing like a dumb broad," Bobby said. "You probably read that witty little drama in Greek."

"Spanish," Harry said.

∽

THE DISTINCTION between reading and performance was left intentionally unresolved. We agreed on clear boundaries: no staged production, no audience, no confusion of roles. The work would remain therapeutic, consent-based, and provisional, with individual sessions continuing alongside one final in-person group devoted to processing the change in frame and the anxieties stirred by working together outside of it.

The idea of conducting full group therapy on Zoom appealed to no one.

This could work as a transitional arrangement: a way of collaborating on a gay art project while I tended to essential relationships in New York, testing the men's mettle and giving me room, quietly, to begin addressing the intrigue they had already set in motion but no one yet dared bring into language.

"I can see Dr. G looks a bit anxious," Andy said. "But you'll hear everything in our individual sessions."

I mentioned that I wouldn't be leaving until mid-December. "So start after the holidays?"

"Why not *during* the holidays?" Andy asked.

"Yeah," Harry added. "Give me an excuse to bag out of *La Familia* and some boring sex parties."

"Last thing I need is to wallow in my depression," John said.

"Ezra will drive me nuts with his latkes," Bobby added. "For eight days!"

"So you guys want to start the week of Christmas?" I asked, disbelieving.

"Fuck Jingle Bells," Harry said.

ACT II — RECITARE

The men stage a queer remix of Plato's *Symposium*—and accidentally expose their own desires.

CANTO 12: ENTERING
THE ANDRON

What follows is a summary of everyone's notes and sessions with me. I did my best to create a sense of a cohesive whole, even though the rehearsals were not so linear.

It's worth remembering that Plato's *Symposium* is itself a relay of memory and distortion—Apollodorus recounting Aristodemus's recollections long after the fact, colored by prestige, desire, and rivalry.

What survives is not transcript but oral history.

THE NEXT WEEK the guys arrived almost in method-acting mode, armed with props: the Penguin and Oxford translations of *The Symposium*, printouts, notebooks, coffee—even a small bust of Socrates that John had ordered from a Greek boutique he had once visited with Carter in more halcyon days.

Bobby had found a photo of Alcibiades and created a

collage that he had framed and set up next to the Socrates icon.

Harry came with his own playlist, which included: "Soy 18 with a Bullet," by Spanish Fly.

The air carried that charged stillness particular to beginnings—and a DJ war between Anita Ward and Lil Rob.

ANDY SET a bowl of black grapes on the low table because it felt right—a small gesture toward an older conversation and a safer substitute for wine, given Bobby's and Andy's recovery.

"These fruits are fire," he said. "Taste like what I imagine Andy's titties taste like."

The laughter cracked the air open.

"Somehow," Andy said, "this man says words that are crude but land almost prudish—he pushes, but never far enough that Dr. Glitter would disapprove."

"What would our dalliance with the classics amount to," Bobby surmised, "without Brujo Baby giving us a thrill? But let's not burden the poor lad with the weight of being Falstaff."

"Wrong book," Andy said.

"If sack and sugar be a fault, God help the wicked," Harry said, already half-performing.

"What did you *not* play in?" Bobby asked.

Bobby pulled out his boombox. *Do Ya Think I'm Sexy* filled the room. Harry got up to dance with him.

"Dr. G would say," Andy interrupted, "let's hold off on the touching for a while."

But having no interest in making Andy cross, Harry took a seat.

AGREEING to have Andy organize the agenda, they sat like "good boys and girls," as John put it, receiving Andy's color-coded binders. And to be sure, what had been their therapy room now shimmered into a slightly different modality. Lamps dimmed; chairs were pushed against the wall; the space stretched wider than it had any right to.

The ambience of the Greek aristocratic *andron*—the men's gathering room of ancient Greece for elites, artists, and philosophers—hovered as both fantasy and field experiment. Ikea couches replaced marble benches; a ring of folding chairs became, somehow, symposium couches.

They had all read *The Symposium*, cover to cover, and listened to a rather campy version I'd sent from Audible.

"Now if a white person had suggested Plato," Andy added, "I'm not so sure I'd be down."

Bobby blinked, then tilted his head. "Why's everything gotta come down to race?" he asked, his drawl half-playful, half-earnest, deciding not to involve Dr. Glitter, who was Jewish.

"Bear with me," Andy said. "I'm moving from being a Model Minority to an angry person of color."

"People of all cultures should be assigned this shit," Harry said. "Yeah, it's fucked up how they treat women, and the pederastic thing doesn't give us homos today such a good look, you feel me—so you need the POC lens, but don't throw the baby—"

Even Bobby had to clap at the clarity of the articulation.

"But," Harry added, "in the hands of a non-gay or white Karen—like my dumb-ass professor—you could miss that these Athenians are all flamers. Ain't no pussy lovers in this dialogue, no sirree Bob."

Bobby jumped up, dropping his knitting to the floor, clapping his hands together as if he were at a Mariah Carey concert.

"Harry is a Gay, Gay, Gay man, after all! Never doubt Mother's intuition!"

"Call me whatever the fuck you want," Harry said. "But call me."

ANDY THOUGHT we should name the main players. Bobby countered with sound. Harry stole crayons from Clara. John moaned, but, with Andy's help, compiled the below:

Queer Plato Remix Music Play Collage

SLIDE: Phaedrus rising rhetorician.
Love as the oldest of gods, source of courage and virtue.
The boy who wants to sound wise and almost manages it.
The first toast belongs to the idealist.
Cue: **"Macho Man"**

SLIDE: Pausanias— lawyer, lover of Agathon.
Two Loves: Common and Heavenly.
The former grooms boys for babies and money;
the latter grows souls in each other.
Cue: **"More Than a Woman"**

SLIDE: Eryximachus— physician.
Love as cosmic doctor, balancing humors, planets, and passions.
The kind of man who thinks desire can be charted.
Cue: **"Love's Theme"**

· · ·

SLIDE: Aristophanes—comic playwright.
Love as myth of the round beings, split in half,
rolling through the world in search of reunion.
He turns pain into punch line, loss into laughter,
theology into stand-up.
Cue: **"Ring My Bell"**

SLIDE: Agathon—newly crowned tragedian and host of the
party.
Love as youth, symmetry, perfume, and performance—
the kind of beauty that makes intellect look overdressed.
Cue: **"Do Ya Think I'm Sexy"**

SLIDE: Socrates—philosopher, barefoot and penniless, yet
desired above all.
Love as daimon: spirit climbing from flesh to form,
from form to truth, from truth to Beauty itself.
His poverty makes him magnetic.
His abstinence makes him dangerous.
Cue: **"Don't Leave Me This Way"**

SLIDE: Diotima—the priestess who never appears,
speaking only through Socrates.
She carries the teaching he can't quite own:
that love is born of lack, lives by inventing,
and procreates in spirit rather than flesh.
Cue: **"I Will Survive"**

· · ·

SLIDE: Alcibiades— general, notorious beauty.
He crashes the banquet drunk,
confesses unrequited passion for Socrates.
He is both the hangover
and the proof that even divine love wants a body.
Cue: **"Born to Be Alive"**

MARGIN NOTES (SCRAWLED Later by Andy)

Disco is not decoration. It is collective eros. Philosophy without bodies lies. Performance reveals what interpretation hides. Alcibiades is not an example—he is an event. If Socrates is the ladder, Alcibiades is the rung that snaps.

CANTO 13: BOBBIFYING
THE SYMPOSIUM

"Bobby had a hard time realizing he was not the only actress among us," John told me in his download. "When Harry recited his lines in Spanish, English, and a dash of Greek, Bobby melted like Margaret Hamilton."

"How did you calm Bobby's tempest?" I asked. "Don't tell me—you gave him full artistic control."

"Despite what some of us say," John said, "you were not born yesterday."

"So now Andy must consult when making syllabus changes? And what else?"

"We gave Bobby full reign in casting?"

"What?"

"It's okay, Doc. There's only four of us, and Bobby may need a bit of correction every now and then, but he's not BPD. DB comes through as a last resort."

John shared the slides with me over Zoom.

∽

SLIDE 1: Plato (c. 428–348 BCE). Student of Socrates, teacher of Aristotle. Wrote in dialogue. *The Symposium* stages a drinking party where speech becomes revelation.

Bobby, looking happy as a lark, arrived to rehearsal before anyone, trailing Clara, his bewitched duffel. Out came fabric, beads, gold lamé, scissors, glue pens, and a rhinestoned tape measure he swore could detect hypocrisy to the eighth of an inch. He put on "More Than a Woman."

SLIDE 2: The Setting.

Agathon's house, celebrating his first big theatrical win. Philosophers, poets, physicians, and the notorious Alcibiades gather to praise Eros, god of love.

Harry arrived next, and that's when Bobby made his first costume changes, draping him in a makeshift toga that Bobby sewed to expose his arm tattoos, but nothing else. Harry, being Harry, lit what he swore was Blue Lotus and took a drag while Bobby waved the smoke like Glinda clearing a tornado.

"Pooh! What a smell of sulfur."

Then Bobby had the idea that this "smoke" could give the group the feeling of something otherworldly. To John, Bobby seemed a bit too happy, and he and Andy exchanged looks.

SLIDE 3: Agathon — The Host.

Young, handsome, newly crowned, the latest of Socrates' philosophical crushes.

As John explained it, he arrived last, setting a small

Turkish journal with gilt edges on the table, then a photo collage of Malik.

SLIDE 4: Some of These Speeches Still Bring the House Down.

BOBBY HAD BROUGHT in bean chairs to be turned into the couches that would adorn the *andron*—the men's room of ancient Greece—as it seemed to materialize

SLIDE 5: Comedy or Tragedy?

BOBBY LIT up at the Aristophanes slide. Assigning himself the Aristophanes speech, he proceeded to rhapsodize:

"ARISTOPHANES'S SPEECH is the one we remember the most— the myth of the round beings cut in half. We used to be double-bodied, rolling in bliss till Zeus sliced us apart. Ever since, we've been looking for our missing piece. That's love. Not Hallmark. And the first humans? Male-male, female-female, mixed. No heteros! Amen!"

THE DIVA BUILT A LITERAL STAGE, comprised of three cardboard cutouts of Siamese twins: male-male halves, female-female halves, and male-female halves

SLIDE 6: Pausanias — Two Loves.

Bobby assigned Pausanias to Andy—"for this is the most crucial intellectual point." Andy gladly accepted his role and told us, briefly, why:

"Common Aphrodite gives us babies and property. Heavenly Aphrodite gives us soul-making. She's the first queer theologian—older, purer, born of Uranus alone. She makes love between men sacred, not sinful.

SLIDE 7: Alcibiades and the Unruly Heart.

Bobby and Harry had a bit of a tussle over why Bobby thought Harry should play Alcibiades rather than anyone else.

"You are type-casting me," Harry declared.

"You are going to ask John to play the drunk general," Bobby reasoned.

To coax Harry's cooperation, Bobby had sewn him a toga of unbleached linen threaded with gold, cut asymmetrically to bare one shoulder and fall low at the hip. It hung loose and imperfect, catching the light when he moved and refusing to stay entirely in place. Harry paced, fully in it now.

"Occupy your role, Thespian," Bobby said, letting Harry know that Bobby could now see what a profoundly good actor Harry was, by virtue of his having been well read by people and by books.

"People act like Alcibiades is comic relief," Harry said, accepting the crown Bobby placed on his head. "But he's the truth bomb. He crashes the party drunk and says what no philosopher dares: love isn't a ladder; it's a breakdown. It's a confession that could start a revolution."

Then John sped through the rest of the slides, as our time was running out.

~

SLIDE 8: From Athens to Christendom. ("Like a Prayer" — Madonna.)

Monasteries keeping desire alive under God's nose.

SLIDE 9: Muslim Scholars and the Dark Youth. ("Rock the Casbah" — The Clash.)

Love reborn as mysticism, poetry, danger.

SLIDE 10: Sor Juana and Sacred Eros. ("Don't Leave Me This Way" — Thelma Houston.)

A nun reworking Diotima in New Spain.

SLIDE 11: Renaissance Revival — The Body as Temple. ("I Will Survive" — Gloria Gaynor.)

Michelangelo's *David* as theology in marble.

SLIDE 12: Alain Locke and the Harlem Renaissance. ("Ain't No Stoppin' Us Now.")

Beauty reborn in Black modernism and queer vision.

SLIDE 13: Gay Liberation and the Search for the Sacred. ("Born to Be Alive" — Patrick Hernandez.)

~

Almost as delighted by John's rendition as if I had been there myself, I finally asked why none of the slides had included Socrates.

"Oh," John said, embarrassed. "I knew I couldn't get one over on you."

"What happened?"

"Saving the best for last," John said. "Bobby insisted that I was the right and only person who could play Socrates. But before giving me a chance to explain why I had always loved him, Bobby took center stage to give the whole thing some context."

John then reproduced Bobby's speech, in Bobby's tone:

Now, girlfriends, Socrates was an Athenian man in the fifth century BCE who simply refused to write anything down, which already tells you he was either wildly confident or chronically inconvenient. Everything we know about this apparently wise but wizened man survives because other men simply would not shut up about him afterward, most notably Plato, who took his teacher's voice, gave it good lighting, and cast him as the leading lady of Western philosophy.

Socrates lived right in Athens, wandering the marketplace barefoot and underdressed, asking questions with a smile so sweet and so surgical that powerful men would start unraveling mid-sentence, because he had a talent for exposing that most so-called knowledge was just opinion in a respectable toga.

He claimed to be guided by a *daimonion*, an inner voice that didn't tell him what to do so much as when to stop, which meant he trusted conscience over ambition and instinct over applause—who does that these days? Well, maybe John, now that he's a dead man walking. Plato presents him as ironic, magnetic, and dangerously charming, especially to younger men, turning conversation into a kind of intellectual foreplay where certainty dissolved and desire for truth took its place. As for any hanky-panky—who can say?

When Athens finally charged him with corrupting the youth and disrespecting the gods, what they were really saying was that he had embarrassed the wrong people in public one too many times, and democracy, bless her fragile little heart, does not like to be questioned when she's about to become an oligarchy. Sound familiar? Offered a chance to flee, Socrates refused, insisting that breaking the law to save himself would betray the very ethical order he'd spent his life poking, prodding, and polishing. And so he drank the nasty hemlock calmly, still talking, still teaching, still making a scene of restraint so elegant that Plato turned his death into philosophy's most enduring curtain call.

"Not too bad," I said. "I mean, your performance of Bobby."

"Ha."

"Did you get a word in edgewise?"

"Once Bobby introduced me, I did."

"He introduced you?"

"Yes," John said. "The Diva did—and took his sweet time."

"How did that go?"

John again took on Bobby's voice:

Now before we all start clutching our pearls and pretending we don't already know how this ends, we should name who's gonna carry the burden of being Socrates in this room, because that man does not just ask questions—he survives other people's answers. John's got the temperament for it: the patience, the irony, the moral spine, and that way of listening that makes you feel seen right up until you realize you've been indicted by your own words. Socrates wasn't loud, wasn't flashy, and didn't need props—just nerve and an unshakable faith that truth could hold its own in mixed company. And if that ain't John after a heart attack and a divorce, I don't know what is.

"Oh," I said, a bit worried.

"Don't worry," John said. "As we figured, once we gave Bobby the semblance of being in control, all of us had a lot of fun doing things our own way, which suited Miss Thing just fine."

"Ahhh," I mused. "I guess, all's well that ends well."

I was aware the guys were kicking the can down the road—and that the can was heading towards someone, and I hoped that someone would be me.

CANTO 14: MORE SEQUINS, LESS SOCRATES

The next week I heard that the men arrived at what they were calling "Healing Theatre" subdued. Bobby's sequins dulled under the fluorescents; Andy clutched a sheaf of notes; Harry kept his hood up.

Why so blah this week? Ah—John had sent everyone his dramaturgy for the Socratic operatic speech.

John, proud of his scholarship, read from his summary of the famous Ladder speech given by Socrates—guided by an ascent toward heaven, propelled by the love of beautiful boys —as though delivering a keynote at APA rather than a crescendo.

Bobby broke it. "Jobbie John, I admire the erudition, but this was drier than my mother's pound cake."

Andy adjusted his glasses. "Maybe that's what we need— less jazz, more score." Then, after a beat: "Though I do own a whip and a Venetian mask, should the pedagogy require props."

Harry muttered, "You gon make world-changing philosophy into a recovery meeting."

Bobby groaned. "Then let's dance instead. Let's feel the symposium again. Ficino didn't just read Plato—that Neo-Platonist staged him. Made philosophy a drag ball for the gods."

"Not sure what's worse," Andy said. "Plato as drag show or as sobriety chip."

"I have an idea," Harry said, fiddling with the toga Bobby had sewn for them all—but which only Harry proudly wore: unbleached linen, threaded with gold, never quite staying where it was told.

"I'm going to do an Alcibiades—and pull out my meat. About time you gawkers saw my sausage."

"Don't you dare," Andy said.

"I'm texting Glitter," Bobby said.

"I'm not looking," John said.

"It's too late," Andy said, breaking into a rare laugh.

What Harry grasped in both hands was a fresh pork sausage from the *carnicería*, picked up for his mother's pasta later that night.

CANTO 15: STAIRWAY TO HEAVEN (WITH CHER)

The next week, the sequins won.

The room had been rearranged. Chairs angled inward like a small amphitheater. The lights dimmed. A silver goblet sat where a coffee mug should have been.

John stood center stage — steadying himself on a rickety chair as the frail, elder Socrates.

Andy sat poised as the sharply handsome Agathon, criss-crossed by a leather harness, as he held up the Jowett translation of *The Symposium*.

Bobby fanned himself with a rainbow fan, nerves hidden beneath layers of multicolored nail polish.

Harry slouched apart from the circle, arms crossed, drinking wine from the silver goblet. He burped loudly. His eyes drifted — again and again — not to the stage, but to Bobby and John.

Andy (addressing the room, as Agathon):

Before Socrates turns to the great Priestess, Diotima's, teaching, he first takes Agathon to task — the pretty boy, newly crowned tragedian. Through questioning, he exposes an unwelcome truth: love is not abundance but absence; we pursue someone to fill a void.

John (as Socrates, sharp, relentless):

Tell me, Agathon: does Love love something — or nothing?

Andy (as Agathon, poetic, tentative):

Of course he loves something.

John (Socrates):

You don't say.

The Chorus cuts in — raw, overlapping.

Chorus:

The gay boy feels empty because his father does not hug him.

John (Socrates):

Does he love what he lacks — or what he has?

Andy (Agathon):

What he lacks, I should say.

Chorus (harsher):

He feels "in want" because the other boys mock him as a sissy.

John (Socrates):

And does he desire what he is in want of and does not possess?

Andy (Agathon):

Certainly. Someone he cannot have?

Chorus (low, almost whispered):

He feels empty because his mother made him her little husband.

John (Socrates):

Then Love desires what he lacks and does not possess?

Chorus (building):

He loves what he does not have — sometimes a straight bully.

John (Socrates):

We have agreed that Love is also love of Th Beautiful?

Andy (Agathon):

Yes.

Chorus (breathless):

He feels ugly because he is always ten years behind, or more, 50 going on 15.

John (Socrates):

And also of The Good?

Andy (Agathon):

Yes.

John (Socrates, closing the trap):

Then Love is in want of the beautiful and the good, and therefore is neither beautiful nor good.

Andy (Agathon, barely audible):

So it appears.

Chorus:

He feels empty on the DL.

He feels it after the trick leaves.

So love is in want of what is ugly.

John (Socrates):

Not even a god, if gods are good and beautiful?

Andy (Agathon):

It seems not.

Chorus:

By this reasoning, Eros — in his work of healing lack —
is not a god but a *daimon*.

A dark teacher of the shadow self.

Images flash: a father's belt on carpet. Donuts. Guillermo. A
fat boy eating pie. An Asian boy in the ER. A Black boy
looking into a crystal ball.

Andy paces, fanning himself with Agathon's laurel.

Andy:

Socrates grows bored with the pretty boy, because — as
Bobby once said — beauty without truth is a drag queen
without a wig.

Andy evokes the Priestess Diotima

HELP! We need a new idea! We are trapped in assimilation
or postmodernism. Diotima of Mantinea, Priestess.

Foreigner. Philosopher. Prophet. She can teach us about the magical nature of Gay Love. We're dying here. Agathon is a boring twink and Socrates doesn't know what the fuck he is doing with him!

Music cue: Cher, "Song for the Lonely"

Bobby crowns the Apollo bust with a Cher wig, polyester teased into priestess couture. He turns — not to the room — but directly to John.

Bobby to John
    Put the wig on, honey. Serve prophet drag.

John (dry smirk, donning wig):
    No, you put it on, you're a better Diotima that I could ever be.

Andy Wait, we agreed John would play both roles.

Harry Yah.

John takes the wig off the Apollo statue, tries it on, doesn't fit, hands to Bobby

Bobby resists but John will no take "no" for an answer

Bobby as Diotima (applying the wig a bit too easily, and checkin in his compact for adjustments)

Okay, well , then. Deep breaths. Okay, I'm here, you poor lost gay boy. Gay Love is is a great spirit, Socrates, an intermediary between the divine and the human.

Harry stiffens.

John (as Socrates):

What does this great Spirit of Gay Love want of us, dear Diotima, great Priestess, and teacher of homos?

Bobby (as Diotima):

He wants you homos to learn this, as you let your love of cock, balls and ass take you back and forth from the divine to the human, remember: Love is the desire for the possession of the Good.

Andy (to the audience) Back in Plato's day, "The Good" was a True Form and is a bit like how people think of Jesus, but that is an approximation. Anyway, back to the story.

John (Socrates):

So, then, tell us, dear Diotima, because all we have is the White Picket Fence or the Grindr App, What happens when men join — not from lack — but from wanting possession of the Good—for what you call a higher gay calling?

Bobby (Diotima):

They come into a greater understanding about the exact nature of their attraction.

John (Socrates)

And what of this nature?

Bobby (Diotima):

Due to the doubling aspect that the great Aristophanes showed us, and the Heavenly nature, that the great Pausanias showed us, the two men (or two women but Plato had no time for lesbos) feel an urge to procreate. But it's not the penis and vagina form, and has nothing to do with making a family in the typical sense.

John (Socrates)

So they come tougher to procreate but not in the biological sense.

Bobby (Diotima):

They do become pregnant but not with an embryo but with the spirit of other kinds of children. Children of thought, of art, of science, of freedom, of consciousness, of new paradigms.

John (Socrates):

So there are two pregnancies. One for straight people — and one for us?

Bobby (Diotima):
Yes!

John (Socrates)
Who knew?

Bobby (Diotima): Those pregnant in body beget children to preserve their memory. Those pregnant in soul conceive wisdom, virtue, art. Poets. Inventors. World-makers. I'll show you.

Harry (half-laugh, half-sour):
Must be nice. Getting pregnant together.

Silence ripples.

Bobby (as Diotima, voice sharpening):

Now listen, Socrates. This is not just poetry. To get to his new undersatanding, you need to climb up a ladder, No skipping rungs, baby.

John (as Socrates) I have a bad knee.

Bobby (Diotima)

I'll hold your hand, here.

John takes Bobby's hand, as they both make way to ascend.

Bobby (Diotima)

First — you love one body.
One ache. One obsession.

John and Bobby climb.

Bobby (Diotima)

Then, as you boys follow the Good, and go from Grindr to the next rung, you learn the beauty was never owned or enslaved, as we saw the heteros do.

John (Socrates)

Our feelings of beauty are but visitors. They never stay in one place, or person.

Bobby (Diotima)

So you love many bodies —not carelessly, but with your eye on the higher rungs of the ladder, upward, towards The Good. Desire pushes you forward, like when your lover inspires you to pull through.

Harry

Hello?

Bobby (Diotima):

Then ascending to minds. Climbing towards souls.

Harry:

A good mind outlasts a good ass, it would seem, if one doesn't mind eating ass in the process.

Bobby Shhh. We'll lose our place.

Bobby (Diotima):

Then Gay Love takes us to laws. Then Justice. Then structures that hold more than two, but the many.

John (Socrates)

My knee. My knee.

Bobby (Diotima)

This is where boys falter. If they can't recreate the heterosexual couple, they don't know where to go next. No MAP, no Guide, No Compass. So knees give out.

John (Socrates)

No one survives — without a MAP.

Bobby (Diotima)

But if you do survive, if you do climb—you glimpse Beauty itself.

Andy (to the audience)

Back in Plato's day, "Beauty" was another form of what we would call God)

The room shifts as people try to see Beauty yonder.

Harry Yo, I'm here.

Bobby (Diotima)

Shall we climb further still? Together? Stairway to Heaven?

The two proceed, but before they reach the top, John's knee gives out. He collapses, falling off the ladder, tumbling to the floor. Bobby races down, calls for his help.

Andy grabs ice from Dr. Glitter's frig. Where is Harry?

John (Socrates)

I can't go on. I am over whelmed by a life I left behind, loveless, failures. I'll never make it to the top.

Harry: Someone is losing their shit.

Bobby (catching him): Rest here, wounded healer. It's not your knee. You just got inseminated, honey. We popped your cherry. You left the mundane world of chasing boys to the higher realm where boys and men make love to The Good and The Beautiful. Before you fell down, you got a nut inside of you.

John (holding his expanding tummy):

Oh, you are right! I feel the baby growing in me. I couldn't have procreated my new child without you. We carried it to term.

The wig lies on the floor. Harry steps forward — then stops.

Harry (low):

>I carried you.

Music cue: Aretha Franklin, *Natural Woman.*

Andy (texting Dr. Glitter):

>Something is happening with Harry.

Dr. Glitter: Andy?

Harry (breaking): I'm finna out of here. Take your fucken show, and stuff it. Let the goddess-worshippers have each other.

>Socrates forgot he loved me. He forgot I taught him how to want.

The door slams.

Andy (out of character, loud):

>We lost Harry.
>
>He left right after the speech.

Bobby:

>I didn't notice.

John:

>He didn't strike me as upset.

Andy (furious):

>You drove him out, you two sisters — drunk on each other, as always.

John (sad):

>We killed the baby.

Andy (steadying himself):
    Let's gather.

Bobby Perhaps he'll come back.

Andy Maybe—but not to take the same shit.

CANTO 16: ALCIBIADES CRASHES THE PARTY

The *andron* falls away; it is only the therapy room again. Bobby tidies spills of fake wine, folds books, gathers loose pages. John has gone gray and inward. Andy writes notes, trying to leave a message on my phone, voice catching. Everyone is distraught.

Andy: We chased out another one. Harry's not answering—

(A crash in the hallway, then a shout, then dishes and footsteps, then a fist at the door.)

Voice (bellowing): Diotima, save the dumb ass prayers and get the hellie outta my way before I fart on your rosy lips!

Voice (feminine): *Amigo,* you've had too much to drink. *Cálmate.*

Voice (gossiping): I heard a party and came to find the revelers—and favors.

Harry bursts in—shirt half-open, a gold lamé sash turned toga. One boot, one bare foot. Glitter streaking chest and cheek. A wreath of tired roses tilting in his hair. He carries a half-empty rosé and a dented hand mirror that throws stray light as he sways. His swagger is divine and ruined at once.

Harry (as Alcibiades): I came to see if the philosopher bleeds — or just blabs.

Andy (whisper): Oh my God. He's back?

Bobby (soft): Dionysus in a Forever 21 toga.

John (looking relieved and almost delighted): Harry—

Harry (booming, half-drunk, half-performed): Don't "Harry" me. Don't you fucking dare, yo. You are NOT my daddio, baby! Tonight I am ALCIBIADES—General of the Wounded Heart, Patron Saint of Drunken Interrogations, Interruptions, Intermediate Types, and Returner of whatever and whoever you thought you had fuken transcended. BOO! And fuck the Death Card, you bitches. I am here to bring— *(burping)* LIFE!

(He slams the bottle; pink fizz freckles the carpet, and vomits into Dr. Glitter's New Yorker *piles.)*

Harry (as Alcibiades): You preached a holy divine god-foreskaken ladder, and I climbed until the rungs cut my hands and tore at my callouses. Any foot pigs here, I need a human footstool. At the top, I found a ghost in a goddess wig with a bloody pig. I'm funny, haha, almost as funny as your Cher, which is funny but in the wrong way—like we say in the hood, "What up with that clown? He funny, AF."

(He laughs, staggers, rights himself, ruffles the script, spills wine—or grape juice, not clear—on it.)

Bobby (anxious): Baby, not on my scripts.

Alcibiades *(rifling through the pages of Andy's script, but not tosses it aside)*:

I bleed with style, ladies. My heart bleeds with less style.

(He lifts the mirror. He offers the goblet to Socrates, but he's in Recovery)

Alcibiades: Look at your pretty philosopher. Drunk on Beauty, but won't drink the bottle in front of him. Spits out love like it's pee from a dehydrated cock.

(He catches John's eyes; the humor drops a degree.)

Alcibiades: Oh, I forgot. Andy, I mean, Pausanias, is the Piss Queen.

Bobby: I'm sure Alcibiades had his fair share.

Alcibiades (to Bobby, miming Bette Davis): Wake Up, Pearl! I mean, Cher!

(quiet, to Socrates): You forgot me.

Silence holds like a chord.

Andy (worried, reaching out a hand): Come sit. Have some water.

Alcibiades (grabs the hand, then pulls away): Alcibiades doesn't sit. Alcibiades bursts in, shames the party, and tells the truth no one invited.

(Roses slip from the wreath as he gestures at the lights.)

Alcibiades (grandiose): The gods brought me, to break y'all outta your trauma bubbles. Mean Girls cock-blocking energy. High-key codependency, all that.

Bobby (paging through his journal): I bet he rehearsed some of those lines.

Alcibiades (winking, clever):

Instead, you called on Diotima. I can see her sitting over there, OVER THERE, wearing the Cher wig, yoo-hoo. I called on the bruised god—the one who teaches without scrolls, the one who knows how love smells when it costs a night in jail. You people never been in jail, yah don't know what ya missing—all those loud noises, no, the toilet over-flow, they don't clean up the feces and the food stinks like John's shit—but wait, oops, John, I mean Socrates—his shit don't smell, right, Fam?!

The bitterness thins; a human tone returns.

Alcibiades: Here I am—the body you made a metaphor, the hunger you tried to make holy. But I'm profane! BOO!

(He drops the mirror. It cracks and scatters light like a dying disco ball. Out spill post-its, rolling papers, and colored pens.*)*

Bobby (running to pick up the pieces): Oh, honey—

Alcibiades No *te preocupes*

Andy (looking at John and then the rest): I can't tell if this is acting or we should stop. Let's stop.

Alcibiades looks up, eyes bright and wet (booming): Do not Stop the Chicano. Would be a MACRO-aggression.

Alcibiades: Yes, I'm being dramatic, doctors, so not to worry. But how else could I inform Socrates over there to keep his lame-ass ladder up to the stars to himself? Some of us live at the bottom rung, and the wine still tastes good down here. *(taking a swig and burping)*

(He collapses onto the couch, crown awry. Violet light in the mind, a ghost of Donna Summer pulsing from nowhere.)

Andy (still worried): Either you have been holding out on us that you are such a good actor, or you are drunk as a skunk.

Alcibiades (as himself, shaking off, the drunk affect): Give me a moment, fools. I am trying to keep faith with the text. Not Bobby's text, which is bullshit. But so many translations, so little time…

Alcibiades (paging through books, he tosses them to the floor, but finds his own)

Silence, slaves!

I am not your modern-day Caliban, or your modern-day Falstaff.

I am not your Samantha!

I am not your Regine!

I am not your Toto, Too!

I am not your Satan!

I AM ALCIBIADES REGAINED!

Bobby I don't think this was part of our rehearsal?

Alcibiades

Who can rehearse a drinking party, especially one drunk on rejection? I looked for Socrates snoring in the street to rest my handsome head on his arthritic shoulder. He barked at me to go—he needed sleep. So I wandered to Agathon's, heard the boy won a prize. Pretty, talented. My FOMO knows. Here you all are, celebrating life without me. As always!

Alcibiades (to John): I rose fast on eloquence, pedigree, and face.

Alcibiades (to Andy): I studied under Socrates and came from noble stock.

Alcibiades (to Bobby): I helped plan the Suck—uh, Sicilian —Expedition, 415 BCE. Promised glory, found disaster.

John (correcting Harry): It's Sicilian. Sicilian.

Alcibiades: Suck Sillian.

Alcibiades (to the audience):

I made friends with Sparta, Persia, and Athens—diplomacy and drama. All beside the point. Why compare, when everyone already calls me the dom top and that twink Agathon the pig bottom?

Sit on his face and he'll tell you lies; lie with him and you'll get lice; lay with him and he'll show you—through his gaping hole—whose lies lie low. Low life. Tragic poet. Where is Agathon?

(Wine dripping down his wrist)

Alcibiades (looking for Agathon): He told me to come by and fuck him raw. I will stand rather than lay with him so as not to get lice from that low life.

I am early and plastered; if he's not here, I will choose someone else. C'mere, piggies. I came prepared. I have poppers, dog collar, nip clamps, weed, lube, mask, K, X. No one turns you down when you have party favors—

Andy (annoyed, to Harry): Maybe not go too rogue?

John Maybe let him shine?

Bobby Best bet.

John to the audience: All the world's a stage, and Harry, it turns out, is not just its show runner — he's an accomplished actor, a lover of the classics, a technician of perfect timing, a superb memorizer and extemporaneous showman. Who knew?

Bobby (whispering) I told you to look at his work on Tik Toks and YouTube. We have all the connections in the world.

Andy So modest yet so grandiose.

Alcibiades (to the audience): Could you tell the members in the peanut gallery to shut the fuck up. I shoot a big wad so they might want to put on their goggles.

(He swigs, lifts a fist, then lowers it on an IKEA table.)

Alcibiades: I will punish Socrates through praise, which he loathes. I will honor that lily-liver'd, action-taking knave, a whoreson, glass-gazing, super-serviceable finical rogue.

For this, Socrates traps me with his wisdom. Against my will, he makes me ashamed of how I waste my life with stupid boys like Wes, and years pining over a boy who would not have loved me, and projects started and never finished, and more angels than can dance on the head of a pin. He says, "Know thyself," and so now I tell you: I do not yet know myself.

Andy. John and Bobby look at each other, fully Cher Horowitz lost, the freeway roaring, no exit in sight.

Alcibiades (to all): I try to return to my fun-filled, drug-induced, cum-bucket life, but I can't. (Crying) the minute John—I mean Socrates—leaves my sight, I fall back to my old habits of forgetting to do my homework for the G+Q MAP. Did I just time travel? Did I just speak to the men of the future? Look, I do not imagine that Socrates as totally innocent. He flirts with Agathon, and Glaucoma, and who knows who else.

John: What a scoundrel.

Alcibiades (pointing directly at John): And he led me on—oh, how this scoundrel led me on. I thought he wanted me. I cooked him dinner, sent the servants away, looked perfect, studied the ancient texts, boned up on my pre-Socratics. After I proved myself to do everything he would have expected, I expected ravishment. What did I get? Not even a pat on the head. Not even a touch with the hand. Not even a look of hope and desire. Men of Athens, what did this so-called generous and good-hearted philosopher of the ages give to his noble prince, Alcibiades? Nothing. N.O.T.H.I.N.G!

Alcibiades (forlorn, talking to an imaginary theater audience): So I invited Socrates to wrestle—sweat, pressure, breath—and still nothing. I fed him lamb and libations and kept him all night talking ontology. I made a bed. He agreed to sleep over, and I thought we would finally know bliss. It was winter. I threw my coat over him and slid under his threadbare cloak, holding the monster in my arms. I would not be denied, I told myself, of my great love and passion for this man, for never, ever before have I loved someone as I love Socrates.

John (looking very rapt): We all say we want Aidan—but somehow, we keep falling in love with Big.

Bobby throws some Tarot cards for guidance as Dr. Glitter is responding to the voice memos unable to suppress a giggle at the dialogue.

The Lovers. The Devil. The Tower. The Hangman.

Alcibiades (glancing over to the throw, back to the audience): But what happened when I made my pass for the Lovers? What happened when I made my feelings known? Nothing happened. No kisses, no sucking, no fucking, not even mutual relief. The Devil upside down. I went to his feet; he giggled. In the morning I rose as if from the couch of a father. So many choices laid out — and still, not chosen. The Tower. Tied to him anyway, like I know better and do it all the same. He is not straight—even straight men cannot keep their hands off me—but Socrates can. He just hangs there in his virtue, seeing everything, touching nothing, while the whole room comes down around us. The Hangman. Socrates cannot love me. And what am I to do? I can't live without him. He represents my salvation. Oh, woe is me. Where is the Death Card?

(He tears the toga, storms out, then staggers back, barefoot and shaking. Not fully Alcibiades, not fully Harry.)

Bobby (uneasy): And I thought I was the drama queen.

Andy I have a feeling this is NOT what John was thinking when he suggested we do a Queer *Symposium*.

Alcibiades (approaching Socrates): So, Socrates. Here is your one last chance, papa. You gonna sit there in your lovely holier-than-thou philosophical echo chamber where all the boys worship you but can't touch you—or are you going to let real love in? Your last chance. Pick Job's lot, or mine?

Bobby (gasping): We should take this on the road!

Andy: No cap.

John (turning towards Bobby, putting his finger to his lips)

John as Socrates (standing up, removing his Diotima wig): I hear you, Alcibiades—and you are right. I have been hiding here under my spiritual bypass. Let this day be the day when I stop turning my back against the men I love—and the men after whom I lust.

Bobby Be more specific, John!

Alcibiades (still acting, moving closer): Once a Socrates, always a shut down Socrates.

Socrates I can change.

Alcibiades: By what means?

Socrates (crossing his arms, thinking twice, uncrossing them): The ladder should not only go up?

Andy Where else should it go?

Socrates Down, as well.

Bobby (despairing) Back to hell? Wasn't Alcibiades supposed to be our Beatrice?

Socrates: Down so far, it goes back up. More like a circular motion than a straight line?

Bobby No more straight lines.

Alcibiades If we go down, and gag, we have to come up, for air, and kiss, you feel me?

(Grabbing the *carnicería*). And whatever goes down, must get a hard-on!

Andy What if we get stuck in the shit or burnt by the sun?

Alcibiades A therapist cooks and *Carnicería* between its highs and lows.

Bobby I wish I had Dr. Glitter on Face Time to hear that!

Alcibiades So, Socrates wants his *carnicería* or Cher Wig?

Socrates Why so either/or.

Andy put his head in his hands, then leaned against Bobby's shoulder, who absorbed his groan.

Harry rubbed a tear from his eye and collapsed into a chair, exhausted and aware they only had the room for another thirty minutes, Andy tapping his watch.

Harry Okay. Good enough for now. Rome wasn't built in a day.

So, Papa John—wanna take a bow or some shit like that?

John bowed, then curtsied.

Harry motioned for the others to bow as well, then took one himself, visibly startled by the standing ovation.

PROGRESS NOTES FOR
THE PURGATORIO

What unfolded following the group's reworking of *Plato's Symposium* was not, strictly speaking, insight—but exposure. The dramatic structure allowed certain truths to emerge without requiring immediate ownership: longing, rivalry, idealization, age anxiety, and the fantasy that desire can be safely staged without consequence. It could not.

In particular, Harry's identification with Alcibiades and John's position as Socrates revealed a dynamic that had been circulating for some time beneath the group's discourse. The performance did not create this dynamic; it named it. The group's task afterward was not interpretation, but containment.

What followed in the days after was a period of heightened affect, humor, and intellectualization—much of it productive, some of it defensive. The group demonstrated an increased capacity to think symbolically about shame and desire, and to situate their personal struggles within a longer queer lineage. At the same time, it became clear that the group was beginning to strain against the limits of a traditional therapeutic frame.

This shift was not driven solely by the members' ambitions or relational entanglements. It coincided with significant changes in my own life: the reemergence of a long-standing relationship, my partner Marco's cancer diagnosis, and the increasing demands of caring for my ninety-five-year-old mother in New York. I knew I would need to spend extended time there in the coming months, though the duration—and its impact on the work—remained uncertain. These realities required a re-evaluation of how, and where, I could responsibly continue.

In subsequent sessions, we began to speak openly about the difference between therapy and collaboration, between treatment and collective inquiry. The group's interest in developing something public did not signal an ending of the work, but a transformation of it. What had begun as group therapy was gesturing toward a different form—one that would require consent, structure, and a redistribution of authority. Their commitment to individual work deepened, and they voted not only to continue individual sessions via Zoom, but to add a final in-person session devoted to processing the change in frame and their shared anxieties about working together outside of therapy. The idea of conducting ongoing group therapy on Zoom appealed to no one.

ACT III — PURGATORIO

The men set out to build on the Plato psychodrama to construct the ABCs of the emerging G+Q MAP—and precipitate their first major rupture.

CANTO 17: INFORMED CONSENT (OR, MAKING ART WITHOUT KILLING EACH OTHER)

When we met for a post-mortem on Zoom, it was clear that the way the men deferred to me as Group Leader was mostly muscle memory. It didn't feel organic.

"You've actually been running your own group without me," I said.

"All hail the Dorothys," John replied.

"We didn't kill each other," Andy said. "Yet."

"He almost had a nervous breakdown when he thought we'd lost Harry," John added.

Harry grinned. "That part was real."

I asked how they'd managed the handoff—how Andy and John hadn't quite known what was happening.

"We got two Dorothys," Harry said, referring to Bobby's Dorothy Z. "The second one gave me direction at *El Garaje de la Ascensión.*"

Andy raised an eyebrow. "Did we just get breaking news? Bobby and Harry cooperating?"

I told them that my mother's health—and Marco's—had both taken a turn for the worse.

"As long as you don't take away our individual sessions," Andy said. "That's what keeps us from going off the deep end."

"The Diva Mother stops taking her medication," Bobby said, sketching a worst-case fantasy. "Files a restraining order on Ezra Pound."

Andy paused. "Is that a joke—or a prediction?"

"Let's get some paperwork taken care of," I said, balancing the guys' organic systems of self-regulating with some house-keeping we all needed.

"As the group is in the process of of altering its structure," I said, "we require a revised Informed Consent."

I read aloud, with judicial clarity, the following:

> …that each member would remain in individual therapy; that ruptures, outside affections, and unspoken tensions must be brought to the circle rather than buried; that departures would be processed, not swept under the carpet; and that secrets would fatally compromise the therapeutic contract. The experiment could destabilize as easily as it could advance. The G+Q MAP adjunctive experience might accelerate individuation—or reopen old lesions of shame. It would require vigilance, reflexivity, and a weekly accounting of what each man was holding in order to succeed as a container rather than become a disrupter.

The documents were sent via email, unsigned for the moment.

I added a special addendum: that the project of self-regulating the group would take more of their time. Adding rehearsals, organizing administration, communicating with me, processing complexities and political problems—that was a big commitment.

"You guys up for more work?" I asked. "Before we sign, this is a good time to share second thoughts."

Andy, who had started to become an "observer" at ICE demonstrations, blew his whistle. "I'm in," he said.

"Hollywood's Titanic is sinking. Time to jump ship."

"My life killed me," John said quietly. "But making a play revived me."

"I can do my day job in my sleep," Bobby said. "During my downtime, I say, let's make art, not war."

"Hello," Andy said dryly. "My name is Andy, and I'm a frustrated activist."

Harry said his parents had trapped him with love, money, and guilt—all welded together.

"I also hate my job," he said.

"Job?" Bobby asked. "I'm sure posting on OnlyFans takes its toll."

"They are educational," Andy said, but Harry motioned for him not to take the bait.

I DISCUSSED how the project could advance therapy by extending it beyond the dyad, by reintroducing community into what had become a privatized ritual of confession.

But the new frame could fracture boundaries if they mistook disinhibition for authenticity.

"We'd need to evaluate its impact weekly," I said, "and recognize the first signs of disorganization that would signal us to terminate."

"Disorganization?" Andy said. "We're already vastly disorganized."

"If you all had come up with a structure or a syllabus, that might help you stay focused?"

"How much did Andy pay you?" Bobby asked, joking.

G + Q MAP for the Gay Man's Hero's Journey

A Provisional MAP for the MAP (each person's expertise weighs in, Harry for the earth, Bobby for the fun, John for the shadow, Andy for Integration)

G — Getting Grounded: rooting in the body; breathing, eating, sleeping; integrating goodness.

Q — Queer Spark: the awakening—first crush, first kiss, the shimmer of the true self.

S — Shadow Selves: the underworld—where the bullied child meets the internalized homophobia that shaped him.

H — Helper Selves: the archetypes of repair—the inner beloved, the good mother and father, the erotic god who does not punish.

I — Integration: the capacity to hold opposites without splitting, to live in paradox without paralysis.

F — Fucking & Feeling: sex, touch, movement, sensation, and affect—pleasure that is conscious rather than compulsive; feeling that is embodied rather than dissociated.

T — Technology: the praxis and the transmission—therapy, journaling, dreamwork, embodiment exercises, queer imagination, digital tools, and the evolving technologies of connection and consciousness.

"NOTHING TURNS me on like bullet points," Bobby said.

Harry laughed under his breath. Maybe this time they'd get *la revolución* right—if not more Marxist, then at least more goofy.

John said that a map—even a provisional one—was better than an argument.

I took a minute to print Andy's map for a map while attaching his file to my Informed Consent, preparing to email the revised Magna Carta over to each person.

Bobby cleared his voice.

"I'd like to amend the informed consent," he said, rummaging until he found his purple-ink and blood-orange fountain pens,

"Okay?" I asked.

"Of course we need a roadmap," Bobby demurred, peering at the screen. "But, if y'all don't mind, I'd like to add a bit of neon pink by the Queer, charcoal bruised purple by the Shadow, give Helper robin's-egg blue, Integration beige, and Fucking & Feeling some velvet rope."

"Sounds good to me," Andy said. The others muttered "sure," and "no problem."

"If it's okay, and while I have everyone," Bobby added, "I'd like to request that Mother have veto power over the color palette for our content. Andy's a doll, but he had other priorities than taking the Orozco seminar at Yale."

Even though Andy had gotten an A in Mexican Muralism at Yale, no vetoed the motion for Palette Oversight.

So we lived to fight—and color—another day.

CANTO 18: PRIVATE LIVES

"I give Harry and John a few months of playing a tired version of *Pride and Prejudice*," Andy said, "before one or both get bored with the ambivalence. And then—if they break up—what happens to our project?"

He paused.

"Which brings me to Jim."

"I understand that asexual does not mean trauma, but it's too easy to say there's no trauma there. "And Jim is so devoted that I think he will consent to go to therapy—and I need him to, not for any reason other than I want to touch the man I love without him feeling I'll cross any boundaries."

I remembered that Jim and Andy shared a leather interest.

"Not yet," Andy demurred. "Ever since my big reveal— that I was beaten by my father's belt—we've both been shy about going near the leather at all. But yes, Doctor, that's one place where we feel electricity."

"My worry is how narrow Jim's circle is. If it's not work, or the program, or me, that's it. He's met Bobby and John and is terribly fond of them. He'd get a kick out of Harry. Harry

—he's so leather without the leather, actually rather wholesome."

He paused.

"Would you talk to Jim?"

"I thought Jim didn't want therapy."

"He doesn't want to drop $450 on a couples therapist who pathologizes him. "He'd be open to talking with us about how to find a really good couples psychologist."

"You sure this isn't more for you?" I asked. "A way to share your thoughts in your therapy?"

"That's why you are the doctor and I am not," Andy said.

"Just in case this moves too fast," I said, "I'll forward you a release."

"Take that home," I added, "and give it a read."

Typical Andy: he speed-read it on his iPad and signed on the dotted line.

LATER THAT AFTERNOON, the phone rang with a blocked number. I recognized Jim's voice before the voicemail finished loading.

I hadn't clarified whether this would be therapy or simply a conversation. Too late now.

He thanked me, briefly but fervently, for helping Andy survive. He asked whether I might consider meeting with them—not for ongoing couples work, he said, but for a session or two, or for a referral.

"I don't want Andy to think I don't want him to touch me," he said. "But I need him to touch me in a particular way, and I've been too shy to say so. We're stuck."

I suggested we meet once, first, to clarify what he was actually seeking.

He sent me $450 for thirty minutes.

Who does that?

John's Private Session

"Have you ever had a situation in therapy where one patient falls in love with another?" John asked.

"You mean, who are individual therapy?"

"A group."

"Just feelings, that's one thing the therapy can address."

"If it's not just feelings?"

"What then, if it's not just feelings?"

"I am not sure."

"You mean, like dating?"

"No, not so much."

I was reluctant to tell him what I was learning from consultation with supervisors and the Ethics Board. Therapists who were also lawyers provide a great to support to many of us. Their guidance was refreshing and a bit supposing. Group Therapists can have a vision of holding the container for just Group Work, but they can't require it. If people want to see each other outside of group, it would be unethical to shame them or disband the group for the reason. The best that could be done is to use the outside engagements for Group Process. Discourage outside relationships, but don't pretend to control them. Protect the group container. Bring anything external back into the room.

"Are you asking for yourself," I said, "or for a friend?"

"More for a friend," he said. "And for the lawyers. In groups like ours, it must come up."

"Frequently."

He nodded. "Transference doesn't have to be romantic."

"No," I said. "It can be about power. Or testing limits."

"That's what I thought," John said. "The group I'm

thinking about already has enough to manage. And my friend —he's older. He's been through enough. Not in his interest to get entangled. Once you're in, it's hard to get out."

"And the younger man?" I asked.

John shook his head. "There's no way to know what he actually wants. Pretending otherwise would be irresponsible."

I smiled. "Tell your friend he's lucky to have a lawyer friend."

"Oh, I'll tell him, alright," John said. "But he won't thank me."

LATER THAT WEEK, as I half expected, I heard from the hidden demon of Bobby's marital life—Mr. Ezra Pound, as we had been trained to call him. Not because he admired the modernist poet and fascist sympathizer (he didn't), nor because he favored Bobby's pound cake (he was on Mounjaro), but because it served as a disrespectful shorthand for dismissing the man's concerns—as if Bobby's subjective assessment could qualify as validity and reliability. As if Ezra's form of emotional overload—as hard as it is to believe, or perhaps because it makes perfect sense, Bobby had chosen a mate who talked and cried more than he did—could be reduced to a poisoned recipe from Mother, neither of them eager to taste, let alone digest.

The voicemail lasted for three minutes:

Hello, Dr. Goldstein. I know you know me, and you know I know you. But of course, we don't know each other, because we've never met—or been invited to meet.

I know Bobby has told you I wouldn't see his therapist, but Bobby chooses to take only the things I say in anger seriously—and the things I say with love and a calm tone, he makes a joke about. So yes, I'm sure you've heard I have a temper.

As a Jewish eldest born, as you are, you'll agree we're not the calmest people on the planet. If you fuck with us, I'm not being political. I know Bobby probably depicts me as some myopic fellow regressive tendencies, but nothing could be further from the truth. Yes, I'm supportive of Israel—what Jew wouldn't be?—but I'm not a fan of war, and heart goes out to the Palestinian people, not that Bobby can tolerate me explaining the facts to him.

He started asking me the other day, and when he didn't hear me being thoughtful, I raised my voice. That's when he asked me to leave. Leave my own home? But what could I do? When Bobby makes up his mind, there's no talking to him. I packed my bags. But I am up all night missing him.

Anyway—I just wanted you to know the only reason I raise my voice is that it's the only way I can get this very entertaining man—who is a real laugh riot—to listen to me. But of course, he yells back. So no one listens to anyone.

I know he also gives the impression that I'm inflexible sexually, but I'd be open to trying new things if he didn't assume I didn't want to—and then get me angry for assuming I don't want to do something I may actually want to do. Help me, guide me. I'm not Mr. Know-It-All, as he thinks I think I am.

By the way, I'm not a fan of secrets. No need to call me back. But you have my permission to play this to Bobby or the group. I've tried to give a balanced view.

Thank you for your time. Over and out from 'Ezra Pound.' I know that's what you call me. I don't like the poet, nor the cake—but be that as it may. 'What thou lov'st well remains,' right?' Even an idiot can quote that. Good day to you.

I've gotten some calls in my day, but that took the cake.

DURING HARRY'S SESSION, I half expected him to bring up the big scene with Alcibiades and Socrates, but he had other things to discuss.

He was still hung up on Wes—who, after love-bombing Harry and introducing him to his circle of cool friends, just stopped returning calls. All because Harry had decided to bottom for a change—and expressed real feelings.

This made me sad, and I found myself tearing up.

I tried to learn more about his father. He stiffened at the mention; something had happened.

This led to his complaint about his life-of-the-party mother. According to Harry, he could do no wrong. She called or texted a few times a day—and if he didn't share his location, the calls came faster.

Because she was infallible—never angry, never curt, just lovey—Harry's occasional explosions (always understated, never loud—he was, after all, his mother's son) had no effect whatsoever.

By the time the session was nearly over, we'd come up with no plan around Wes or his mother—and barely touched John.

At the mention, Harry smirked and blew off the topic like secondhand smoke:

Oh, I'm not tripping. The brother talks a big line, but he's been too hurt by—Cartier, like the jewelry. We should call her Cartier—the nerve. You put a ring on my finger, yo, I'm not looking nowhere else. A ring is a circle, the alpha and the omega, a symbol of the freakin self, you don't fuck with a ring. Someone gives me a ring, that clown better be ready for meaning what he says.

Harry laughed at my look of shock.

"Bro—I mean, Doctor—you should've been in silent movies. You must suck at poker."

"You would get married?" I asked.

"Hellie yah!" Waving his ring finger in the air. "The right stand up man comes around. I'm sick and tired of living the single life. I want a man's love morning, noon, and night."

With that, Harry—realizing he was overtime—grabbed his satchel, Venmoed his fee, and ran to his motorcycle.

He called me from the 10 freeway to apologize for talking so much. At least, that's what I thought I heard—between the engine and the wind, and what his earbuds permitted.

CANTO 19: ALL THAT GLITTERS—IS GOLD

In the following weeks of transition, we met with me on Zoom saying hello at the beginning and returning only to check in at the end.

I made arrangements with my officemates to let the men use the Group Room for the next month, before they arrived at other plans.

They were mostly on their own.

ANDY ADJUSTED a thick accordion file containing a color-coded syllabus for each person.

Harry placed a Himalayan singing bowl from El Garaje on the low table, the felt mallet beside it.

"All right," Andy said. "Since we've already checked in, let's start on page three. Recall a dream, fantasy, or childhood moment when queerness first shimmered."

"We've got to start this shit somewhere," Harry said, nudging the bowl.

"Speaking of starting somewhere," Bobby said, unzipping Clara like a diva unveiling a secret weapon.

The zipper purred open. Color spilled out—paints, brushes, scarves smelling of eucalyptus and club smoke; stickers of pride flags, kissing men, Lady Liberty, Harvey Milk; false lashes, broken rhinestones, feathers, ribbons, glue, glitter labeled *Faith*; lipstick—crimson and corpse-rose—poster board, crayons, gold lamé, a sachet of lavender gone gray. The floor became a bright disorder, ecstatic and excessive.

"Before we quote scripture," Bobby said, already kneeling in feathers, "I vote we make a mess."

John sighed. "Andy's here to keep the train on the tracks, not derail it onto *Drag Race*."

"Spoken by the man who drags us into the Inferno every week," Bobby shot back.

Meanwhile, Andy emptied a brown paper bag of John's quotes onto Bobby's art supplies. "More material for the vision board," he said.

Harry unrolled his yoga mat, stretching slow and feline. "C'mon, Papa—or Mama—let me stretch you."

"See?" Bobby said. "Our opener could be yoga."

John half-laughed. "I haven't seen you this labile in months, honey."

"Amateur diagnoses," Bobby said. "Andy's rubbing off on you."

Harry patted the mat. "Come stretch, baby. Chivalrous Chicano won't bite."

He stripped off his shirt to audible gasps, crossed to Bobby's spread, and pressed stickers—pride flags, flowers, fruit, Harvey Milk—onto his chest and belly. He bent toward Bobby.

"You wanna do my back?"

Bobby applied them like a mother diapering an infant.

"We're supposed not to idolize Harry," Andy warned.

"I never subscribed to John's religion," Bobby said. "And I pray Harry doesn't either."

"Maybe we get back to the writing exercise before Dr. Glitter returns," Andy said evenly. "He's not going to like all this chaos. Or—fine—we can make a vision board for John. Or do an Active Imagination about our grouchy, bitchy, resistant, cutting, mean, nasty, pearl-clutching teething infants who, when they can't stuff their mouths with Chick-fil-A, make others eat their rage-shit."

He divided the room into two zones—yoga on one side, vision boards on the other.

Bobby watched, impressed.

"Maybe I misjudged him," Bobby said. "So nasty! Maybe he's the real leather daddy."

"Trust me, Scarlett," Harry said. "He is."

John, now shirtless on the mat, invited Bobby to stick quotes to his chest. Andy, from a distance, named some greatest hits:

I am invisible, not because I am unseen, but because people refuse to see me.

I will say unto God, Do not condemn me; show me wherefore thou contendest with me.

"How'd you remember all these?" John asked. "I don't even remember saying them."

"Andy remembers everything," Bobby said. "He's actually a perfect person. Yale took him, Hollywood took him, Jim took him, and now therapy's taking him—not for his IQ but for his emotional intelligence. He can even fight a Grand Diva. He'll lose, but he'll fight."

"But in one area, he's not so perfect."

No one followed up, but Bobby continued anyway: "I don't like our title—GQ + MAP. It's stale. We should define our terms."

Andy handed out markers. "Define these: *Mythic Bitch. Judgmental.* Not funny."

Bobby laughed. "Well, look at you, competing for Top Bitch."

Everyone got markers and poster board.

While painting, Bobby mused that *Mythic* belonged to Harry—his OnlyFans was practically legend.

"OnlyFans?" John asked.

"You subscribed?" Harry grinned. "Friends-and-family rate."

"At 25 dollars per month?" Bobby fanned himself. "I did help myself to the free video. Teaching boys how to stretch their arses. Tempted to send to Ezra."

"Which means you did send it," Andy said, trying to keep everyone focused on their Vision Boards.

"Isn't Andy doing a great job regulating me?" Bobby said brightly.

Harry reached out gently. Bobby jerked away.

"Unsolicited touch isn't informed consent," he snapped.

The air froze.

"Bobby," Andy said, steady, "if you don't talk to Dr. Glitter, I will."

"Cute," Bobby shot back. "Teacher's-pet energy. Did someone hand Andrew a license? Last I checked, he was wheeling and dealing in Hollywood, not assessment."

Andy dropped his clipboard.

"Maybe I need to look at why I want control," he said. "I don't want a power struggle with you, Bobby. We've never had this before."

"Don't apologize," Harry said softly.

"Yeah," John echoed, relaxing as Harry pressed on his belly. "Stand up to her."

"I'm not tripping about you trolling me," Harry added. "Keep the cards and letters coming."

"Who cares about control?" Andy said finally, handing Bobby the clipboard. "Here—you run the meeting."

He crossed to Harry and John and took off his shirt. Three bare chests. "Give me some stickers," he asked Bobby.

"You realize, gang," Bobby continued, "that Harry's getting rich online while poor Dr. G's Botox fund ran dry."

"He does look a little jowly," John mused.

"I will give him a cut," Harry said, joining with the diplomacy of Andy and John.

Bobby, temporarily humored, went sprinkling glitter on their shirtless chests, and moving their Vision Boards closer to their Yoga mats.

No one was fighting him.

So, he decided, fuck it, to take off his shirt for the first time in front of gay boys, and braved everyone looking at the folds of fat from having lost 150 pounds over five years.

And he laid down besides them, following Harry's gentle direction to breath and stretch.

WHEN I RE-ENTERED THE ZOOM, feathers floated in sage smoke. Half-dressed men; Clara gutted across the carpet. Andy clutched the bell mallet like a scepter; Harry's yoga mat lay open.

"In two hours," I said. "You've reinvented ritual. I see Clara's out—and by the look of it, you boys are ready for After Hours. Walking Vision Boards?"

"We were good gays," Bobby said, chin proud.

"With these fire stickers," Harry added, tugging on his shirt.

"And no shirts?" I asked.

"Part of the method," Harry said. "*Lo hablaremos el miércoles. Alguien chismeó mi OnlyFans.*"

"OnlyFans?" I repeated.

"We were angels," Andy cut in. "Classic resistance. Bobby tested me; I stayed present. Everyone found their role. Bobby ended up being quite the lamb."

"*María tenía un corderito*" Harry hummed.

"Sounds like we are moving through our transition," I said. "Curious what guys come up with. I understand you will be meeting almost daily during the holiday. I wills you for another supervision next week. If you need more before, you know where to find me."

Bobby blew Andy a kiss—half affection, half dare—grateful to live another day until Dr. Glitter called the paramedics.

CANTO 20: COAT OF ARMS CONTROVERSY

Although Harry had offered the guys use of his infamous El Garaje de la Ascensión to inaugurate their first post-therapy G+Q MAP workshop, I noticed an open office in the building they could use for the transition without involving me. It seemed more neutral, at least in theory.

In practice, the experience was anything but neutral. Andy and I had already discussed how my unconscious preferential bias toward him had allowed me to appoint him substitute teacher—something Andy did not want, and something that had quietly complicated the group's internal balance.

Andy wrote a text then and there to Bobby, titled *Why Don't You Run the First Inaugural Meeting*, which Bobby received with a flicker of apprehension. Was Andy humoring me, or was this a genuine handoff?

~

After a run-of-the-mill Check-In, and a flurry of emails in which Andy coached John and Harry not to polarize with Bobby, Harry was given the task of heralding the path forward.

"Blobbie the Beautiful," Harry said, warming to the role.

"I'll keep my ideas about the embodied gay hero's journey on the back burner. John's got the fire ancestor rap for next week. Andy can chop it up about shorty Urania at a moment's notice.

"Today, though, we're all your children. We want to draw, paint, and regress. So spill, Clara, the bad bitch. Tell us what you and she got."

"Well," Bobby said, almost breathless with recognition, "I think any gay man embarking on the Hero's Journey needs some protection—some armor. It's not good to call my mammy, or engage Ezra, Dr. Glitter tells me, without putting on my Hazmat suit."

"Shit," Harry said, glancing toward me. "Can we get me a Hazmat suit to deal with my mammy too?"

"So we gays need our own inner bouncer," Bobby continued, leaning in, "our own protective covering."

"Indeed," Andy said, neutral but attentive.

"So I did some research," Bobby went on, "and I came up with a Gay Coat of Arms project."

"Say what?" John asked, already bracing.

"Yes," Bobby said, trying to contain his excitement.

"A Coat of Arms was traditionally forged on a shield—signals of identity, honor, and values, often inherited. In our context, designing our own armor becomes a playful but sacred way to remake ancestry, speak desire plainly, and imagine a queer self no longer at the mercy of ritualized fag-bashing.

"The old forms—Mesopotamian scales, Greco-Roman

leather and metal—can, and should, be re-signed for modern queer boys and girls."

"Military tone in a healing frame," Harry said carefully. "Could low-key start a TikTok craze."

"We reclaim the form," Bobby countered. "Much like you boys use the word queer."

"That's a Harry thing," Andy said.

"Feudal symbols related to war," John said, coughing slightly. "Like we are fighting internalized homophobia."

"Precisely," Bobby said, visibly pleased that the men were finally treating him like a serious intellectual.

"Symbols mutate," Andy said after a beat. "So appropriation is not off the table."

"Exactly," Bobby said.

"Where I live," Harry added, "shields and armor read as cops or gangs. ICE bullshit. But I think Bobbie the Beautiful is saying that we clowns are going to expunge the patina of state violence from these emblems of war, clocking you right?"

"Claro que sí," Bobby said. "I cannot wait to show you the mockups for *Your Own Personal Coat of Arms*.

The blinding screen revealed dozens of digital collages.

"Holy moly," Andy said, blinking, overwhelmed not just by the brightness but by the operatic density of color and form.

Harry — The Tower (Lightning at the Crossroads)

"Fire. Summer. South. Samantha. Gambit. Blanche on loan.

The door stands ajar, a hand-wrap caught in the hinge. An obsidian river stone bears a pressed jacaranda petal; breath marks rise like incense. The air sparkles with something about to break.

"I gave Harry this motto—*sin vergüenza, con espíritu*—alongside Sor Juana, the 1968 Walkouts, and a boy holding the Huelga eagle, stepping straight into the fracture and calling it freedom."

Motto: Sin vergüenza, con espíritu.

"Shit," Harry said, motioning for Bobby to swipe slower, taking in his new feudal uniform rendered in an Aztec register.

John — The Hierophant (Order in Shadow)

"Earth. Winter. North. Miranda. Dorothy. Cyclops.

A compass rose bends toward the text, "Invisible Man," like a lawyer drafting prayers. A fountain-pen nib rests across an empty legal scale; an ironwood ring casts an eclipse-shaped shadow. He builds meaning where others plead for mercy, sovereign even in doubt. A shirtless African tribesman holds a fire stick."

Motto: Sovereignty begins inside.

"Christ," John muttered. "I look like the Vatican's notary."

Andy — The Magician (Fire and Air)

Air. Spring. East. Carrie. Rose. Nightcrawler.

A red thread crosses a paper lantern and disappears into the sprocket holes of film—tied off, not knotted. Andy never resolves; he frames. Sparks of irony light the sky. Laughter edits pain into a scene. Every cut is clean. Every emotion color-graded."

Motto: Get that fucken belt back, bro.

"I suppose focusing on my child abuse ad infinitum can be inspiring," Andy said, dryly.

Bobby — The Empress (Leather and Honey)

Water. Autumn. West. Charlotte—repressed, darling, and therefore my twin flame. Sophia, short and savage. Jean Grey, because if I'm going down in flames, I intend to resurrect beautifully.

A cracked crown repurposed as a planter—wildflowers forcing their way through florist mesh. A spool and needle paused beside a honeycomb. A swatch of oxblood leather that might be Clara. Home and history in the same breath. Tenderness—sweet, brutal—the force that holds the hive together.

Motto: Tenderness is a heavy thing to lift.

Silence followed. Even Harry did not wisecrack.

"You nailed yourself, Bobby," John said softly.

Bobby nodded, small and proud. "I always do, darling. Eventually."

Bobby, looking extremely excited, asked if the guys were ready about his new idea for inaugurating the G+Q MAP Project?

"Yes!" Everyone said, unanimously.

"So my idea is to finesse this into a three-day workshop that would give every participant a Queer Coat of Arms— something you can wear on a fashion walk. Traditionally emblazoned on shields, these symbols of honor, identity, and legacy could be reanimated as people sashay. And what do we gays need if not legacy, if not the power to stitch our broken ancestries into myth?"

"Ambitious," Andy said, the irony only half-dissolved.

"Sensational," John added, careful but sincere.

"I can see why you make a lot of money," Harry saiid. "You know how to use violent images to make an artsy point."

ANDY WORRIED. In the past, this kind of gentle ribbing would have summoned Bobby's inner figures who could bring him back to earth. Bobby, like anyone who had survived HIV, ultimately prized reality over fantasy.

Was Bobby unable to handle all the freedom granted to him?

Now that was a new way of thinking of internalized homophobia.

Andy watched Harry—the Fool—step off the cliff.

"I'm not in love with you using my images without asking," Harry said evenly. "Low-key Karenesque of you, even if your Blobbie heart's good."

"African tribesman holds a fire stick," John said.

"Cultural appropriate," Harry said.

John, already flushed, followed him in. "You are asking men of color to wear symbols Europeans used for the Crusades?"

Bobby's threw his iPad to the floor and dumped Clara's contents across the room.

The rain thickened.

Then, Bobby spoke.

Before I say something I will regret, I am going to step out for water and ask you three to sit with something while I am gone. Since Harry joined, there has been what you might call projection toward me. You do not have to agree with that. Just look at it.

I am not going to throw around 'reverse racism,' especially right now, when people of color are under attack by ICE goons. And I am not going to trot out *White Fragility* either. The white man's feelings are hurt, cue the violins, everyone rush to comfort him. Spare me, and spare yourselves.

My point is simpler. I am overwhelmed, and I am reacting badly. So instead of asking you to educate me, or pretending that I am the aggrieved party, I am going to step away and see what my guides have to say.

ONCE IN THE CAR, Bobby called Ezra.

Ezra: Hello, baby.

Bobby: Don't sweet-talk me. I do not want to go over what happened. I am in trouble. I am so upset by us that I took a shit on the guys.

Ezra: Oh no.

Bobby: I let them get to me. I accused them of reverse racism.

Ezra: You did what?

Bobby: …

Ezra: Go back and talk to them. If it was not for these boys, you would have left me long ago.

Bobby: Oh, so you are cosplaying therapist now.

Ezra: Please, Bobby, do not say such mean things. The guys need you.

Bobby: Thanks for the advice.

Ezra: Go back on your meds, honey.

Bobby hung up.

BOBBY RE-ENTERED the group therapy room with red eyes. His phone buzzed in his hand, and he dropped it to the floor.

He spoke:

I could have walked out and let you worry you had offended me. I could have complained to Dr. Glitter, who might or might not have the gall to call me on my not-so-unconscious racism. And despite my sob story that no one is more sinned against than me, I know perfectly well that I enjoy more privilege for being as pale as I am than I can even fathom.

So I am not going to play the you-boys-misread-my-art card either.

My real issue is not humility. My real issue is I feel humiliated, all the time.

So no, I am not staying to hash out race, art, or my failing marriage tonight. I made the terrible mistake. of canceling my session with the good doctor yesterday.

He exhaled, long and shaky.

The Doc tried to reach me, and I let it go to voicemail. So I am going back to him, on hands and knees, to sort this dizzy brain.

Let it be on the record, Master Scribe, that Bobby spoke with Dorothy and did not walk out.

Being of relatively sound mind and body, I will consult my therapist and my psychiatrist—cute, daft, bless him—and proceed accordingly. And with that, to quote another great mind, see you fools in the next lifetime. Ta ta.

CANTO 21: AFTERMATH

The room felt empty—the way a full room does when the life of the party leaves. The three remaining men looked not just sad, but stranded.

They felt the guilt of knowing they had not done everything possible to prevent the breach. They had pushed Bobby, and Bobby had pushed back just as hard—but they reassured themselves, perhaps unsuccessfully, that they had avoided the cruelty of his acerbic tongue.

Each man—despite seeming active in the world—guarded a deeply introverted nature. They preferred listening to shouting, asking to asserting. Harry could seem extroverted, the way people gathered around him, and his friend Gloria loved to tease him about his "entourage."

He was his mother's son in charm, perhaps—but in temperament he was his father's: letting the noise pass while quietly counting what mattered.

On their own, none of them could match Bobby. Maybe no one—not even Dr. Glitter—had ever gotten far enough beneath Bobby's skin to rewire his nervous system from fight-

or-flight into something steadier. But together, they might have had a chance.

"It took race to penetrate him," John said. "That's complicated, because now we might spend weeks processing race and never get to the armor underneath."

Harry had grown uneasy about how convincingly Bobby had cast Ezra as a monster when he wasn't.

"A man might have to raise his voice just to survive Bobby's tantrums," John said.

"Maybe we didn't teach Bobby how to calm Ezra," John said quietly. "Maybe we taught him to escalate."

"Maybe we owe Bobby an apology," Andy said.

"Not before we get one from him," Harry replied.

HARRY UNROLLED HIS YOGA MAT, then reached into his satchel for leaves, a grinder, and what he called tree. Andy watched as John—without ceremony—helped break down the flower, drained the sweet tobacco from the backwood, and rolled with practiced ease.

Andy hadn't seen this before. He marveled that they had forgotten he was sober. Of course he didn't mind. The Program lived inside him like sustainable architecture—one beam among others, alongside Jim. He found the guys' ease almost sweet. Being included still mattered to him, despite everything.

Yet part of him wanted to go home. Jim would be hungry by now. They were both Capricorns, as Bobby loved to remind them—men of structure. It might be good for Harry and John to be alone, to cool down.

"I'm going to head out," Andy said. "Text me if you hear anything."

Harry, who was a hugger, and Andy, who was not, finally

found a compromise: a fist bump.

"Good night, guys," Andy said.

ALONE TOGETHER, Harry and John felt awkward—like boys untrained in quiet. John rolled another joint, took a long pull, let the smoke drift out and back in, then passed it.

They got high together for the first time and did nothing dramatic at all. Harry rested his head against John's chest. They talked softly—about Bobby, about Andy, about the doctor they all relied on. Outside, the rain came down, an early autumn Los Angeles rain, washing dust from the air.

Harry fell asleep first, snoring gently. "Well, I'll be damned," John said—and drifted off too. No trazodone. No Carter. No guru. Just rain and another man breathing.

Later that night, Andy realized he'd forgotten his phone—something he never did. He drove back.

The smell of weed greeted him immediately. He smiled. On instinct, he grabbed a blanket from his car.

He laid it over the two sleeping men, retrieved his phone, and closed the door so quietly even a mouse wouldn't have heard. Then he drove home to Jim.

CANTO 22: BOBBY
TELLS THE TRUTH

By the time a deflated Bobby reached my office, I had already received texts, sessions, and a rarely a voice-mail, rather unnerved.

Bobby carried many burdens, most of which he believed were no one's business: mild bipolar disorder, ADHD, pre-diabetes, clogged arteries, HIV; a history of alcoholism, overeating, and recovery.

He arrived by Zoom sitting in the dark. Bad sign, I remembered going through severe depressions with him, before the Group and Ezra provided structure, that necessity a few hospitalizations.

"Mail order glitch," he said, about why he hadn't been taking his medication."

I didn't scold.

We revisited old battlegrounds he had won—his weight, his mother's intrusions, his preacher father's infidelities, the bullying, the loss of Alfonso, his identity as a longtime HIV/AIDS survivor. Framed that way, he dropped the mask of cattiness and adopted his personal coat of arms: Survivor.

Still, he felt overlooked.

Andy's the smart one. John's the wise one. And Harry—hell, who can hate Harry? I'm glad you brought him in, Doctor, but it's not lost on me that you coddle that boy. His mama did too. He's gotta learn charm ain't the same thing as character.

I didn't say what was true: Bobby had us all wrapped around his charm.

His voice softened.

Tell me why folks of color assume that just 'cause I'm white I'm carrying racist bias. I bring a playful art exercise into the room and suddenly I'm waving a MAGA hat. I married a Jew, for God's sake. My friends growing up were all Black girls. But the minute I bring beauty into the room, it's like I'm back home—too fancy for my own kind, too country for everyone else.

I steered gently.

"Let's talk about the meds," I said. "And maybe why you've been avoiding me."

He hesitated.

"You firing me? Have I become too much?"

"Honey," I said, "I'm worried about your health. Something's off. We can all feel it."

"Damn you," he said. "You remind me of my mother when she was in her right mind. Couldn't keep anything from her."

He looked down.

"The doctor found a spot on my prostate. Probably nothing. But my PSA's off the charts. Biopsy's next week. Looks like I might have cancer."

We both reached for tissues.

I can't believe after everything I've survived—AIDS, addiction, grief—that God would throw this at me. I'm not dead yet. I just need to fall apart for a while, on my own terms. And what really pains me? I'm pushing topping Ezra— which is probably why we're fighting—because I want the pleasure of owning that man, missionary style, before I lose my erection.

"Have you told Ezra?" I asked.

I barely told you," he said. "You think I want that invasive helicopter of a man screaming at Cedars-Sinai staff for lab reports? You think I want the whole nuclear and extended family—the *mishpucha*—showing up from Manhattan and Miami with notes from Uncle Sol and tasteless kugel?"

Could he share this with the guys?

"They're already mad at me for being a bratty Karen. I don't want to add Dying Diva to the list. Not this week."

"You should tell them," I said. "They'd show up."

I'll call my psychiatrist—I'll give you that. You'll see. I'll be back on my meds before you can say caramel macchiato. As for Ezra—leave the Jew boy for another day. I don't want him letting me top him out of pity. I need to think.

He pulled a small waitress notebook from Clara, uncapped a navy pen, and began to write.

"Talking points for tomorrow's group," he said. "Can't let the homeboys see the queen sweat—gotta take their anger up my pussy like a man."

"Are you sure?" I asked. "It may be rough."

"I like it rough."

"Bobby," I said. "We know you're tough. But the guys are

worried—and so am I. You've come through so much. My first job is to keep you safe. The next is to help you grow."

He dropped the mask.

Doctor, you've kept me safe for many years, and Ezra and I are grateful. But it's time for Miss Thing to grow some balls. I love those men. I have no interest in misreading their reaching for me as anything but what we now call gay love— or, dare I say, the Gay Hero's Journey.

If it gets too hot in that kitchen—not hot in the Harry way, but hot in the Carrie way—Beautiful Blobbie will let you know before she melts.

Unable to stay morbid long, he shifted—precise, restrained diva mode:

You cursed brat! Look what you've done! I'm melting! Oh, what a world! Who would've thought a good little girl like you could destroy my beautiful wickedness? Oooh—I'm going!

CANTO 23: THE MEN WHO STRETCH

The sound rose from the street like trouble—low, sleek, expensive. A BMW M5, tuned for ego, not comfort.

Harry froze mid-stretch, helping his mother prepare tea and coffee for the incoming yoga students, before his mind could name why. The growl deepened, prowling closer, filling the quiet house with a vibration he felt in his ribs.

He moved fast out the back door—bare feet on cool wood, the air tight around him—and reached his old man's cedar chest by the window. The lid gave with a sigh, the smell of gun oil and cedar rushing up like a warning.

Outside, the engine cut. Silence followed—wide, waiting.

Gloria lingered nearby, telling him not to worry; she'd walk out with him to see.

They spotted the driver, a tall stranger—an inch or two taller than Harry—with reddish-brown hair streaked with gray, Einsteinian in its chaos. His shoulders were loose, chest open; he hit his vape with practiced languor, sweet smoke curling around him like incense punk. His sweatpants, overwashed to the softness of tissue paper, hung low on narrow hips; the drawstrings frayed into tiny gray tassels.

Even from the porch, Harry could smell him—bergamot, salt, and money.

Gloria, who was signing about ten people from the Eastside into class, stepped away to have a word with Harry.

"It's rare we have grown white people here," she said.

"He's olive," Harry mused.

"You staying out of trouble?" she asked, paranoid from olden times—before therapy.

"Yeah," Harry said. "Well, I slept with John two nights ago."

"Don't clown me," she said. "If you slept with the old man, you'd have told me."

"He's not an old man."

"Oh, you *did* sleep with him."

"And I yelled at Bobby for being racist—and difficult."

"You in the doghouse, bro."

They watched as the curious man drifted into the open-air garage where Harry held weekend classes and filmed content.

Instead of going through the back door, the man meandered through the front of the house, where Harry's mother held court with friends and women buying the jewelry she made at Pasadena City College. Mrs. González could be seen chatting with the stranger, no doubt to suss him out.

"I can't do nothing without my mother involved."

"That's your mom," Gloria said. "She's the sun."

"I need to get away."

"You gonna take your garage with you?"

As Harry greeted Isabel, Maria, Francine—all wearing his mother's jewelry—he introduced himself to the stranger.

"Are you here for the sex magick class, bro?" Harry asked. "Come this way."

As the two men walked toward Harry's space, his mother yelled, as a singer might, "You want your coffees hot or cold?"

"Both," he answered.

"Sex magick," she said in Spanish to her gals, while taking their credit cards.

"WELCOME TO YOGA," Harry said. "I said sex magick to give the ladies something to write home about. How'd you hear about us?"

The man extended his hand in an over-eager shake. He said he had a yoga coupon good anywhere in the county, was driving home from Orange County, needed to get back in shape, had bought a Peloton that just sat there.

Harry listened intently. The man's diction reminded him of the guy buying his videos on anal health and pleasure.

AFTER CLASS, as people filtered out, the man lingered.

"Why can't I stretch more than this?" he asked, wincing.

"This is fine," Harry said. "Just breathe."

"Kinda hurts."

"Go gentle, man."

"What if breath doesn't help?"

"It's not supposed to help. It's supposed to be what it is."

"Feels numb."

"You just said it hurt."

"I guess I can't be numb and hurting."

"Ask your freakin' hamstrings."

"They're annoyed with me."

"Are you annoyed at them?"

"Yes, that's terrible."

"Don't add meanings."

"My hamstrings are making me feel ham-strung."

They laughed.

Harry studied him. "You remind me of a guy stalking my OnlyFans."

"Oh yeah?"

"This cracker thinks he's a top, but his lover's tired of being the one who takes it lying down. Sound familiar?"

"I have a friend in that position," the man said, laughing. "Maybe he's curious about another position."

"So your friend's a homo."

"Card-carrying."

"Life at home?"

"High conflict. He prides himself on not losing his manhood."

"Only straight people think getting fucked means losing manhood."

"I need to talk to my friend."

"How did your friend find out about my *Ass Stretching Instructional Video*? My OnlyFans page isn't exactly searchable, brother."

"I wouldn't know," the man said. "But I'm sure whoever it was, they were well-intentioned."

Harry swept the studio floor and blew out a candle.

After a pause, the man asked, "You wanna get a bite?"

"What you in the mood for?"

"Anything's fine—except ham."

"And pound cake," Harry said.

At the driveway, Harry stopped to admire the man's BMW. The man tossed him the keys.

And just like that, the two—who could talk, who could see—became friends.

CANTO 24: WHO HOLDS WHOM

During what the guys would later call the *Bobby Coat of Arms Uprising*, Andy grew increasingly aware of what he had begun to think of as his true calling.

His journal became a "person" in between sessions with Dr. G.

Why would anyone as energetic as you keep pouring that gift into other people's projects?

For money? You had enough to live modestly if you stopped chasing boys who loved you only for your class.

For power? You already had the program, the reputation, the belt.

Between therapy and meetings—sometimes daily—Andy began to see the gap between how faithfully gay men suffered in private and how unaware they were that no one required it anymore.

Why did it take me so long to realize we need to help one another?

The journal broke into tears.

～

WHILE WAITING FOR JIM, Andy dug through the books he'd packed in anticipation of selling the house and moving in together. He found his worn Rilke—*Archaïscher Torso Apollos*—a gift from Bloch during their hot-and-heavy, post-Yale continental romance. They'd always called it a gay anthem.

Du musst dein Leben ändern.

You must change your life.

Bloch's marginalia still flared: notes on ripening fruit, dark centers, orgasms bursting like stars. For Bloch, the poem had always been a call to come out.

Fun fact: Jim had given Andy the same poem during his first week of sobriety.

"Oh, fuck," Andy said. *Scheiße.*

Not Jim. The contract.

～

ANDY AND JIM READ TOGETHER—*THE Tale of Genji, A Portrait of the Artist as a Young Man*—talking books in bed, sober and careful. Jim admired Andy's intellect, even when he couldn't tell whether Andy was mocking him or himself.

"What's so wrong with safety?" Jim asked, when Andy pressed about the engagement. "Especially when it's never been granted to us."

Andy found the answer unbearably tender.

But their sex life, what of it? Andy had sworn off the belt until he understood his father's pleasure in administering it. Jim wrote about everything else in the weekly emails they exchanged at their therapist's suggestion, the therapist they had discussed during their one session with Dr. Glitter.

Everything except Jim's unspoken fears.

With the boxes packed and the move imminent, Jim knew

Andy might use tonight to call off both the engagement and the company.

So much for safety.

WHEN JIM ARRIVED—SUITED, harried from Century City— Andy skipped the usual affection.

"I needed to talk," Andy said. "I put this off too long."

"I got into USC," he added. "And UCLA."

"For your master's?"

"No. For yours."

Silence.

"I'm going the Ph.D. route."

Jim nodded. "There's a reason you didn't tell me sooner."

"It's full-time."

"You can't just walk away. We have a company."

"I can do whatever I want."

Jim thought of the years he'd held everything together: the deals, the damage control, the apologies. He thought of Andy half-pickled, brilliant, uninsurable. He did not say any of it.

"You don't burn the bridge while you're still on it," Jim said softly.

ANDY DIMMED THE LIGHTS. Lit a Cuban cigar Kofi had sent after Andy's first Golden Globe.

"Get on your knees."

Jim froze—then obeyed.

"Who's your master?"

"You are, sir."

"We're engaged," Andy said calmly. "I'm not leaving. I'm not abandoning our projects. I'm practicing both/and."

He paused.

"I'm not moving in yet. That doesn't mean I don't want to marry you. It means I don't know who I am."

Jim nodded.

Andy slipped off his Gucci belt. The sound was unmistakable.

The night was still young.

CANTO 25: RECONSTRUCTION

Rain came steady against the windows, turning the city into a smear of gray lights and dripping palms. I logged on, but the guys also wanted to try to process their first fight without Daddy being too involved.

Inside my office suite, the group gathered—Andy by the bell, John sunk back in his chair, eyes keen but tired, and Harry restless, his bracelets making small metallic noises.

Then the door opened.

Bobby lumbered in last—no sequins, no boas, only dark circles under his eyes and a peace-sign pendant swinging low over a black T-shirt.

"Rough morning?" Harry asked quietly.

Bobby shrugged. "Just morning."

He took off his glasses and set them on the low table, a small ritual of surrender.

"Well now," he said, voice half church hymn, half blues riff. "Here I am, babies. And truth is, I almost didn't make it. A voice in my head this morning—mean as a rattlesnake— told me to stay home, pull the covers up. But I got dressed, brushed my teeth, packed Clara, and hauled my ass through the rain because something in me wasn't about to let shame have the last word."

Andy leaned forward. "Can you, for once, give us you sans Blanche DuBois?"

Bobby smiled faintly. "You think this is Blanche? No, sugar. Blanche was Louisiana—perfume and tragedy. I'm Mississippi—mud, magnolia, and blues. We don't faint on couches; we build 'em from scratch."

John broke in. "You left us in the lurch, honey. Now it sounds like you're doing us a favor by showing up."

"How you faring, Bobby?" I asked.

"Doc," he said, "I pulled the Knight of Wands. That little salamander walks through fire without being destroyed. I'm ready."

"You want fire?" Harry said. "Here you go. When you said 'reverse racism,' my stomach turned. I trusted you to hold me and my people, and it felt like you yanked the rug to win a round. That cut keeps bleeding."

Bobby's hand twitched toward a fan that wasn't there.

"Stop with the fan," Andy muttered.

"Please, sugar. Don't give me agita about my fan."

He pulled a peppermint from Clara. "Mama swore a peppermint steadies the nerves. Doctor says it steadies the blood sugar. Guess I'll test both."

"You got diabetes?" Harry asked.

"Someone give our Chicano Curandero a medical degree already," Bobby shot back. "Not like I haven't been dropping cues between the pounds."

Andy, clinical: "Maybe you lost too much weight too fast. You never talk about your HIV. Or your meds—psychiatric or otherwise. You on Lamotrigine?"

Bobby froze. "Who told you?"

"I'm not a psychologist," Andy replied. "I just play one on TV."

John, to Harry: "He's getting as snarky as us—and as bitchy as Bobby."

Harry: "Bro's coming into his own. He'll be the biggest top of all of us."

"How could I not notice?" Andy asked. "The sleepless energy. The irritation that flips to charm. The 3 a.m. texts about re-editing your Coat of Arms? You're not manic-manic. You're Bipolar II—just enough lightning to feel alive before the thunder caves in."

Bobby exhaled. "A girl can't have any medical privacy from Spock."

Andy: "Said Lamotrigine just to see if you'd flinch—and you did. Mousetrap."

"That was inappropriate," I said.

"Fire me," Andy shot back.

Harry and John high-fived.

I sighed. "No touching."

Bobby shook his head. "Doc, stop worrying about me. I feel cared for by Andy. That was the most loving—and accurate—diagnosis I've had."

Harry said, "Still, what happened with you and Ezra?"

"Can we not?" Bobby said quickly. "Yes, I stopped taking my meds. Got over-excited about the MAP project. Life stressors. I'll own that."

John pressed. "And the race thing?"

"I didn't say *reverse* racism straight. I said *revere* racism. Irony lost in translation."

Andy: "Still white fragility by another name."

Bobby sighed. "I was scared, cornered, tired of being framed as the problem. Doesn't make it right. I reached for a word that hit back."

Harry shook his head. "You study racism doesn't mean you're woke. Study don't cleanse the wound."

Bobby: "Didn't we just lose an election over the word woke?"

"Bad jokes aside, I do have one burning issue."

"Go on," John said.

"My fear was that you brown boys would form a clique, ice me out, hold secret orgies I wasn't invited to."

John laughed. "Funny—your walkout made us a clique."

Harry: "And we had the orgy."

Andy: "So there."

John: "You got your wish."

Bobby could not help but laugh at the irony of it all.

John grew quiet. "Truth is, we were sad. You've always come back, Bobby. Don't leave like that again."

Bobby nodded. "I won't."

They teased, joked, half-lied about blankets, toothpaste, and catnaps that replaced orgies. Under the laughter, something softened; something mended.

Then Harry asked, "So what about Ezra?"

Bobby stiffened. "Leave him out of it."

"Call him," Harry said. "I have an intuition that you should."

Bobby looked very sad and grateful and angry—all at the same time.

Despite himself, he picked up his phone and sent a single text: *I apologized to the guys.*

"That's it?" Harry asked.

Bobby nodded. "It's enough for today."

PROGRESS NOTES
FOR PURGATORIO

Hearing how the group navigated its most significant rupture to date reduced my concern that the convergence of strong personalities and unintegrated shadow material would overwhelm or destabilize the group. Instead, the members demonstrated a growing capacity for affect regulation and relational containment. Notably, they were able to tolerate one another's emotional reactivity without defaulting to retaliation, responding instead with empathy, patience, and direct confrontation when needed.

The conflict involving Bobby temporarily eclipsed the developing intimacy between Harry and John. That connection currently presents as cautious and largely platonic in tone, reminiscent of an early adolescent attachment. Both men appeared reluctant to disrupt group equilibrium and relied on individual therapy to process the excitement and anxiety associated with emerging creative and relational possibilities. Each articulated that these developments were connected—both metaphorically and concretely—to the project's stated aim of healing gay sex and love.

At present, the group remains in the early developmental phase of the G+Q MAP Project. My sense of stabilization may therefore represent a temporary equilibrium rather than a sustained resolution. To date, the group has not yet engaged the external world through enactment or public-facing expression. Such engagement—particularly with audiences beyond the familiar and affirming circles that comprise Harry's social milieu—will likely introduce additional clinical and relational stressors.

Overall, the group demonstrated increased cohesion, reflective capacity, and tolerance for conflict. Further observation is required as the project moves from internal exploration to external enactment.

ACT IV — CRUCIBLE

The men attempt to salvage gay love, gay sex, and gay pro-
creativity—during a debacle.

CANTO 26: ANOTHER OPENING, ANOTHER SHOW—OR CLASS

"Paging Dr. Glitter," Andy texted, unable to wait even an hour before the Zoom session. "It took a few weeks of arguing, but the first G+Q MAP workshop is scheduled."

He had to wait—but the moment I logged on, there he was. And he looked a bit… different.

"How's Marco?" he asked. "Your Yiddishe Momma?"

"That's a snazzy leather jacket," I said, noticing how Andy had been bringing more of himself into the Zoom lately. "I can smell its history from here." Then I added, "Everyone's hanging in there, but it's bitter cold and I could use a jacket like that myself."

"Italian motorcycle jacket—Belstaff. Middleman find. Le Meatpacking District… *tu te souviens?*"

"Those were the days," I said.

"We miss you," he said. "But thank God we still have you. I'm a bit anxious—but here's what we've got."

Andy nodded, flipped open his laptop, and—with the insouciance of a man casually dusting imaginary cocaine from his jacket—showed me mockups of the possible venues for the workshop: Harry's *Garaje de la Ascensión* or Bobby's Powder Room. He had been unofficially appointed location scout, and this was his report:

First came Bobby's Red Room—a sewing den dense with gowns, capes, and refitted menswear. Backstage Paris revue energy. Chalk marks still ghosted his campaign to shrink a former fat-boy wardrobe into Twiggy proportions. Nearby, the Power Room doubled as dressing room and drag battle-field: bright mirrors, wigs by decade, sequins, glue guns, and the faint acetone tang Bobby treated as incense. In a sunlit corner sat Clara's Room of Her Own—glitter, thread, and cosmic clutter—named, Bobby claimed, for an imaginary woman who "gets pregnant here and has her Uranian babies." Andy didn't ask what that meant. He suspected Bobby didn't know either.

Andy had only ever heard tall tales about Harry's four hidden rooms, but walking through them in sequence felt like entering the man's internal architecture.

First, the Iron Altar: the old garage still ribbed with its original beams, every tool and length of rope hung with priestly precision. Then the House of Breath and Body, where the punching bag swayed like a metronome of discipline and the weights gleamed under a single focused light. Beyond it waited the Incense Room—a sanctuary of meditation pillows, Mexican fabrics, and the faint sweet-ness of copal masking discreet hooks and silk restraints that hinted at Harry's more devotional practices. And at the deepest point of the corridor lay the Cell of Rest: a dim lavender chamber where a down comforter and ceramic keepsakes shared quiet space with a folded sling

—a room equal parts bedroom, confessional, and spell book.

Closing the laptop—and fake bowing in response to a few quiet claps—Andy added that Bobby had been crestfallen when the Diva realized Harry's Ascension boasted more inches than Clara's Room of Her Own.

"Like losing a title in the Miss Universe of square footage," Andy said.

"He mentioned that Ezra and he own a small apartment a few blocks away they have been renting out for Airbnb that he might move Clara's Room to. I got to thinking that Bobby was plotting and planning for us maybe to use that as an alternative space to rehearse in that's not all the over in Altadena and when we can't use the open space in your office."

I asked Andy when he had mentioned that, or why he looked so earnestly deep in thought.

"Oh, nothing," he said. But I knew that Andy was plotting and planning himself, because he had decided to either sell or rent out his own Silver Lake cottage to support him should he decide to go to school full-time."

On the issue of cost, opinions diverged. Andy and Harry strongly discouraged charging at all—each, for different reasons, committed to attracting people without many resources. It wasn't that John or Bobby were desperate to make a hundred dollars or less from the workshops.

"People will not value what we offer," Bobby declared, "if they don't have to pay anything."

John agreed, which put him at loggerheads with Harry, who accused John of being a capitalist—prompting Bobby to snap, "Look who's talking, the most spoiled boy alive, who can work or not work because he doesn't have to pay rent!"

John, still smarting over how Carter had taken advantage of him, already had a bone to pick with Harry. Harry responded by showing what he made as an influencer—not a fortune, but not nothing either—along with the amount he paid his parents for rent, leaving out that they deposited it right back into his private account.

I found their capacity to fight—and even to dislike one another—reassuring. It marked real progress from the days of storming out. They could now tolerate conflict without my constant refereeing.

That made it plausible—if still a little foolish—that they might manage the leap from talk to action: taking their modest show off the page and into the world. If not on the road, then at least into Harry's garage—within the month.

THE PERSON I expected to be most excited—Harry, who had won the battle to host the first G+Q MAP Hero's Journey Workshop—seemed the most anxious.

Gloria—his *mano derecha*—had just gotten engaged to her Arizona girlfriend and was spending less time at Harry's place. She alone could switch effortlessly from *la butchona chingona* to *la morra más linda del mundo*, and she knew exactly how to run interference between Harry's world and his *jefita*'s.

Being kind to Harry's mother was easy—she came off *bien dulce*. Gloria's own mother, by contrast, would spit and mutter *mira esa cabrona, queriendo ser vato* every time she saw Gloria in work boots. Staying close to Harry's house met needs Gloria couldn't afford to neglect.

Without her around, Harry had lost his shield—Gloria, the bridge between worlds. Which meant Harry's mother

might be extra mindful of the four men she suspected—
correctly, according to Harry—had come to take her
momma's boy away.

I asked why he seemed off. His individual sessions—still on
Zoom—had continued uninterrupted, but the group structure
had shifted.

"I'm a scared, sad boy," he said. "It'll take time to trust
things without you in the room."

"What are you most worried about?"

He didn't answer right away. Then: "That I'll be happy."

"Happy?"

"No one ever stuck around for that," he said. "They liked
me better when I played POS. Pump you full, spit in your
face, pretend I didn't need you to let me live."

"So something's changing," I said.

He shook his head quickly. "We can't say that yet. If I get
happy, it'll be a mess."

CANTO 27: HARRY'S UNFINISHED FAMILY BUSINESS

When Bobby, Andy, and John said they'd arrive at 9:00 a.m. for a noon workshop in Altadena, they meant 8:00.

Harry, by contrast, believed that if a brother says 9:00, only a tweaker shows up at 8:00. So, like a normal person—by which he meant someone who'd dropped out of the matrix— he set his alarm for 10:00.

John's driver let Andy and John out at the curb while they confirmed they had the right place. Andy appreciated the wide street, the old oaks forming a canopy overhead. Craftsman porches, Spanish-tile roofs, careful landscaping.

Folding chairs spilled across the front lawn. Kids zigzagged between cousins. Juan Gabriel drifted from a hidden speaker, mixing with bass thumping from a parked car down the block.

Set farther back on the oversized lot, partly hidden by hedges, sat another structure—what Andy guessed must be the ADU Harry and his father had rebuilt. In Altadena, these back houses often felt like separate properties altogether: their own walkway, patio, and privacy shaped by distance, trees, and fences.

"Are you sure we're in the right place?" John asked.

A woman in a butter-yellow cotton sundress appeared, embroidery catching the light. She carried a platter of *pan dulce* and freshly cut fruit. She seemed instantly youthful to Bobby, who whispered *Sophia Loren in Houseboat*, to which John retorted *Elizabeth Taylor in Cleopatra*. She glowed in the morning sun.

"You must be the boys Harry has spoken so much about!" Mrs. González said, beaming.

"Oh—I'm his mother, in case you didn't know," she added, offering pastries, fruit, and linen napkins.

"We know," all three men said, feeling happier by the second under the force of her warmth.

"Hand me your key," Mr. González said, shaking hands. "I'll park your Porsche between the Ford F-150 XLT and the GMC Sierra Denali. Once night falls, they could steal your alternator. There'll be about ten more cars for the *convivio*."

Andy pulled John aside. "Once night falls? I thought we'd do our three-hour workshop and be out of here by two or three."

He added, "Jim and I have an important dinner. Can't miss it."

"We'll be in and out," John said. "It's just a very casual G+Q premiere—five or six people. Harry will run it."

"What is a *convivio*?" Andy asked Bobby.

"Small family gathering," Bobby supplied.

Sensing their nerves, Mr. González offered cigarettes or more sweets.

"Gave up smoking about two years ago," John ventured, even as Andy took one.

"Um... where's Harry?" Bobby asked. "He was expecting us at—"

"He's still catching *zzzzz*," Mrs. González interrupted, powdering her nose in a compact. "He's not pleasant in the morning. Please—have a *pan dulce*."

Then she retracted the platter. "Oh! I iced initials. Who's A and who's J?"

"A regular demon," Mr. González said, making little horns with his fingers. "*Un diablo*."

"A darling," she corrected. "We spoiled him. Same sun sign, same good looks—and oh well—he's also our… problem."

"Pric—" Mr. González began.

"Say it, honey," she finished. "He's a prince. Who else in the family is getting a degree? UCLA. *Bendito sea Dios*. I'm so glad he has you boys to help him stick with his studies, settle down, find a nice girl."

Bobby winked discreetly.

Oh, so that's where the DL comes from.

Mrs. González took a closer look at Bobby. Used to women in tank tops and boots, tattooed biceps gleaming as they unloaded gear, Bobby was a horse of a different color: multicolored silk scarves, light pink slacks, elegant sandals, Rainbow Glasses.

"*¡Qué bonita!*" Mrs. González exclaimed, clocking that Bobby—her contemporary—was not only wise but radiant.

Bobby's heart recognized where Harry's charm had been minted.

John and Andy exchanged looks.

Where the hell was Harry?

THEN CHAOS.

Curses inside. A chair shoved. Dishes crashing.

Harry burst from a side door, half-dressed, boxer shorts

barely decent, tearing across the lawn, scattering children and folding chairs, muttering under his breath.

"Mother!" His voice cracked. "So you're up to your old tricks again—making this your *convivio*? I told you—*te lo dije*—this is private!"

"*Cálmate, mijo*," his father said gently. "It's not what you think."

"And what the hell are you doing wining and dining these men of honor?" Harry snapped.

The men had never seen him like this.

"I'm getting my own space—*Jesús Cristo*! And then this bull —acting like Bobby is your long-lost daughter when your real daughter won't speak to you cuz you smother your kids with Catholic love."

Bobby moved instinctively to make peace.

"Do not," Andy said.

"We're sorry," Bobby murmured.

"¡BOBBY!" Harry snapped. "Stop—*ahorita*. This is my shit. *Mi cagadero*. You want shadow? *Pues aquí está*. Don't touch it."

Bobby stepped back, even though he knew what he was doing.

"*Mamá*—coffee. *Papá*—cigarette," Harry barked.

His mother scurried. His father lit a Lucky Strike.

Harry kept talking, motioning for his father to go—*déjame en paz*.

At this point, John put his arm around Harry and drew him close, waving the smoke away. Bobby gave John a thumbs-up as Andy took a hit of Harry's cigarette.

"Do you even know what this couple does—these two?" Harry began again, much less angry and more sad. "My mother makes mole *poblano, birria, tamales*—each one exquisite. And if that wasn't fuckin' enough, she sends free food all over the neighborhood. She even goes to ICE protests and hands out her delicacies."

"Doesn't sound good," Bobby said.

"There's no one on this godforsaken planet who doesn't worship my mother. Does she ever sleep? She's up when I come home—even if I'm fucked up at five a.m.—and awake when I wake."

"Overbearing," Bobby added, quietly.

"I'm not cappin' you. It's like God gave her a sixth sense. I can't do anything without her knowing. I don't even have the heart to turn off my phone's location! She knows when I'm going to the group and when I'm leaving it—I kid you not! And if she starts to look sad and lonely because I haven't shared with her the contents of my day, I fall down on the job completely and tell her everything. She's at once my confidant and my backstabber!"

"We will have to do an updated version of *Psycho*," Bobby said. "And you can play Anthony Perkins. I can direct."

Andy bit his lip not to laugh, curious to see Bobby choreographing a kind of family therapy.

"And you know what he does?" Harry asked, able to stay on track and smile at Bobby's joke. "My father brings the brandy, the cigars, the carne asada, and the game on Sundays. They feel so guilty for how they spoiled me—and ruined me— after the whole Guillermo fucked-up shit, but also keep their eyes on me so I don't become who they think I really am: a dead-ass sociopathic *bad hombre*. They fault themselves entirely —for not observing us kids better—while my father was out whoring and she was crying like we weren't supposed to hear!"

"And yet, you remain," Bobby said so quietly, Harry didn't have to hear.

"And my father lets her be *La Reina* because the world passed the old *Rey* by, and his bastard son won't even go to MEChA, and no one knows where his great love—the one he kept secret—is at. The Virgin cooks for the poor; the Whore lies to the family. And Harry—her holy fool—loves them both, or feels sorry for them, or I just get so confused, so I cry with her still."

"Crying with mom," Bobby said. "That's why I left Clarksdale."

"And now he's tryin' to make up for lost time, giving me that 'go into business with me, *mijo*' shit again. 'I'll buy a condo, make it an Airbnb, you fix it up and rent it,' he says. I said, 'No, *papá*, I'm moving out to make my way on my own.' So what does he do? He builds me this—this little kingdom! The garage, three times the size it should be, so I never fuckin' leave the compound! I even have a fucking hot tub. It's for the whole family, but no one dares use it."

Altadena is so far away from all the rest of us, Bobby said to himself.

The three men stayed silent. Late-morning light spilled through the open door. Andy's eyes narrowed, analytic; John studied Harry like a case study come to life; Bobby fanned himself slowly, mesmerized, half-smiling at the revelation.

Harry's voice softened but still carried heat. "I need to move out. Breaks my fuckin' heart. The garage they made me is like a fuckin' palace—gym, yoga studio, sex-magic hut—but the more I fuck with you boys, am home too many days a week, they're starting to hover like they did after we lost G."

From the kitchen, Mrs. González's laughter rose again— bright, unstoppable, like a radio that never quite turns off. The scent of coffee and fried masa filled the air. Andy took a breath. He watched Harry's fury dissolve into his parents' noise.

～

"Why are we stuck here in the middle of the yard on these rococo chairs?" Bobby asked.

Andy got oriented. They had first met Mr. and Mrs. González at the front of the house. Then, under Mrs. González's jurisdiction, they were escorted to the Big Lawn, where the *convivio* preparation was already underway. Two servants, a few relatives, and three friends clustered around a wooden table and lounge chairs beneath citrus trees. Breakfast had begun: plates passing, chairs scraping. From here, Andy could see that Harry had his own enclave: a never-never zone of rococo chairs, crystals, ashtrays, and cushy blankets, all laundered by Alejandrina—Mrs. González's "maid," which really meant favored sister.

"Where's *El Garaje*" Andy asked, given that the one time he had seen the space had been a night and through the back, private alley way driveway.

Harry, almost delirious, due to having suffered emotional expenditure before coffee, cannabis, and morning meditation, pointed to the back of the property.

Andy spotted a series of lemon and olive trees that led to small walkway. Andy pointed John to the area. He saw two possible pathways and decided they should head to the closest one now.

We need to get there," Andy said. "Now."

John heard Andy's Senior command and led the boys led them past the lounge chairs and casual traffic of cousins toward a narrow stone walkway.

The path curved behind the house and opened onto *El Garaje*.

First came the Iron Altar: the old garage itself, still ribbed with its original beams. Tools and lengths of rope hung with priestly precision. Black-metal shelves held lumber, gym gear, boxing gloves, jump ropes, water jugs, and art supplies. This was where events were held, and filmed.

To one side lay the the Breath and Body Space. A punching bag swayed gently. Weights gleamed beneath focused light. The room smelled faintly sweat and rubber.

Beyond was the Incense Room. Meditation pillows rested on woven Mexican fabrics. The air carried the sweetness of copal.

At the far end of the corridor was the Cell of Rest. A down comforter lay folded with care near a futon. Ceramic keepsakes lined a low shelf. Hooks for a sling held a linen blanket.

"It's where I can find peace," Harry said, as he motioned for people to find a comfy cushions or love seats arranged in a circle. He lit candles and sage. As the care of Andy and Bobby remained his priority, he refrained from rolling a backwood.

He moved his cushion close to John, to lay his head near John's lap.

A few minutes had passed when Harry asked what time it was.

Bobby said, 11:00 a.m.

"Shit," Harry said.

"What now?" John asked.

Harry looked pale.

"Not good," he said, quietly.

"I think I made a big boo boo."

And that's when they heard the clamor.

CANTO 28: THE RIOT AT ASCENSION GARAGE

By now, Andy and Bobby—having peeked out first—heard car horns, raised voices, and what sounded like about forty people: some with boxing gloves, others with yoga mats, some wearing very skimpy clothes, others who looked like mechanics.

The duo stepped out along the quiet path Harry and his father had built. The winding walkway, laid with sun-warmed stones to steady one's gait, was flanked by desert blooms—bursts of magenta and gold against pale sand.

A small fountain murmured nearby, its basin guarded by a humble sculpture of the Virgin, her robes painted in the colors of the Mexican flag. Beside her, an image of Jesus shimmered beneath an LGBTQ rainbow glaze. Wind chimes made of turquoise glass sang softly in the breeze. A lemon tree leaned toward a fig tree like an old friend, their branches arching above the path.

This is what they saw a few yards yonder:

A wiry, commanding woman stood at the center, marshaling the crowd alongside Mrs. González.

"I bet that's Gloria," Bobby said.

The moment Gloria spotted Bobby and Andy—especially Bobby—she ran right over. She had clocked that the queen who floated an inch above the ground was the "Mother" Harry spoke of so warmly.

"I feel like I know you both," she said, extending her hand.

Singing a few bars of "Gloria," Bobby grabbed her hands and snapped into action.

"Andy—rush back and tell John and Harry to stay put. Grab the folding table I saw in the garage. Grab my Clara. Then run back here."

At the same moment, Bobby texted Ezra:

I saw you lurking back there. I have no idea why you're here, but I think I figured it out. In any event, meet me by the front driveway. I'll need your help. On two matters.

BOBBY FOUND himself irritated that he was wearing sweatpants to an elegant workshop and hadn't shaved. The impulse to make him feel bad about this rose in his chest, but he managed his best to tell that "Hurt" that Papa would attend to Judy in a second.

"It's good to see you," Ezra said. "What's up?"

His voice, however, was lovely. Bobby hadn't realized how much he had missed its nasal tonalities.

"Oh, honey," Bobby said, "before I tell you the plan about helping to manage this mess here, there's something you don't know, and I need you to hear it without trying to fix me. I have prostate cancer. It's early, it's fast-moving, and it scared me enough that I started acting like a lunatic."

Ezra went still, his mouth opening and closing again as the

old reflex—to erupt, to interrogate, to demand—rose up and stalled,.

But Harry had drilled this into him: listen first. Ezra swallowed hard, his eyes filling against his will.

Bobby kept going because stopping now would undo him.

"I didn't tell you because I thought I could manage it, that discipline or control or style would save me, and instead I just made everything worse."

Ezra nodded as tears slipped free, silent and humiliating, pressing the heel of his hand into his eye while breathing the way Harry had taught him to breathe when he wanted to scream.

"I'm listening," Ezra said finally, but fearing an asthma attack.

Bobby exhaled, the smallest loosening. "Good. Now help me with the chaos in front. If anyone knows how to help Diva do her thing, it's her *balboosta*."

"Will you take me back?" he asked, and then, remembering how Harry had taught him to stretch one hamstring at a time, he proceeded to do a yoga salutation, to Bobby's amazement.

Then he asked, "Where to?"

Ten minutes later, Bobby, Ezra, Andy, and Gloria gathered with Mr. and Mrs. González, who were struggling with the now-unruly crowd—which had not, in fact, grown to forty.

"One moment," Mrs. González said, "and we will have everything settled." Then, to her husband: "Why is Harry not answering his phone? And I wish I had that tall woman's phone number."

"213-314-4343," Bobby said, motioning for Andy to set up

the table and Gloria to open Clara, while also giving Mrs. González a discreet hug.

"Thank God," she said. "We have a riot."

Bobby handed Mr. González and Gloria a stack of half-by-eleven-inch crème card-stock.. Each received a pair of scissors. He instructed them to fold every sheet in half, then cut along the crease. On one side, Bobby wrote *Ascension's Garage Fall Sale*. Inside, he added: *A Special Two-for-One Deal for Those Who Made the Trek*. Beneath it, he sketched a vehicle—a car, a boat, or a plane—whatever image his hand felt moved to conjure.

The crème paper held the ink like skin taking makeup.

Working fast, and as only Bobby could, he produced twenty handmade Two-for-One Ascension coupons—each poised between whimsy and craft. Even Gloria looked stunned. They felt less like coupons than small acts of faith.

"Quite the husband-and-wife team," Mrs. González said. "Do you lovebirds have children?"

"We're working on it," Bobby answered, then pointed to Ezra and said—"*Todavía es virgen*."

Gloria got the joke. Harry, apparently almost as bad as Bobby, was a real yenta.

"Does Harry give you different emails with clear instructions?" Bobby asked Mrs. González, once they had gotten everything under control.

"He gives me different email lists with no instructions."

"I will take that to HR," Bobby said, to Mrs. González's relief.

WHILE SOME OF the attendees who had driven from as far away as Venice and Riverside remained angry, the combination of coupons, Mrs. González's finger foods, and their enduring love for Harry sent most back to their cars, vowing to return another day.

Six remained—ages seventeen to seventy—carrying books and journals, mostly Latino, but not all.

Afterward, Mr. and Mrs. González fetched folding chairs and lemonade so everyone could relax before dealing with Harry's quiet wrath. Noticing the matching wedding bands on Ezra and Bobby, they arranged the chairs so the two "lovebirds" sat together.

"We should go back and get the workshop going," Andy said, winking at Bobby not to get too chummy with the parents.

Bobby winked back, removing Ezra's hand from his.

"Hang around," Bobby said to Ezra. "If you can. In about two hours, I may need you again."

That's all I ever wanted—to be needed, Ezra wished to say. But substituted: "Roger, Roger."

BY THE TIME Bobby entered the garage—smelling of weed and telling himself boys will be boys—he realized he was emotional about seeing Ezra. *He did seem changed, but I don't know, he's so needy.*

But, he made a grown-up decision to have a firm talk with "Punch" and "Judy," his nicknames for Rage and Hurt.

"Everything is handled," he said, smiling.

Then the tiny jab: "Ezra's here."

Harry put his head in his hands.

"Oh—that's Ezra!"

"Do you know him?"

Harry danced nervously in place, begging his body for elixirs.

"Not so far, Mister," Bobby said. "I figured out our problem. Harry's mother sent the invitation to the wrong email list. Out of thirty people who showed up, we have five brave souls who—if they haven't left—are eager to participate."

"Let's just cancel," Harry said, utterly deflated.

"Cancel?" Bobby said. "That's like Lexi Featherston dancing at the party and falling out the window. That's the end of the It Girls."

"Over my dead body."

JOHN STEPPED FORWARD.

"I have a better idea than suicide," the elder said. "I treated this little cosmic joke as a dream—one that explains exactly what we're doing here."

"Pray tell," Andy said, pleased not to be the only shrink in the room.

"Better still," John added. "I'll run the meeting. Bobby— may I have some paper and colored Sharpies?"

"Run the meeting?" Harry groaned. "It's not a meeting."

"You forget I used to run meetings between directors, actors, studio heads, and agents. Call it dream analysis if you prefer. Here's your agenda—your script. Your lines."

"Mr. DeMille, I'm ready for my close-up," Bobby intoned.

John reached out a hand for Bobby and Andy to pull the him off the yoga mat to standing position.

"Follow me, you clowns," he said. "You, too, Harry. We're about to have our premiere."

"When the Saints Go Marching In," Bobby sang—pointedly not *Send in the Clowns*.

CANTO 29: JOHN
INTERPRETS THE RIOT

The Premiere

At John's suggestion, Harry led the crew to the part of El Garage called the Iron Altar. Black-metal shelves stood in perfect order: tools, lumber, gym gear, ropes, boxing gloves, jump ropes, water jugs, art supplies.

John nodded to Gloria to put something on—"Brought Up in a Small Neighborhood" by Lil Rob.

Bobby danced his way into the space. The six devotees who had paid for the G+Q MAP Premiere filed in and sang along.

The ice had broken.

~

GETTING GROUNDED

At John's cue, Harry introduced Bobby, John, and Andy, and invited the attendees to grab some cushions and settle in.

Harry blessed the four corners and lit sage.

"My brother, John, here," Harry ventured. "Give him

your respect. He has an idea about how to see the debacle, you feel me, as a dream within the dream—seriously."

JOHN SPOKE IN A QUIET VOICE. He pointed with his eyes for Bobby, Andy, and Harry to sit in different places in the circle, marking four corners, with Andy closest by.

"So we had, as you all know, a bit of a mess out there," John said, laughing slightly.

"But as we were collecting our thoughts, it occurred to me that this mess wasn't a catastrophe. No, using our 'technology,' Bobby's Rainbow Glasses, which he's wearing, we could view this imbroglio as a metaphor for the Queer Hero's Journey: how it starts, how it stops, and what can be done about flowing with the cycle."

Andy, Bobby, and Harry met each other's eyes. They had not expected this to be John's moment to shine.

"We were rather excited," John added. "At least to start with."

"We thought we were prepared. Damn near. Harry had warned his moms and pops to go to the Pasadena Farmers Market. Didn't want those snoops to be snooping."

The attendees giggled. Each had endured the invasive eyes of Harry's *mamacita*. But no one had discussed the price her time exacted.

Queer Spark

"However, nothing is as it appears," John continued. If you think of this this Meet as a dream, we can interpret the wish for the launch of our G+Q MAP Workshop Premiere as no different from our original queer wish for love and acceptance when we are born. That is, if you can harbor the thought that each of us was born with *The Queer Spark*. Maybe even before we felt homosexual or bisexual yearnings, we knew of this Spark. Who knows how spirit and sex work, or interact? But if you feel it's real raise your hand.

John asked Bobby to distribute white paper and colored markers.

"Andy over here will invite you to do some writing on your Queer Spark. You all ready?"

AS THE PARTICIPANTS WROTE, John asked Bobby to hum "Amazing Grace" which bled into "Aint No Mountain High Enough" with Bobby able to anticipate when he might upstage John, so brought it down. John nodded kindly.

SHADOW SELVES

"But like the iconic Garden of Eden story," John added, "our best-laid plans got waylaid. The Queer Spark hope went to shit. What caused us all to feel so confused and lost was that Harry's mother and father, out of their idea of heterosexual love, took us hostage with their charm offensive. And Harry, who is more susceptible to them than we are, was felled. He lost his stability.

How many of you have considered the price you pay for living in a heterosexual world?

Before I go on, and bore you with ideas, Andy over here will give you some paper to write just one memory of how you have had to reduce yourselves when you are with family.

"I can't talk about my boyfriend when my father is home," someone said.

"My own boyfriend hates it when I act queen."

"My mother won't say the word, 'girlfriend.' She can only say 'friend.'"

John made sure to go over to each person who talked and look them right in the eye and even hug them if that is what they felt they needed.

The man you all look up to as a Brujo Bro, cannot, without the help of others, and that is a big theme today, the help of others, stand up to thousands of years of organized heterosexuality."

"How did this happen? Well, on the conscious level, they wished the best for Harry and his friends. But the unconscious level—this is just my guess—they did not trust what we were about to do.

"My guess is that, deep down, they saw us like the Jedi taking Anakin from his mother to train with the Master Jedi, and they weren't gonna let their spoiled Anakin out of their hands."

"So when Andy, Bobby, and I arrived, they swarmed us and tried to get us hypnotized—not with poppies but *pan dulces!*"

The crowd laughed, themselves having gained a few extra pounds as the cost of doing business with Harry.

"This angered Harry," John narrated.

People stopped laughing. Each recalled the one or two times they had seen Harry upset.

"And, well," John went on, "we had known that Harry had some issues about getting close to another man—you know, despite him being the leader of the pack. He's actually pretty lonely. Now we see why."

Harry lay his head on Bobby's lap. As Bobby caressed his hair, his gaze met Andy's, who stood as sentry near John.

"We saw how the heterosexual family—and this is a nice and accepting family—could overwhelm and thus annihilate the Queer Spark with which we were all born, ya hear me?"

"And these are nice and well-meaning parents, Mr. and Mrs. González. I'm sure some of us had Mommy Dearie parents who would *not* go out of their way to spend a small fortune in a garage in which Harry could host his training classes and fisting ceremonies."

"Only did fisting once," Harry said to Bobby, "but whatever."

Bobby agreed, "Whatever."

"But mark my words," John continued, raising his voice, sounding like a pastor, "heterosexuals cannot teach the queer child about his original parents—his homo Mother, Aphrodite Urania, and his homo father, Lord Seth, which predate the biological."

"Bro's fuken erudite," Harry said, looking up at Bobby. He then whispered, "You got an Airbnb goin empty?"

Bobby listened as that information could only have come from Ezra.

"In fact," John continued, his voice rising as if he were Socrates climbing a ladder, "their entire system of holding little Harry when they first got him, made his gay child feel like he some kind of monster. His Queer Spark got shoved underground, into shame."

Harry sat up, shocked. But John wasn't done.

"We cannot survive under those conditions," John said. "True as we may want to make excuses for our well-meaning mothers and fathers, *they did the best they could*, we have to stop turning to the Ten Commandments. The Higher Power in the mind must not be the heterosexual parents. They must be the

Gay Royal Parents. Only they can summon our long-lost Queer Spark."

Harry took out his journal and jotted that line down: *The Higher Power in the mind must not be the heterosexual parents. They must be the Gay Royal Parents. Only they can summon our long-lost Queer Spark."*

"Even Dr, Glitter didn't talk that way," Harry said to Bobby.

"Dr Glitter doesn't give sermons," Bobby answered. "Or host revivals."

JOHN ASKED Andy to come forward and asked Bobby to ring the bell.

Andy offered this prompt:

Can you write a few words about the time you realized you could not be yourself—when you were bullied or queer-bashed? This will help you uncover the long-lost Gay Child, your Shadow Self.

ONE PARTICIPANT TOLD the story of being beaten so badly by his mother, after she found him performing fellatio on a neighborhood boy, that he had to go to the emergency room. She broke his nose and cursed him, and he chose to report her to Child Protective Services rather than return home. Until he turned eighteen, he lived on the streets, until Harry took him in and secretly gave him safe harbor, lest the authorities (including Harry's parents) find out. He slept in this very room.

People clapped.

"Did you do that?" Bobby asked, wondering why Harry never brought that up in the Group.

Harry looked at Bobby, of course.

Helper Selves

"Harry is a person who helps. We all must be people who help. We live in sociopathic times. I should know. I worked in the film business, and I was cutthroat. I made a lot of money for a lot of people. I thought I was helping them. But the jury is out.

"But it is also possible to honor that help comes from within. For us, help comes in the form of dreams. For most gay people, the major helper comes in the feeling of falling in love and wanting to have sex with another man or woman. Each of you can also turn to this person who lives in your heart and pray to him or her. You do so when you are intimate with yourself."

"While it's very important to be a person who helps," John added, "it's even more important that we also learn to ask for help. Giving and receiving are really two sides of the same coin. I learned this in therapy."

Andy will come by and give you pictures from magazines of people you could say are your inner helpers.

"If he weren't so depressed," Harry said to Bobby, "we could make him like a preacher type, get him to monetize this shit."

But Bobby, whose mind was elsewhere—actually on Harry's last request—shook his head in disapproval. "That's not what he needs," Bobby said.

John's last words hung heavy on Bobby.

While it's very important to be a person who helps, it's even more important that we also learn to ask for help.

"I don't ask for help," Bobby said.

"No," Harry said. "You really don't."

"That makes me sad."

"Makes me sad, too."

INTEGRATION

"So here is a big understanding," John said. "Because when we do not learn how to go with the shadow, feel our bad feelings, or reconnect with our ruined child self, each crisis either marks a death knell—or we use drugs, or people, or food, or consumerism, or social media to numb ourselves out. But we just gotta look at the Jesus story to see that with death comes a new birth."

"That came for me in the form of my own death experience after losing my husband—not having noticed that they were trying to live life in a different gender—but also through the bummed-out feeling we all suffered when our little G+Q MAP premiere didn't turn out the way we had hoped."

"A presence inside of me told me to die unto the experience, and then a dove settled on my shoulders, and it said, 'Here's an idea. Step up. Learn how to be the real Son and Father to your new boy Harry, and in his own home, rise up and make meaning from this—for meaning begs for integration.' Also, for help, big boy. And so, here we are. Simple."

FUCKING

"And what that integration did was take my depression—which, as the guys know, can act like an addictive drug, because I can wallow in it—and reframe it. If I just collapse, as Harry did, that's not going to work for me. I am sixty-six years of age. I can collapse, yes, but only if I see the collapse as a metaphor—a child, a boy, a cripple. Once I see the image, I can then keep the feeling from killing me. It's okay to see Harry all collapsed. He needs us to help him. There are some people who take a whole lifetime to ask for help."

John pointed to Bobby. "There she is, Miss Thing. Wave to

the audience, Bobby Blue. I can see clearly now—or my daimon can sense—you are holding something heavy."

Bobby waved.

"I lost my libido," John continued. "I lost it before my heart attack. But when I do something courageous for myself, when I work with my Shadow Selves and integrate what I have learned—like I am doing right now, right as we speak.

"I don't want to use crude language, as I don't know you yet and I want to win your trust, but no one knows that the libido works in mysterious ways and seems to like it if you penetrate its defenses to find your long-lost Queer Spark. And that gets me a bit—how shall we say—into a fucking feeling, which means I just feel good about myself and want to make love not just to my man, but to the world. Kind of like 'Ode to Joy.' You feel me?"

Harry was taking notes. If Bobby were not holding Harry, he'd probably jot a few tidbits down, too.

"THESE ARE JUST SUGGESTIONS. And the honest truth? I recommend you get your asses to therapy. Low-cost therapy exists—community nonprofits, LGBTQ centers, all that. Andy's workbook will list places.

"But here's the problem," he went on. "Your therapist might not be trained in this particular gay-affirmative psycho-analytic world we seem to have fallen into. So the first piece of technology isn't a method. It's learning how to see from your True Self, even if you're still caught up in your False Self."

He asked Bobby if Clara still had the Rainbow Glasses. Bobby wasted no time fetching them. John fixed them above his eyes, then took them off again so he could see the room.

"These don't make you fabulous. They let you see your gayness as a gift. Once you get that—and if you need a metaphor, think midichlorians in *Star Wars*—you've got the technology.

"From there, you can reread your whole damn life: your wins, your fuckups, your disasters in love, your fantasies, your dreams. You can talk back to your dream figures. You can do Active Imagination. You can listen to your feelings like they're actual characters instead of problems you're supposed to medicate away.

"And you don't erase your race, your culture, your family shit to do this. You bring it with you. You synthesize it. You make something new out of what you were handed."

"That's it," John said, setting the glasses down. "No magic. No guru nonsense. Just learning how to see—and then not looking away."

FINAL MOMENT

And that's when Harry—no longer shattered, but better consolidated and cooked through by John's interpretation of his unhealed family bruises—rose to his feet and told the crowd,

"So let me introduce you to my new man."

No one—ever, ever, ever—had heard Harry make such a proclamation in public before.

Bobby searched Clara for Kleenex.

CANTO 30: WHEN QUEENS COLLIDE

When Mrs. González spotted the retreating army making its way toward her outdoor dining bench, she asked her maid, Alejandrina, to increase the number of hands. They simply had to improve the floral settings so they looked more like Saks Fifth Avenue than *el barrio*, please, dear, and make sure there was enough food for ten, eleven, twelve, thirteen, fourteen people—for the men had huge stomachs and would eat her out of house and home—and also, lest we forget, her sisters and their children had promised to arrive by 1:00 p.m. at the latest. "¿Dónde están ellas?" she called, half to herself, half to God.

Bobby, meanwhile, had already approached the woman he now called "The Other Queen," his arms open with grace—and, of course, she thought the same thing of him.

Offering, with her own arms extended, her infamous *albóndigas*—as she really didn't like hugs and kisses as much as she let on—Mexican meatballs, she clarified, placing a colored toothpick in each.

He gasped upon ingesting one. The almost otherworldly

array of spices and textures explained why this woman ruled her roost.

He asked for the recipe and then joined Alejandrina arranging the flowers: *rosas rojas* and gardenias mixed with baby's breath and bright *cempasúchil*, carrying the scent of home and altar at once.

Ezra remained outside the inner sanctum, lingering near the portico between the garage and the gathering. When he caught Harry's eye, he signaled that the space could now be opened. As Harry relayed the message to Andy and John, Ezra winked at the group. They were witnessing a side of Bobby they had not known—domestic, gracious, disarming— working easily alongside his husband, without friction.

When Bobby managed to break free, he drew Ezra close, keeping his voice low, angled away from the table.

"Oh, honey," Bobby said, "I can't thank you enough for your help before. But I have another request."

"I hope it's not about you telling me you have another fatal illness."

Bobby cracked up. Almost no one but Ezra could make everything in life, even dying, a comedy.

"Because here's the part you're not going to like. I'm going to manipulate Mrs. González, I'm going to let her feel sorry for me, and by way of that sympathy I'm going to get Harry out of this house and into our orbit. It might blow back on me, and I don't have the energy to clean up another mess, but I don't know how much time I have, and I'm done pretending I can do this alone, so I need your help to help me help the others."

"Manipulation is your strong suit," Ezra said. "That's not a compliment."

Then he gave the matter more thought, after some tears. If they had more a "family feeling" at the house, they might not get in each other's way so much.

"If I help," he said, his voice rough, "will you go with me to couples therapy and actually tell the truth?"

Bobby looked at him, and felt the cost of being loved this way.

"Then let's join the convivio," Bobby said.

AT THE MOTHER'S Table

When Harry's mother saw that Harry and his friends would join the *convivio*, she relaxed. Watching the group march toward her camp allowed her to better control her party crew and issue calmer instructions to her husband.

Harry busied himself helping Alejandrina. But Bobby motioned for John to get his boy to sit down so Bobby could make happen what he was about to make happen.

Mrs. González, however, was one step ahead. She grabbed Gloria, who was picking up debris, and asked her to sit next to Harry.

"Isn't Gloria such a help?" Mrs. González said to everyone, but especially Bobby. "She keeps the trains running on time, dear girl. She and my youngest boy are childhood friends. They used to date. Wouldn't they make such nice Mexican children? Think of the photos I could send to Harry's *abuela* in Guadalajara!"

Bobby's eyes bulged—not just at the audacity, but at the humor and the irony. He might have laughed, but he remembered that his job here was to be the other queer mother.

"But they're both gay," Bobby said, now playing along. "They don't have sex, so how could they make you children?"

"Since when did people have children because they

wanted to?" she asked, laughing, though not wanting to laugh too hard at her own wit.

"And sex—well, whoever said a happy marriage meant good sex was not married."

Even her husband—who was, in fact, rather sexual with his wife—could not restrain a good belly laugh.

"Oh, Bobby," Andy whispered to him, "I think you've met your match."

That's when Bobby, looking for backup, turned to Gloria, who clarified to the matron that, as nice as marrying Harry might sound, she was marrying her girlfriend Rosalinda— didn't Mrs. González remember?—and that the two of them were moving to Arizona in a month.

"Rosalinda," Mrs. González said, pulling a strand of angel hair from Gloria's eyes, gazing upward as if dialoguing with Jesus. She could not retrieve the index card from her otherwise photographic memory, suggesting that Rosalinda had barely registered on a mind that was, if nothing else, an impression-making machine. Translation: You'll be back.

John—who had been distracted by workshop members addressing him as if he were a great teacher whose canon of gay wisdom they were eager to study, even though it had hardly been compiled—had just arrived at the luncheon table.

When Gloria rose to make room for John, Mrs. González turned to her and said, "Oh, so you will be moving to Arizona? You can't be serious, my dear. Your family and your family's friends are all here. Sit. Tell me your plans."

"Oh, I'm happy to share," she said sweetly, "but I'd love Harry's new *novio* to weigh in, because"—and here she looked directly at Mrs. González—"because he's a very rich and powerful lawyer who apparently runs Hollywood and—who knows—might even help your son get a job,"

Mrs. González took a second look at John. Her gaze

lingered, almost against her will, on the weight of his gravitas, his class, and a fear she felt but couldn't place.

"Harry would make a wonderful camera man," she said.

"Husband," she added to Mr. González, "pull up a seat for this distinguished gentleman."

Director's Notes

Now that the seating had been rearranged—and as Gloria looped her arm through John's and Harry's without breaking eye contact with Mrs. González—she winked at Bobby.

The wink said: Stage set. Lighting good. Proceed.

Bobby motioned to Ezra, who was keeping a polite distance. "Come sit, darling Ezra—I have news for everyone. But first, Andy—did you invite your Jim?"

Andy explained that he hadn't wanted Jim around, partly because of lingering tensions, and partly because he hadn't wanted Jim to witness what he and Dr. Glitter had privately predicted might be a flop.

"Oh?" Harry said, still a little butt-hurt. "You guys knew I couldn't pull it off?"

Bobby winked back: Play along.

So Bobby—who had been exchanging texts with Jim for the past two years and had invited him without anyone knowing—sent a message: "Linger by the picnic tables in case you're needed."

The man Bobby had once met years ago at a drag show— in drag, his face camouflaged—tipped a leather cap from across the courtyard, as if this had always been the cue.

Mrs. González saw him too. And for the first time since the *convivio* began, she did not look like the only Queen on the board. She even thought to herself, who does HE belong to?

Bobby whispered to her, "Andy's."

Bobby almost felt a pang of sympathy for her as the "common Aphrodite." There was nothing common about her. In another life, she might have been a glorious actress, dancing and singing in *West Side Story*, microphone in hand, coaxing Bobby out of Art Direction to his true love, performing. Both were comprised Divas. Neither had truly lived their dream. That fueled Bobby's resolve even more. John's words reverberated in his gay soul.

~

THE BARGAIN

As the plates were passed and Mrs. González's sisters arrived—each younger and more beautiful than she, though none with her stage presence—and Mr. González spoke of his heart disease while Mrs. González catalogued her gallbladder, Bobby decided it was time.

"So," he began, "I knew something was off. I was running to the bathroom too much. Turns out I have an enlarged prostate. And, yes, prostate cancer."

Everyone stopped eating.

Ezra stood abruptly, losing composure.

"What the hell," Harry said.

"Language," both Andy and Mrs. González said.

Ezra stepped in to steady the moment before it tipped.

"Bobby didn't want to burden anyone—especially after the mess with the Coat of Arms and how much he'd already disrupted things."

"I don't like to be burden."

Harry broke into unrestrained laughter. Everyone looked at Harry, for it was out of place for him to laugh during solemn moments.

But the combination of how much of a burden Bobby,

had been together with his engulfing sadness, made him unable to stop laughing, until the tears came

Mrs. González gasped, clutching her rosary as if it were the last solid thing in the room.

"You have cancer?" she asked, allowing her mascara to fall. "It is in your breasts?"

"No," Bobby said. "It's where men's private are."

"Men's," she asked, and then realizing what was going on, she only sobbed quietly more.

Harry moved toward his mother instinctively, then hesitated and turned back toward Bobby. His face crumpled. He pressed his forehead briefly to Bobby's shoulder and whispered, almost without sound, *Please don't leave me. I need you.*

"Oh, sweetheart," Bobby said gently. "I'm not planning on dying."

He looked at Mrs. González, then back at Ezra, letting them flank him.

"But it is fast-moving," he added. "And that scared me more than I wanted to admit. Enough that I tried to manage it alone. Enough that I forgot I don't actually have to."

Ezra stayed beside him, hand firm at Bobby's back, the two of them unmistakably aligned now.

""What can we do?" Mrs. González said. "Anything?"

"There is something you can do for me," Bobby said, steadying himself, "and, oddly enough, it will help your family as well."

Mrs. González leaned forward, rosary looped once around her fingers, her expression sharpening into the look she used when contractors tried to overcharge her.

"Ezra and I have a small place near our house," Bobby continued. "An Airbnb. It's empty right now, and it's close enough that Harry wouldn't have to ride his motorcycle back and forth every day, which frankly terrifies me."

"That motorcycle terrifies *me*," Mr. González said, seizing the word like evidence.

"It would only be temporary," Bobby went on. "A few months. Harry would be safer, and also Andy is selling his home and wants some time before moving in with his fiancé, Jim. There are two bedrooms and two baths, and the guys get along. Andy would have a quiet place to work, and we could rehearse without turning your garage into a refugee camp."

Meanwhile Andy was glowering, not only at Bobby, but at Harry. Was Harry sharing Andy's private confessions with Bobby? Harry refused to meet Andy's gaze.

Mrs. González blinked. "You are telling me," she said slowly, "that instead of riding like a delinquent and filling my house with strange men, my son would be living quietly in Beverly Hills?"

"Quietly is a strong word," Ezra said, before Bobby elbowed him.

Mrs. González ignored this.

"And you would be watching him," she said, pointing at Bobby, "not turning him into some kind of loner who forgets to call his mother."

"And father," Mr. González said.

"That part I can't promise," Bobby said. "He would forget to call me if we didn't have work to do. But we'll keep an eye on him."

She considered this, then nodded, satisfied.

"But Beverly Hills," Mr. González said. "That's pricey. And we spent a lot of money to give him his own empire here."

"Oh," Ezra said. "Not to worry. The Airbnb is dormant for a reason. We are thinking of selling that property, but the rates are not good right now. So please, it's on us."

"Well," Mrs. González said, turning to her husband, "that sounds very generous of *them*, and very responsible of *us*. And if it keeps him off that motorcycle, I am willing to allow it, but for a short period of time. How long is the recuperation? A year?"

"I hope not," Bobby said. "But a year at the most."

Harry stared at Bobby, stunned. Andy looked down, already doing the math on freedom.

"And I will come clean the place myself," Mrs. González added. "Airbnbs are never as clean as people say. I know you own it. But no one cleans like Alejandrina, isn't that right Harry?"

Harry was modeling to Ezra how difficult but fruitful it is to keep one's mouth shut. He had found some masking tape in Clara and taped it across his mouth.

"*Sí, Reina Madre*," he said in Spanish, through the taped-shut mouth.

"And if you want to come over and cook some enchiladas," Bobby said.

"Oh, my dear," Mrs. González said. "I'm already coming up with a cancer recovery menu."

Ezra, about to inform the table that Ezra—and Ezra alone —was the cook, grabbed a piece of masking tape and affixed it to his big mouth.

"Harry," Mrs. González continued, "let's get started packing your favorite clothes. It will only be a few months, and I've been dying to go back there and empty those ashtrays."

When the negotiations were over, and Mr and Mrs. González began to prepare for their midday luncheon with relatives, Bobby found a lounge chair and collapsed, utterly spent. "These are the days when I used to go for a drink," he said to Ezra. "Or maybe I would start a fight with you. All good ways to NOT feel how much anxiety all that cost."

"You did it, honey," Ezra said.

"We did it." Bobby said. "And what were we fighting about. And how did you get so non-reactive."

Ezra pointed to Harry, who also looked exhausted. "He's been coaching me," Ezra said. "And he helped me find a therapist who wasn't going to sit back and let me yap, but who could confront me for being, well, you know."

"Thank you for helping me," Bobby said. "I couldn't have done that without you."

AT THAT MOMENT, Andy walked over holding Jim's hand.

Jim gave Bobby a polite hug.

"Who don't you know, Bobby?"

Jim spoke. "I think Bobby wanted everyone to hear the plan all at once, and to make your life easier, Andy. You still fear your father's wrath and you worried I would be that bad father."

"Even though you are a good slave," Andy said, but in a whisper, so that only Jim could hear.

"It takes illness to realize you're not a Queen or a King," Andy said.

Andy didn't raise his voice. That was the difference.

"And I don't mean that in some inspirational, Hallmark-card way. I mean it strips you. It shows you exactly how much of your confidence was borrowed time."

Andy felt he had every right to go full Freud on Bobby.

"You didn't want to face your fear of death, and that you needed us. So instead, you orchestrated, kept moving the furniture so no one would notice you were bleeding out underneath."

Andy shook his head—not cruelly, but not gently either.

"And don't get me wrong—I'm angry. I'm angry because you dragged us into it without consent. You made us all extras in a scene we didn't audition for. And you almost made us complicit in your refusal to ask for help."

He paused, breath tight.

"But I'm also angry because I recognize it."

He gestured to himself, then vaguely to John, then to Harry.

"We all do versions of this. We all decide that if we just hold it together *hard enough*, we won't have to face the truth— that we are not in control, that bodies fail, that love doesn't protect us from loss, and that needing people is not a character flaw."

His voice cracked, which seemed to irritate him more than anything.

"Fuck you, toxic shame."

And Bobby, so grateful to have this man in her life on a more regular basis, echoed, "Fuck you, toxic shame."

CANTO 31: THE NIGHT OF THE TWO KINGS

On their way back from Mrs. González's to Harry's *El Garaje de la Ascensión*, Harry insisted that John hold his hand—ostensibly because dusk was still falling and the walkway lights, timed for sundown, had not yet flickered on. The cobblestones he and his father had laid—a rural Mexican garden rendered in stone—could be treacherous. Harry had learned long ago to keep close to anyone he cared about when the ground was uneven.

At the far northern corner of El Garaje, bordered by a white picket fence and dense shrubs, Harry unlocked a thick oak door and ushered John into a room few men had entered. The bedroom extended the rural calm of the garden: mahogany walls, cotton linens in white and cream, and an altar that mixed incense, a stylized Sor Juana, a Chicano *Jesús*, and small photographs—one of a Latino youth John did not recognize, and one of the four men together, taken while waiting for the rain to pass outside Dr. Glitter's office. Seeing it, John understood how long Harry had been half-aware of what had begun.

The bed itself rested high in a loft, too far removed for comfort, and without comment Harry unfolded the futon below, pulling sheets and comforters from a drawer where everything lay in precise order. The transition was fluid. They fell together onto the bed before Harry could offer a shower or a drink, the waiting having stretched long enough.

It was not perfect—no first time ever is—but it carried a relief known only to men who have postponed desire long enough to let it deepen, rather than burn out. They resisted the urge to rush toward release, not out of restraint but out of instinct, wanting the encounter to last.

What followed was shared without aggression or role, without urgency, as natural as entering warm water. Their long courtship had taught them how to stay present without surrendering entirely, veterans of grief careful not to over-whelm what had only just begun.

Release came from a secret they both shared but had never dared mention to anyone else: gentle fingers on the face while taking care of oneself—shocking in the quiet internal shifts and electrical outages that such tenderness produced.

When John woke, still wrapped in Harry's arms, he checked the time: 9:45 p.m. Panic flickered—old panic, familiar panic—and he worked to separate the pounding in his chest from the voice that called him reckless. He roused Harry gently.

"I have a call coming," he said. "An important one."

Harry understood at once.

"Take it," he said. "Here."

John did, and told the truth plainly: that he was with Harry.

Carter laughed—warmly, freely—and spoke of Atlanta, of parents, of courage. When Harry was addressed directly, he said nothing—only waved. After the call ended, John returned to the bed and felt Harry pull him close, silent, firm.

Later, while John slipped easily into deep sleep, Harry lay awake, irritation simmering as it sometimes did when tenderness arrived too close to loss. He felt it in his body and in his chest, and for once did not act on it. Instead, he spoke inwardly to the younger part of himself and made a pact to bring the feelings to the group, trusting that he could hold them until morning.

Sleep came.

They woke to a rooster, the smell of *huevos* and *café recién hecho*, and a text from Harry's mother inviting John to a *desayuno de rey*—and reminding him, gently, to come hungry.

CANTO 32: THE RECKONING

After the Big Premiere, everyone asked for a Group Consultation with Dr. Glitter.

As I admitted them into the Zoom, no one looked like their usual selves. During the check-in, it became clear that the silence wasn't the result of lingering resentment but of something heavier: the group had crossed a threshold. The tone had shifted without prompting. Something had rearranged itself.

"It's like we took acid," Bobby said, fanning himself, "and we're still figuring out where we went, what we saw, and how the cookie's gonna crumble."

"The bro has cancer," Harry said flatly. "What kind of fucked-up shit is that?"

"It's fucked-up shit, Prince Harry," Bobby replied. "No cap."

"I hate cancer," Harry continued. "My grannie had that shit. Lost her boobies. Still alive, still kicking—still kicking my father's ass for working too hard and not paying her no mind.

So I hear prostate cancer is low-key treatable, but you gotta tell us more about what's actually going on."

I tracked the rise in intensity and stayed quiet, watching to see whether the men could hold it without splintering.

At one point, I noted that the group had begun to self-regulate more consistently, and that sometimes my role now was less conductor than lifeguard—present, alert, letting the waves crest unless someone went under. There were too many issues to resolve today, to say nothing of the success of the workshop itself and the way Harry had allowed power to circulate in the Garage.

The group clapped.

"Well," Andy said, ambivalent screenwriter voice sharpening, "there it is—the emerging hero arc. John auditioned for 'born leader' and booked it."

"Very *Dumbledore-escapes-the-Ministry* of him," Harry added.

"That man gave 'I woke up like this… in charge' energy," Bobby chimed in.

John bowed. "I thought Bobby showed real leadership too, *après le déluge.*"

"I must say," Andy added, "watching Bobby and Harry's mother together—that was a summit of sovereigns. Two queens, one kingdom. I'd call it a draw, which says a lot."

Harry clapped Bobby on the shoulder. "You did good, *cabrón.* She liked you. Won't say it, *pero* she did. I know her tell."

I let the affirmations continue without interference.

When I checked in with Harry, who had endured the most visible strain, he patted his chest and said, "Well. These fools got to see how my mother and—" air quotes "—father can send me into a total crying bitch nervous breakdown. No cap. They get under my skin, and this time was the final draw."

"It was brave," Bobby said. "I already thought highly of you, but watching you fall apart with us mattered."

Andy adjusted his glasses. "Honestly, this made me weirdly hopeful. Like maybe we're actually doing what almost nobody manages to do—instrumentalizing our own shadow material, our *merda interna*, as raw matter for gay healing and gay creativity. *Hoc est praxis*, gentlemen."

I noticed Andy was quieter than usual.

"He's distracted," Harry said, launching in. "Got into all his grad schools, wrote about the G+Q MAP, trying to get his thoughts straight, plus—let's be real—he's about to be my roommate because I'm getting the hell out of my parents' compound, and not a moment too soon. And he's worried that I'll be messy."

Harry didn't pause.

"And he's busy navigating his slave—did y'all know Andy has a slave? Jim knows. Jim knows all too well. Andy's still gonna keep a foot in the *ching-ching* business, and I'm gonna help him unfuck the fascist bullshit in those garbage movies he makes—"

I stayed quiet to see if the group could tolerate the escalation.

"Anything on your mind?" I asked.

Silence.

"John hurt me last night," Harry said. "He actually fucked me over."

"What you talking?" John said. "I fucked you over?"

"After we made love," Harry said, "you took a call from your shawty and sounded chipper as a lark."

Bobby froze mid-fan. Andy stopped writing.

"It wasn't a shawty," John said. "It was my spouse. Carter had gone to Atlanta to come out to their parents. I woke Harry up and told him. I wanted to be present."

Andy murmured, "I think we're about to see our first real lover's fight."

I monitored closely.

"If you were that upset," John said, "why didn't you say something then?"

"Because big blow-ups belong in Group," Harry said. "I need witnesses. So do you."

I thought, not for the first time, that many couples would benefit from this rule of thumb.

"What do you want from me?" John asked. "You sound just like Carter."

Andy made enormous eyes. Bobby snapped his fan shut.

"Carter wasn't unhappy for no reason," Bobby said. "You had an open marriage, but you didn't actually deal with gender. That's the difference. Harry is claiming his voice."

A pin could have dropped.

"We are not dating," Harry said, "because you still have feelings for them."

"We ain't dating," John said.

"We aren't?" Harry shot back.

"Dating is dinners, premieres, Netflix, assimilation. I thought you were past that. I'm not going down that road again."

"Maybe you should," Harry say. "Can you believe the looks we'd garner if you had your little Chivalrous Chicano hanging on your arm. Bobby, what would we wear?"

John laughed, taking in the comedy of eros.

"What else you want?" John asked, hoping to get all the cards on the table.

Harry didn't answer right away.

Silence.

"Don't tell me," John said. "Don't tell me you seriously want a ring."

Harry extended his empty ring finger.

John laughed. No one joined him.

"I'm sixty-six," John said. "You're twenty-seven."

"Thirty-plus years," Harry said. "Did the math week one."

John shook his head. "By the time you're forty-seven—"

"I'll be a young widow," Harry corrected. "I can carry on your legacy."

"I don't even know you," John insisted.

"I know *you*," Harry said. "I've seen you dead, alive, wise, scared. I know you better than Carter ever did. And yes, you're the sexiest man I've ever had flipped with. Actually, the only man's I've flipped with."

The argument swerved, then landed again.

Harry showed his bank balance. "I don't need your money. I need you to take my art seriously."

"What art?" John asked. "And who brought up money? Money is an issue. What kind of art do you do? I saw you act. Actors—don't get me started."

Bobby and Andy exchanged a look.

Andy opened up his computer and shared the TikToks appeared—Egg Theory, duets, remixes, elders weighing in. John stared, stunned.

"Damn good," he said. "Not just your pretty face, but all the ideas we talk about here, but damn near better than I could ever."

"Don't see yourself so short, John," Bobby said. "You could make an interesting team."

Andy leaned forward, no longer joking.

"Let me say this cleanly," Andy said. "Harry is famous—

not on our terms, not on the terms of a dying industry—but on New World terms. Half a million followers across platforms. TikTok, Instagram, Snapchat. We haven't even listened to his podcasts yet."

Harry blinked.

"The thing," Andy continued, "is that he never once used that in this room. Never pulled rank. Never acted like the most powerful person here—which, numerically speaking, he is. And that's why this matters. He actually is too modest, in my opinion. If we don't help him, we only hurt ourselves."

Bobby nodded. "We're lucky to have him."

"And," Andy added, "he's also at risk. He's juggling school, the Garage, OnlyFans, his art, his family, us. He's brilliant, but inconsistent. He needs direction—or someone else will give it to him. We have not dealt with the fact that Harry is a gay youth at risk!"

"Bro's becoming a low-key activist," Harry said, trying not to blush or cry.

Andy cleared his throat.

"I already wrote him an application," he said calmly. "USC. Based on his writing."

"What?" Harry said.

"I'm serious," Andy replied. "Because here's the jeopardy: someone is going to snap him up. A manager, a platform, whatever's left of the industry. I already heard he's talking to one—Jim mentioned it. And if that happens without grounding, it's goodbye Garage, goodbye group, goodbye soul. And John—"

"—John will be sleeping next to Job—alone."

John hesitated. "I don't even know how this works. You're moving fast. And I'm still married."

"That's the catch," Harry said.

"Excuse me?" John asked.

"If you want to ask me out——"

"As me out?" John cut in. "What kind of heteronormative bullshit is that? We already see each other twice a week. We've slept together. I met your parents. I don't need dinner reservations to prove anything."

"I want something normal," Harry said. "Cooking. Movies. Netflix. The boys over."

"The boys are over all the time," John said.

I just watched, as curious as everyone else.

"Okay," John went on, once a lawyer always a lawyer. "So what's the catch?"

"You have to divorce her."

"That's not your call," John said carefully.

No one liked John's statement, and neither quite did John. But he took his sweet time before saying:

"What's wrong with you, you dummy?" John asked. "You think I would have let myself make love to you if I hadn't already had this conversation? If Carter and I hadn't already restructured our lives?"

The room stilled.

"The papers have been served," John said. "Everyone knows who each other now loves. Y'all, this is a tempest in a teapot. So fuck off. Fuck your plotting and planning—the whole lot of you Machiavellian bitches. The wedding bullshit is dead in the water. I'm not playing games. You make me so mad with your needy, childish, prurient demands. Whatever happened to the 'let's just chill' Harry. How I miss him. Bring him back!"

Harry burst out laughing, delighted.

"When I first saw your ugly ass in group," Harry said, "I

knew you came from the street. Don't lose that edge, Baby Daddio. It gets me hard. And almost nothing does anymore. I sincerely lost my boner, due to my trauma. So thanks for bringing me back to life. If I have to be a widow, at least I'll get my hard-on back for ten-to-twenty years, give or take."

"Oh hush," John said. "So childish."

PROGRESS NOTES FOR CRUCIBLE

Over time, a new stage in the group's process crystallized. As the men worked more intensely with one another and their intimate lives grew more complex, they did not always want to process emerging material in real time during impromptu Zoom sessions, and the need for individual sessions increased.

They were working—unevenly but seriously—to distinguish what belonged to older traumatic material (childhood mistreatment, internalized shame, unresolved family systems, raw instinctual feeling) from what genuinely belonged to present-day dynamics. Often, the difference between how they felt before an individual session ("I have receipts") and afterward ("Okay, maybe not a war crime") marked the difference between escalating a rupture and moving toward greater understanding and repair.

ANDY:

Let's be precise. Harry's Garage wasn't some mythic eruption. It was a specific collision—unprocessed rage, old humiliations, and a few inconvenient hopes that should have known better by now.

DR. GLITTER:

"Should have known better" is always my favorite defense, as if feelings read a syllabus we can only write afterward.

ANDY:

You're being defensive. And yet, we could have drafted a better oversight syllabus. What happened was sloppy. We lost Harry in that brush-up with his mother. I'm pissed no one listened to me about being better prepared. I want a group consultation—to process my shit, their shit, your shit.

DR. GLITTER:

Of course. I'll write the guys straight away.

ANDY:

Which brings me to you. Starting something this ambitious in Harry's Garage? Fool-card energy. Cliff's edge with no helmet.

DR. GLITTER:

I could have insisted on more forethought.
(beat)
I'm sorry. I see that more clearly now—through what you're bringing up.

· · ·

ANDY:

It took the entire movie for the doctor to hear the creature and apologize.

DR. GLITTER:

He tried to do a good thing and ended up being a bad doctor. Are you too upset to return to group?

ANDY:

No. Truth is, the cat's out of the bag. We're more bonded. I can see now why we needed to get through this.

DR. GLITTER:

Do you still want a group session with me present?

ANDY:

No. I needed to bring my anger to you first. I needed to know I could curse you and still be heard. And speaking of fathers—I want to talk next time about mine. He doesn't have long, and I need to figure out what to say.

DR. GLITTER:

Sure?

Andy:

On second thought, a group session with you there may be the best way to pick up the pieces.

.   .   .

After I scheduled the Group Zoom, I made notes about how the termination process evolved into a form of launching, which I shared with my supervisor.

Stage One — Seven Years Ago

A buoyant support space for artists: performative, communal. Shows, readings, small happenings. Bobby was part of this early constellation until COVID fractured the world.

Stage Two — The Gestalt/Yalom Turn

During and after COVID, the work shifted toward a more process-oriented, existential model. This coincided with major life changes: Bobby's search for meaning and relationship with Ezra; his dramatic weight loss; John's post–heart attack reorientation; Andy's confrontation with the limits of his success.

Stage Three — Harry Arrives

Harry entered like a fish out of water—except he was also the water. His presence catalyzed confrontation with family systems, machismo, caste, barrio codes, erotic transference, and mythic projection. This marked the beginning of an unspoken court phase: trial by longing, loyalty, and fracture.

Stage Four — Hybrid Creative Praxis

This phase coincided with my year in New York, the move to Zoom, and revised informed consent. The men chose to disband formal group while continuing individual work, with consultation available around the G+Q MAP. They became friends, collaborators, and—between John and Harry—potential intimates. Their first public attempt failed spectacularly and productively, revealing a more modest and humane path forward.

STAGE FIVE — The Current Configuration

What exists now is best understood as a work in progress, bringing together therapy, art, activism, sex, love, and healing.

The group has entered a hybrid phase: no longer a therapy group, yet not a coalition without some form of oversight, which each member is actively requesting. What holds them together is ongoing individual therapy alongside a shared investment in the group and in each person's growth, as an urgent response to lives that have felt deprived of sufficient vision or direction.

While this stage may appear almost too good to be true— a "healing fiction"—my experience suggests that people are often more capable of this kind of self-directed relational work than prevailing models predict. The difficulty is that the broader culture lacks a shared language of queer psychological ethics, such that acting out and projection are recognized as legacies of heterosexism rather than as personal failures.

Practices such as meditation and 12-Step programs can be integrated into this language but are not sufficient on their own unless the unconscious is also addressed. The divide between a True Self and a False Self is often protective rather than defective; if approached with respect rather than force, it may soften. *Open Sesame* is one way of naming what these men are learning.

This work is unfolding amid political instability that exposes the fragility of institutions and the false safety they promise. Clinical tasks of differentiation, containment, and mutual support cannot be separated from material conditions —especially as ICE has entered some of our neighborhoods.

What gives this moment viability is attentiveness: the

men's growing capacity to reflect, repair, and remain grounded during crisis without collapsing into panic or despair. This makes possible a form of psychological activism —one that attends to external conditions while recognizing that failures of governance originate, and are most changeable, in the inner world.

When Bobby, for example, learns to drop into his body—before surgery—and to feel his feelings there rather than racing above them into reactivity, creating distance between initial affect and the cascade that leads to doing the wrong thing, that may not yet be peace.

But this internal conversation between part-selves marks something just as consequential: the emergence of an entirely new form of governance.

ACT V — COMMEDIA

Facing aging, illness, and desire, the men risk one final dance toward meaning.

CANTO 33: THE GQ SHIFT CLASS ON TECHNOLOGY

In their next meeting, which took place at Bobby's Airbnb, the guys spoke about next steps.

"We wanted to save the world," John said. "But we brought damage and incompetence."

"A bit rough?" Bobby mused.

"It's okay to fail," John said, by way of explanation. "But if we agree we bring damage and incompetence, that frees us up all the more to focus on healing, rather than doing our Hollywood shit."

"Despite how I been trying to youth-an-ize you all and get over yo-selves," Harry said, "Old Man River, though low-key depressing, is saying that we fools can take some pressure off us and have a more real experience."

"Be the monster and less the doctor," John added. Andy moved to correct Harry's mangling of *youth-an-ize*, but Bobby delicately put a finger to his freshly Botoxed cheeks, so that when the deliriously hot surgeon removed the spark plug of his youth two months from now, he'd at least have a pretty face smiling back—at the surgeon."

"So, hunnies," Bobby added. "If I have this right, instead of taking a break until I get my pee pee re-circumcised two months from now, why don't we give our project another shot, but do so in new ways. And I see that Spock is writing down what I am about to say, so, dear Dorothy, read us our new strategy."

Andy ripped out a piece of paper on which he had taken a Sharpie and written this down:

1 Go Simple

2 Focus on healing

3 See Joy

4 Journal

5 Hear my new idea

Andy had unearthed my *Gay Liberation as Queer Therapy* seminars for the University I started twenty years ago, grainy on YouTube, but having survived somehow. And he screened a bit on his iPad.

Speaking over my lecture, Andy said, "I say we go to the students themselves and show them what the actual monsters look like—give a talk or something, do a Q&A, or something boring, like a panel."

"Our shrink hasn't changed a bit," John said, referring to Dr. Joy's certain nerdy charm in "going off on tangents, did she just mention Kant," and "laughing at her own jokes."

"Except maybe those bags under her eyes and those awful wrinkles by her forehead," Bobby offered. "I say we start a GoFundMe page for her Botox!"

"But she's no longer teaching there this year, remember," John said, returning to Andy's idea.

"She can still get Botox in New York," Bobby added. "I know the right gal for her."

"I already contacted her replacement," Andy said. "A cool lesbian. She thought it was a great idea. She agreed not to bother Dr. Joy right now, as Mark is having a big surgery this week."

Harry jumped in with an idea of his own.

"Yo, instead of a panel, why don't we give them a Case to explore. What happens when two gay men meet who are in love with each other but one is afraid of making a commitment?"

"Don't forget," John added, not entirely mad at the idea, "to add that the person isn't 'afraid,' but just 'cautious,' and don't leave out the fact that the person was in a ten-year marriage that failed."

"And let us also teach them that, if a person does not face their internalized homophobia," Bobby added, "or the tendency to make a good gay thing into a bad gay thing, they will use words like 'fail' instead of succeed. People change."

Harry and Andy had already taken out their phones to create a little short of the two sisters having their once-in-a blue-moon cat fight.

"What a great panel this could be," Andy said. "No preparation needed. Just maybe a few key words we can throw around."

"Assimilation," Bobby said, rising as if summoned by a spotlight, one finger already wagging.

"Definition?" John asked.

"A deal with the devil," Andy answered.

"Next," John asked.

"Gay identity," Bobby answered, twirling.

"Definition?" John asked.

"Waking up to the true self my homosexuality insists upon," Andy answered.

"Internalized homophobia, anyone?" Bobby threw out, hands wide open to the world.

"Going after only the pretty boys," Harry offered.

"And hating them for rejecting you while you reject the available men."

"Ooohhhh," John said. "Now that is like having a brain orgasm."

"See," Andy said. "We can just go and be ourselves. We'd have a receptive audience and we can chat with them about the monsters of their creative lives in the real world." Bobby made a face, suggesting sudden terror.

"A week from Tuesday," Andy said. "No fee, no mailing list, no social media. What could go wrong?"

I HEARD about the scheming by the four horsemen of the apocalypse from my replacement. When she heard that the guys, out of deference to my struggles in New York City, had decided to "go behind my back," and then asked if we should "call the whole thing off," I laughed.

"It will be, if nothing else, entertaining, and probably rather edifying."

"You sound worried?" my replacement asked. "Will they be okay with you not being present?"

"The question," I answered, "isn't whether they will be okay. The question is, instead, whether you will be okay." "More for you and your skills at classroom management," I added, "than the guys. Maybe warn the students that these guys know a lot about theory but aren't very academic, and that they are probably more like activists than most therapists."

I also knew that some students had studied Freud and Jung more than others, so when John might spout off about the "unconscious," or Bobby might introduce the class to "Sylvia," or Harry's idea of "getting under the hood" as a metaphor for encountering the unconscious, this might seem like Greek to the students.

But since my replacement was also the chair of the program, and it was she who trained me to be a troublemaker, I did my best to encourage her and offer any postmortem that was necessary.

Apparently, the moment the men walked into the classroom, they guessed that the students seemed a bit—how to put it—tense, and had their textbooks open as if about to take a quiz. The divide that exists in all our separate worlds, be it Hollywood, Academia, Serving Food, or Office Work, struck them as real, if unfortunate.

Bobby, of course, began the disruption the moment the instructor turned the panel over to the men, noticing that she had no intention of moderating, except by asking a question so insipid that Bobby sashayed on it.

"My second husband and I met in a backroom," Bobby announced, "before those were taken down—may their memory be a blessing."

The students snapped.

"We knew right away," he continued, "he was a hungry Top, I was a pushy bottom—which, my darlings, Ozempic is in the process of renegotiating—and he was negative, I was positive; he was Jewish, I was a recovering Southern Methodist. So naturally, it was a match made in heaven."

A ripple of laughter.

"We practiced the ethics of Gay Liberation, which we borrowed from the Black Power struggle and our beloved lesbian feminists. We didn't tolerate jealousy, or monogamy, or being acceptable. But age—and boredom with online culture —has given us the freedom to be monogamous. Without," he added, "adopting the assimilationist, 'respectable' gay ethics your textbooks, God save me from social science, keep pushing. I didn't see a word of the delight of receiving a facial from the man you love, or one you rather dislike."

A hand shot up from an avowed queer theorist studying postmodern narrative theory as the orientation of the couch. "So… isn't that essentialist? Saying there's such a thing as gay ethics rather than a series of idea practices by a select group of people who once called themselves 'gay'?" "*Moi,*" John answered, asking to borrow Bobby's pearls so he could clutch them. "An essentialist?"

"Is that what I am?" John said, asking Harry. "A recovering Hollywood power grabber and a card-carrying essentialist." "

Admit it," Harry said. "As cheesy as it sounds, you are what you eat. And my cock is essentially—uncut."

John licked his lips.

"We are queer in disguise," Bobby said. "We come as essentialists, but in fact, we are the disrupters. I was a famous drag queen before you kids were even concepts, and then I buried your forebears—may their memory be a blessing."

Andy sat up straighter, delighted. He lived for academic combat the way drag queens live for a ball.

"I think," he began, "that queer theory has appropriated the 19th-century meaning of gayness as a sensibility—and then demonized gay people when they don't perform queerness according to the theory's own rules. 'Homo-normative' is a term dripping with judgment and, frankly, internalized homophobia."

The student blinked.

"And if we turn to the American founder of modern gay liberation—Walt Whitman—"

(The instructor looked nervous, as Whitman was not on the syllabus.)

"—in *Democratic Vistas* (1871), Whitman describes the sensibility you're trying to call essentialist, but that we see as ancestral inheritance. The 'adhesive love,' the comradely love, the love between men that counters the vulgar materialism of American life."

Andy opened the book, which he had, of course, brought with him, and read:

"It is the development, identification, and general prevalence of that fervid comradeship, the adhesive love, that I look for as the counterbalance and offset to our materialistic and vulgar democracy... Democracy infers such loving comradeship as its inevitable twin, without which it will be incomplete, incapable of perpetuating itself."

(Quoted in Michael Bronski's *Culture Clash: The Making of Gay Sensibility*; see also Whitman's *Leaves of Grass and Selected Prose*, Library of America edition.)

The classroom went quiet.

"So you see," Andy said, snapping the book shut, "what queer theory calls 'essentialism' is often just a way to refer to a series of memories—ancestral, erotic, and cultural. It's the archive our people carved out long before the academy showed up to rename us."

"If that shit don't sound like fucken ethics," Harry said, "I don't know what the fuck does. And I don't even use the word 'gay' to define my sexuality. I say I'm a label-free homo-SEXUAL—haha, get the joke—Queer As Fuck, 'cause I like to FUCK, especially the man I hope will be my husband. And yet I will not turn a pretty woman down, and I have fucked with a trans MTF."

A student raised a nervous hand, eager to participate. "So... are you saying you're both fluid and fixed?" "My sexual identity," Harry said, suddenly code-switching into perfect academic cadence, "is different from my spiritual being. And based on what Andy is teaching us about the 19th century founders, I would say I am, therefore, gay in my heart — essentially. So, you feel me?"

John leaned across the aisle toward the students.

"The way that man just summed up our shit—his words touched my cold heart. Fuck relationship ambivalence and internalized homophobia."

Harry took a step back.

ANDY HELD up one of his new favorite books, *Lesbian Ethics: Toward New Value* (1988), by Sarah Lucia Hoagland, and riffed on its ideas:

"For us to get a sense of how to heal in the deeper sense," he said, "we can't accept the cards we are dealt and think that just being happy, which eludes most people anyway, is the goal of life. Maybe it's making meaning, or contributing, or feeling existentially seen in a gay way, or fucked in a gay way, or loved in a gay way."

Bobby clapped, both to show his joy at seeing Andy step into his own power, finally, and to signal to the students the need to sprinkle fairy dust on all ideas.

"But we can't get that need met unless we do a lot of work first about who and what needs the seeing—a child, a brutal sadist, a victim, a vampire, or a tender, hurt but not destroyed gay man. So we have to, to quote Harry here, get under the hood first and see what the heck is going on. And if we do so, we may find we can love in a way that had eluded us, because all the parts of the engine were not up to par."

"So what, then," a student asked, "is your theory of change? Sometimes you sound Freud, other times Jung, or existential, or multicultural."

"That's a hard one," Bobby said. "As we are not trained, like you, in theory. I do know we gave you some food for thought. But to let you in on a secret: we promised that we would put our healing—the healing of us four fucked-up gay, or queer, whatever world you like—over and beyond performance agendas. So, on that basis, and let me refer to the work of D.W. Winnicott on the 'false self,' or, in the terminology of your texts, on a sense of 'resilience,' I think we performed quite well."

And on that note, the class erupted into immediate applause, save a few naysayers, who seemed quite angry and left during the applause; one or two people even stood up.

CANTO 34: CARTER INTERVENES

John phoned the person he always phoned after good things.

"You had your first success," Carter said, delighted.

"We had some naysayers," John added. "And some jargon I couldn't follow, but Harry gave them hell. When someone asked whether we were essentialists, Harry had the gall to say, 'As cheesy as it sounds, you are what you eat. And my cock is essential—uncut.'"

Carter laughed.

"That Harry," Carter said. "So what happened next? Did you make a move? I hope you did."

"I did as you suggested," John said. "I invited him over."

"You did?!"

"Yes. I invited him to the new house."

"So what happened?"

"He turned me down. Said he had work the next day." John paused. "Made me miss you."

Carter frowned.

Carter had a suspicion, after listening to John's quiet but

repetitive complaints, that Harry—for all his bold claims of wanting something serious—was also hurt.

Harry did not believe that John and Carter had ended their romantic attachment.

And perhaps neither did Carter.

Carter decided to act.

And because Carter, far more than John, knew his way around social media—and could locate Harry's pages across a dozen platforms with the same distracted ease with which he noticed the slight bobble of his own neck on that rubbery spine—he decided, on a morning when John was most wound up (having double-texted Harry, which he abhorred as much as an executive hates an actor's hemming and hawing after getting top billing), to DM Harry directly.

If you have a moment, Carter wrote, *call me—or better yet, meet me at Urth Café in an hour.*

Harry was already there when Carter arrived, early as always, anxiety tucked behind the motorcycle helmet at his side, camera equipment at his feet, jeans slung low with that gleaming Gucci belt, the leather satchel pressing into his chest like a charm bag. When Carter approached—dressed in his basic cottons, masculine in the understated way of someone who refuses to be decorative—the two men regarded each other with a brief, mutual flicker of recognition: different species, perhaps, but of the same genus.

Harry rose, as a man raised by his chivalrous mother and father does. But Carter—who didn't want to bother with pleasantries—gestured for him not to fuss.

Carter took a tentative seat, the way one sits just before the train that's already a few minutes late arrives to take one to the next destination.

"I'm not here to make friends," Carter began, "though I'm sure we could be, one day. And I'm certainly not here to play games or get in the middle. In fact"—and here he fixed Harry with a look sharp enough to cut through every avoidant maneuver Harry had ever rehearsed—"I'm telling you to stop waiting for John. I learned the hard way that the only way to love someone as indecisive as him is to take charge of the pursuit."

Harry swallowed, charm momentarily useless.

Carter continued, his voice almost polite.

"I also want you—someone I've never met but have heard quite a lot about—to know a few things. I'm not sure if John has told you, because for all his brilliance as a lawyer he sometimes lives in La La Land, and not the glamorous one.

He and I are divorcing. We're moving into separate lives, separate homes, separate relationships. And I bless what you two men are doing. Truly. The future is yours—if you seize it, Brujo Bro. If I could give you my hand in marriage, or whatever you lost boys might end up doing, I would."

Then, with a wink—imitating a noir actor—they added lightly,

"And if you repeat this conversation, you'll never work in this town again."

Carter laughed at his own James Cagney rendition, stood, then thought better of being too warm. No handshake, no kiss. Carter simply pointed a finger at Harry.

Then, paying the bill for Harry's coffee and tip, they walked out.

CANTO 35: THE FIRST
DATE IS A DUD

John thought he heard either the rooster by Harry's Garage or the Catholic church at Morehouse at sunrise.

Gong.

It was a cell phone—the sound on which he had not been raised.

Who was calling so early?

A cardinal rule was never to check the phone before morning meditation.

Later, Carter arrived for brunch to make a list of belongings before the mediation.

A text.

"You'd better get that," Carter said, watching John pretend the heavenly sound had not occurred.

The first text read: *Yo, yo, GM, you hung up on me. Hit me when u get up.*

"So unlike him to text first thing."

"Did you answer?"

"No. And then he double-texted."

John mimicked Harry:

Yo, bro, I been low-key thinking… let's do some dumb-ass boyfriend typpa shit—whether we are or we ain't—and go see that movie, grab some din-din. You down?

"Really," Carter said. "So shocking."

"Pushy," John said.

"Well, don't keep that boy waiting," Carter said, making typing gestures with their lavender fingernails. "Must've got something in mind."

JOHN OPENED the door to his "bachelor pad."

Minimal was John's new standard: a mid-century oak desk on which his journal and fountain pen rested, a queen-size bed on a simple Japanese wooden frame, brown oak bookshelves lined with alchemy and literature, and an altar where Malik's photograph rested among a few carefully chosen objects.

John considered removing the framed photo of the group outside Dr. Glitter's office—the first day Harry had joined them—but Malik, as usual, told him to stop.

"Fancy," Harry said.

John nearly laughed, thinking of how far this place fell from his former home.

Harry pushed John onto the bed, gently but firmly. It had been years since anyone had taken the dominant role with John. Even as he wondered whether Harry was playing at something he'd learned online, desire surged through him.

But their bodies moved faster than their better instincts.

Instead of sharing about their experience, they fell asleep.

Harry hadn't slept much after seeing Carter. He'd spent the morning packing the last pieces of his beloved Garaje, filming GRWM TikToks, running boxing drills, running in the rain, filming all of it.

John had spent the day helping Carter move books, dishes, and the quiet relics of their shared life, overworking his bad knee, bracing it so he could pretend he was fine.

At 2:00 a.m., they woke suddenly—separately—aware of each other's breath, debating who needed to pee, whether alarms were set, how to disentangle. Every snore, every shift, every small sound felt intrusive.

They lay awake, startled by how quickly intimacy had turned into confinement.

Get me out of here, each thought.

Neither said it aloud.

As JOHN LOOKED at himself in the bathroom mirror, Malik approached from behind holding the Tarot card of the Hangman. John thought to rifle through Bobby's notes explaining the cards.

"If you continue like this," Malik said quietly, "you will lose what you have just been given."

"WE SHOULD TALK," John said, upon entering the bedroom after a 30-minute reprieve, noticing Harry was also wide awake.

"What about?" Harry added, sad.

"Look," John said. "I've lived my life as a phony and a fake. At the age of sixty-six, I'm just getting that. I had a dream that we should not be doing what we are doing."

"Are you breaking up with me?"

"Bro," John said, almost delighted by this more tender

Harry, even though earlier the CC had pushed him around. "I just don't want to use you for my pleasure."

"But I want you to want me to use me——"

"Are you so sure?" John asked. "I don't think we know ourselves well enough to be rushing into objectifying each other."

"Bet."

"I also have a request," John said. "I'm kind of scared. It's a bit kinky."

"Yes," Harry said, tentatively.

"Will you meditate with me?" John asked. "It would mean the world."

Harry put his hand to his face. "That's your idea of kinky."

John nodded.

"Well, bro," Harry said, "you realize that by asking me to meditate with you, that's even more intimate than fucking you."

"That's why I asked."

THIS IS ALSO the day they had decided to drive together—which neither had yet done—to Palm Springs, where Andy had organized a special meeting to focus on the "F" letters.

"You think there's a dress code for this thing?" John asked.

Harry thought they should drive to the Garaje and grab a harness or some chaps, but he didn't want to stir anything up after their deep meditation.

"So," John said to each other, "I guess we'll come as we are."

"Yup, glamorous sweatpants and weed-smelling hoodies."

Harry opened every car door for John and inquired about the music, and made mention of the wobbly way John walked, for he had seen his father receive both a hip and a knee replacement.

"Maybe it's time to get that bitch replaced," Harry said, with the same poise with which he might refer to an alternator.

As John was getting strapped in, Harry offered Mexican Cola or water. In driving, he held the wheel with his knees to roll his backwood. He held John's hand—which Harry had not done—and kissed the two knuckles by his thumb.

Then he invited John to pull the seat back and "take a nappy."

And in Harry's hands, John drifted off into sleep—but not before Harry, with the roof down, took a few selfies, lip-syncing to "Pound Cake / Paris Morton Music 2," and blowing smoke into the camera.

CANTO 36: RANCHO MIRAGE, AFTER DARK

They met Bobby on one of the most sedate streets in Rancho Mirage—wide, palm-lined avenues where bougainvillea drooped over stone privacy walls and wrought-iron gates hinted at Sinatra-era secrets. Harry and John arrived expecting a discreet cocktail gathering. What they didn't expect was Bobby at the curb in a sharply tailored leather ensemble—the sort Europeans call "elegant fetish"—a worn Belstaff motorcycle jacket hanging off his narrow frame.

At last, the host appeared—a rail-thin man in his early seventies in full leather regalia, with the serene smile of a church elder and the riding crop of a man with commitments. His posture was immaculate; his eyes twinkled with private amusement at the sight of such fresh faces.

"You boys seem to be coming through the wrong entrance," he said gently, with an accent that reminded Andy of Ohio, as if correcting table manners. "Guests of Andy use the downstairs door."

They followed him along the side of the modernist house, past citrus trees perfuming the dusk, to a descending staircase hidden behind a sculptural hedge wall. At the bottom, the host opened a heavy, soundproofed door.

What awaited them was not a dungeon so much as a subterranean academy—a cathedral of kink lit in low amber tones, more sumptuous than sordid. Slings hung from polished steel frames; whips and restraints were displayed as art, arranged with near-ecclesiastical symmetry. Water stations and ergonomic seating lined the periphery. Moving through the room were men mostly in their forties, fifties, and sixties—leathermen who had lived several lives and were still interested in collecting new ones.

HARRY AND JOHN froze for a moment before Bobby nudged them with the subtle confidence of someone who had clearly read the invitation more carefully. At the back of the room, rising above the hum of murmured greetings, was Andy—no longer the introspective, shy boy in recovery they had come to rely on, but a figure of composed authority in full leather gear, the kind that did not advertise but clarified. The fitted, open-backed vest revealed the sculpted geometry of his shoulders; the harness beneath framed his chest with near-calligraphic precision; the pants emphasized the strength of his legs and the unmistakable curvature that drew the eye before the mind could censor its own delight. He held a short leather crop with the unselfconscious ease of someone who understood exactly what this object meant—not ornament, not threat, but symbol.

What startled Harry and John was not Andy's attire but the unmistakable authority emanating from him—authority rooted not in dominance but in knowledge, in a sense that he had earned, through long apprenticeship to psychology and desire, the right to speak seriously about the forces shaping every man in the room. The men arranged themselves around him with the alertness of students awaiting a masterclass they hadn't known they needed.

Meanwhile, Andy made two adult decisions: not moving in with Jim until they "figured their shit out," and deciding he was done writing for Hollywood on Hollywood's terms. His emerging assertiveness—once split between model minority and leather stud—now felt like life force rather than pathology. His depression lifted. He recognized that being abused by his father didn't mean he had to shame his own aggression or the way it turned him on to wield a crop.

This allowed him to reconfigure his relationship with Jim and enter the leather world proudly, as healing through both body and feeling. With Dr. Glitter's guidance, he wove his and Jim's material into scripts that retained their radical core. Jim, seeing Andy fight for something real, began to trust him again, as lover and as Master.

The S&M dynamic also evolved. Jim asked not for an engagement ring but for a branding ritual—a hot poker supervised by Andy's friend from Paris, prepared with negotiation and consent. Jim declared his servitude not to Andy but to Master A; he became slave J. These were not costumes but coordinates on the psychic map, giving both men a place to stand without collapsing into numb roles.

This erotic education—combined with long analytic work—made Andy consider leaving Dr. Glitter for classical psychoanalysis. A book he had been reading argued that real analysis wasn't about clever interpretations but about attacking the ego's self-enclosures so that the speaking-listening subject could open to hidden dimensions of experience. Andy felt called to that path—not just as patient but eventually as practitioner.

"In this way," Dr. Glitter said, "you would be going beyond me."

Andy wept, knowing this would be harder than sobriety, because leaving work with Dr. Glitter meant risking changes in his bond with the guys.

"Let's not split the baby yet," Dr. Glitter said. "It will take you time to find someone. I'm here."

And now, in the Rancho Mirage basement, Andy began teaching with a tone that settled the room instantly.

He explained that kink—any understanding of Dom, Sub, Top, Bottom, Master, Slave—had to begin with negotiation, not the rushed "safe word?" many men treat as a formality, but the full architecture: SSC (Safe, Sane, Consensual), RACK (Risk-Aware), PRICK (Personal Responsibility), safewords ("Red," "Yellow," softer variants), and the Negotiation Scene —intentions, triggers, boundaries, emotional terrain. "Without negotiation," he said, tapping the crop, "you're not practicing kink. You're reenacting trauma."

He asked Jim—already kneeling—to adjust posture. The room quieted. Andy circled him deliberately. "A Master begins not with power but clarity. Negotiation is clarity. Consent is clarity. Position is clarity. Clarity makes the unconscious bearable." He tapped Jim's back lightly and grounded the spot with his palm.

He continued with the explicitness of a handout: a Dom exercises psychological authority; a Top handles bodily technique. A Sub yields in trust; a Bottom receives sensation. A Switch adapts because his inner figures require flexibility. M/s is a covenant renewed across time. TPE is disciplined consent, not ego license. Aftercare is constitutive. Health protocols protect psyche and body. Community accountability prevents narcissism.

Andy glanced, almost involuntarily, toward Harry and John. There was more he could have said—about how the psyche speaks in figures, about the way power and surrender live inside every attachment—but he knew better. That material was not for first exposure, not for observers still learning how to stay in the room. He let the thought pass. There would be another class.

He struck Jim again—firmer, contained—and grounded it with his palm. Jim exhaled in recognition. "This is the psyche in dialogue with itself," Andy said. "Kink is active imagination with a body. When bounded by negotiation, these forces don't hijack relationships."

There, he had said it. Andy stood up to his abusive father telling him what he could and could not say. He had not been a hypocrite, hitting people for "fun" when not hitting back against his own violence.

People actually clapped, lightly, until Master A said, "Silence, that will break the spell."

CANTO 37: BOBBY
UNDER THE KNIFE

Behind the bedsheet curtain, Miss Bobby Blue steadied himself in front of the mirror, the wig balanced between bravado and prayer, the lashes heavy enough to tilt his gaze. The sequined dress clung to a body that felt different each week, as if time were finishing a sculpture he had once abandoned.

The uneasy fear came to him that there might never be another night quite like this; not another night when he possessed what felt like the taste of youth and virility he had only just reclaimed, a strength in his loins discovered through going toe-to-toe with the boys.

He could hear the room gathering—queens he had known for a generation and Harry's home boys and girls, who could smell the faint sweetness of hairspray, eucalyptus, cannabis, and wine. And when the cue came from Ezra, he stepped through the curtain as though stepping out of a past life and into a spotlight that had not quite missed him, but certainly had not lingered on him.

Someone shouted, "Bobby Blue is back, honey!" Another called, "She's giving Mississippi Gothic realness!" A younger voice whispered, "This is the queen I told you about," and he let the applause crest and wash over him like the fondness of an old lover who had not forgotten, holding back tears because he did not want what he was about to do to be about his own glory.

"It's been a long time since I came around…" he lip-synced, the words syncing to a memory decades deep, the crowd cheering at the line about Nebraska.

He gave them the drag-queen bravado—shoulder pops, kicks, the mock-seductive half-grin. Beneath it flickered the familiar danger, the moment when performance stops being play and becomes shelter, and he shut that down.

On the line *This time I'm not leaving without you*, he put a hand on his chest, stepped backward, slipped behind the curtain, and left the final chorus playing to an empty square of floor while the room froze in an uneasy, electrified hush.

When he came back out—stripped of wig, lashes, sequins, and spray, he was wearing only a soft black T-shirt and cotton shorts that exposed the contradictions of his real body, where fat had melted too fast, where surgery would leave folds it could not erase, where the blunt fact of his sex refused disguise.

This crowd understood immediately that the performance was over and something else had begun.

"Well," he said, his voice steady, lightly amused, "I suppose Harry isn't the only Alcibiades who knows how to crash a party."

He stood there and let them look—not at Miss Bobby

Blue, not at the bitchy oracle of Clarksdale, not at the survivor who wore rhinestones like scars. Who they saw now was the man who would be waking up in a hospital gown in forty-eight hours, trying to grasp what would remain of him and what would have to be rebuilt from scratch.

"I didn't want y'all thinking this was just a show," he said. "It is, of course—it always is—but it's also me trying to mark something. I needed to feel one last round of applause on my skin before they put me under, and I needed you to see who's actually going into that operating room—the man, not the mask."

He moved to the small folding table where Andy had arranged papers, tape, bits of cardboard, and a half-assembled prototype of the Coat of Arms, and the Airbnb—its cramped living room, mismatched throw pillows, gaudy faux-Moroccan lamps, faint smell of bleach—shifted at once into something like a workshop, a confession booth, and a stage.

"It hit me this week," Bobby continued, smoothing the table's edge as if it were a lectern. "That little exercise—the Coat of Arms—that foolish thing I threw at you boys when I was feeling pissy and superior was more loaded than I knew. I didn't understand why you jumped down my throat, why you felt it reeked of lineage and whiteness and fantasy. But after what happened at the Garage, after the meltdown, after showing up at Harry's former home, something in me broke open."

He opened the folder slowly—not for effect, but because he had lived inside these pages for nights on end.

"I DIDN'T SKIM," he said. "I didn't cherry-pick quotes to sound smart. I went in—to the beginning of the wound, the part I was raised to ignore: Reconstruction, the greatest democratic experiment this country ever attempted, and the one my people were trained to call a mistake."

In Mississippi, he explained, they were given a few sanitized sentences about carpetbaggers and corruption, as if democracy itself had been a failed rehearsal no one wanted to remember. What he encountered instead was a history of Black legislators rewriting constitutions, interracial governments daring to imagine justice, public schools built out of hope and terror, and the immediate white violence that rose to crush it—the chaos he had been taught to misname.

He went further back, into the lie at the heart of Southern thinking—the idea that Black ambition was dangerous and white fear was holy—and saw how so-called Redemption governments were never about restoring order but about restoring white supremacy, a truth that burned because it named the air he had breathed long before he had language for it.

"My great-uncle kept a Klan robe in the attic," he said, without drama. "Folded. Clean. Hung like a relic meant to be preserved. We never talked about it. We just lived under its ghost."

When he brought the Coat of Arms into the room, he admitted, part of him had still been performing that inheritance—symbols without accountability—because it was easier to decorate identity than interrogate it.

He paused, rubbing his forehead. The hardest realization, he said more softly, was that he had benefited from the structure even as it crushed him: a queer, feminine Southern boy cushioned by whiteness even as homophobia tore at him, a contradiction that taught him to reach for symbols when he felt attacked, to defend art as innocence rather than implication.

HE SET the notes aside and pulled from the folder a thicker sheet of cardstock, bowed from use. It was divided into four quadrants—not heraldic but psychic: an oil painting of an engorged child; a prostate gland; a white hooded man; and the image he had first shown weeks earlier—a Tom of Finland figure surrounded by painted faeries, resembling a former Latino lover.

When he pinned it to the wall, he let it speak before he did.

"I realized," he said quietly, "that I've never lived from the center of myself."

He emptied Clara—buttons dulled by sweat, bent feathers, shedding lashes, sequins skittering, a chipped mirror, a rosary missing its cross, snapped lipstick, glitter, glue, crayons—until the space beneath the image looked less like an altar than a workbench.

"So this isn't decorative anymore," Bobby said. "It isn't heritage. It isn't art. It's a diagnostic. A sentinel."

The room went still—not because he explained more, but because he stopped explaining and asked them to see themselves inside it.

THREE HOURS LATER, Andy rang the Singing Bell.

"In two days, I go into surgery," Bobby said. "I don't know what will change. But I'm taking a photo of each of your Vision Boards with me into that hospital. And when fear comes, I'll answer it with what we built tonight."

His voice thickened, then steadied.

"And when I can walk, we're going to Paris."

He waved them toward the door.

"Mother's going home to rest. There's coffee, pound cake, and art supplies. Stay as long as the new tenants tolerate. This old queen needs sleep."

CANTO 38: PARIS: A COMEDY IN FIVE SORROWS AND ONE SURPRISE

When John arrived at the Airbnb early with his luggage, expecting a quiet cup of coffee with the "Bobsey Twins" of Harry and Andy, he paused in the hallway as Harry pulled him into a cascade of hugs.

"Is this a vacation," John said, disentangling himself, "or a mobile production unit?"

John counted the bags—cases, backpacks, tripods, hardshell roller coffins, soft duffels—lined up by the door. He also clocked Harry's outfit, dressed as though air travel were a ceremonial rite of his OnlyFans persona rather than a thirteen-hour ordeal: vintage fake leather, cuffs, polished boots, layers of silver chains.

"Come on—don't I look fly?" Harry asked, unsure why John was counting instead of looking.

John felt a flicker of bitterness—having always been the worrier with Carter, and now again with another younger man—that no one had made clear to Harry that the Paris filming was cover for celebrating that Bobby's Pee Pee had survived cancer.

"I almost want you to turn back," John texted Bobby.

"I've brought oils so his carry-on doesn't reek of weed," Bobby texted back from his Uber, then added, "Fear not. Harry will behave as long as I'm there."

That's when Andy emerged from his bedroom, sporting a Hermès scarf.

"Coward," John said, already sour.

ANDY TOLD Harry *en español* that overdressing might flag security, but Harry answered—off to a great start—"No speeekee espanish."

When Bobby arrived, clad in comfortable Adidas, his face more drawn than usual from the procedure and lingering loss of appetite—Botox deferred during a recent depression—the house already smelled of wake-and-bake, and Harry could be heard changing and cursing in his room. Andy had prepared croissants and coffee, but John had apparently lost his appetite.

Instead of letting the irritated Art Director act run him, Bobby forced himself to shift, as he had been practicing in his work with Glitter. The old trauma—of not having had a mother who could help him feel his feelings, because she herself lived in tears and trembling rage, courtesy of her husband's "business trip to spread the gospel," which is to say, his seed—no longer blocked his first clear perception of reality or set off the familiar chain reaction, which he thought of simply as vomiting.

He took an extra moment to breathe, noticing the urge to purge give way to something steadier.

"Harry Enrique González," Bobby called from the vestibule, loud enough to cut through the Meek Mill and resentments muttered *en español*. "Andy made breakfast, and the last thing we need is for Spock to be in a bad mood on the way to the airport. The Chinese emphasize eating well," the Queen Mother added, theatrically waving away the plate with faint disgust.

With bloodshot eyes and a matching dungaree jacket and pants, Harry emerged from the bedroom, seething. But something in Bobby's tender, aging face—and the smell of fresh bread—lifted his spirits. Andy took the cue, plating the croissant with strawberries, yogurt, and honey.

Harry took a ravenous bite, kissed Bobby on both cheeks, and nuzzled against John for one second too long for John's taste, though John still stole a whiff of the man's aura, with only Bobby noticing.

"Now let's liquidate some of these bags," Bobby said, insisting Harry remove his Palestine Liberation pendant and warning them they needed far more time than expected, since Harry did not have Global Entry.

"So let's move it," Harry said, winking as if he were not the last to be ready, removing nothing. "*Ándale.*"

Once the plane settled into the clouds and coffee arrived, Bobby watched Harry and John slide into one of their lover-spats.

"Oh," John said, "so the chivalrous Chicano isn't always so chill—but more of a pill."

Bobby felt a private thrill. *Good,* he thought. *He's holding his own.*

"Prepared for what, *bby?*" Harry shot back.

"For Paris," John said. "Not the City of Light but of filth, rudeness, crowds, and bad coffee."

"We's in reality," Harry said, accepting red wine from the

steward like a prize. "Keeps things lively—not so dull, dull, dull, like a certain Señor Jobbie Job."

"Mr. Chill can be a royal pill," John said again, enjoying himself now.

Harry smiled. "I'm down with royal. And I love me some pills."

"You are exhausting," John said.

"Socrates was exhausting when you performed him," Harry replied. "But we will never forget that ladder bit. The Cher Wig."

Bobby clocked it: Harry wasn't defending himself; he was circling—baiting John into play while matching his crabby tone. *Ah,* Bobby thought. *He's learning.*

Andy cut in. "Can we survive this conversation *en français?* Because right now you both sound aggressively American."

"I got your French lessons down!" Harry said. "*Vraiment. J'adore ma copine—très belle.*"

"Say *beau,*" Andy said. "And don't roll the R like that. You'll be clocked."

Harry laughed and leaned into it, exaggerated, shameless.

"*J'rrrroule mes R comme mes blunts—trop, trop, trop—l'amour de John me fait fumer la langue.*"

Andy winced. John covered his face.

"That," Andy said, shaking his head, "is ranchero. Beautiful—but *wrrrrrrrrrrrrrrong.*"

"What do French Rs want, then?" John asked, arms crossed despite himself.

"To disappear," Andy said. "And have a younger man chase them."

Harry tried again—smaller, swallowed, back of the throat.

Andy nodded. "There. Now you sound like someone who complains quietly and pays rent."

"Rent," Harry said. "Daddy handles that. I pretend not to notice."

"No," Andy said. "I do. And you're late."

THE GUYS HAD AGREED to leave their hubbies at home.

"But John is my hubby," Harry said.

"Slow down, Speedy González," John said.

As a compromise, Bobby would meet Ezra later in Barcelona. Jim wanted time to figure out what Andy was actually asking for; he saw no problem in their relationship and glazed over whenever Andy tried to explain *psychoanalysis*, especially how Andy planned to juggle it with the production company.

"I haven't seen you at a meeting lately," Jim said, when he wasn't wearing the Pup mask.

"Bad dog," Andy said.

"Bad alcoholic," Jim barked.

Bobby, for his part, had taken up meditation again—not only because of the operation, but because of what the Coat of Arms had exposed. For all his feminine strengths and years among drag queens and trans girls, he realized he hadn't done enough work on himself as a man—or, more precisely, as a gay man. Not to abandon being a queen, or a bitch, or a mother to his girls, but handling his penis-in-transition had made him feel sturdier, if also a bit sad.

"Yes," he admitted quietly, more than once. "The canvas still needs filler—and a bit of Cialis—but it could be worse."

Not taking Ezra's bait—and, more radically, taking Ezra in—had neutralized their fights. Instead of blaming Ezra for being "borderline," Bobby could finally see where he himself had been borderline.

It takes time to crack the brick wall so many queer people inherit—the one that says *fuck you, I'm right, you're wrong, I've been fag-bashed too many times to open again,* so I'll perform feeling while actually evacuating it, then blame you for the shitty things I just said. Bobby had lived behind that wall for decades; now a hairline fracture had appeared.

On the plane, his breathing grew deliberate enough that John glanced over.

"You doin' okay, Boo?"

"Given that I am an aging Queen," Bobby almost said, but revised it. "I'm where I need to be," he said instead. "Which is with my boys."

It occurred to the Aging Diva—not as insight but as fact—that this ability to pause past his first reaction was what Andy meant by the *I* in SHIFT: not improvement, but integration—Sylvia no longer scrambling to manage Blobby's urgency, Blobby no longer vomiting his feelings into the room, Harry allowing pleasure without panic.

Or put another way: wasn't it cute to watch Harry get a little soused, John sip merlot to be a good sport, and Bobby and Andy order grape juice like kids at a bar mitzvah?

Later, when Andy got up to stretch, Harry slid in beside Bobby and nuzzled close.

"Show me the scar?" Harry said.

Silly boy—there was no scar. The doctor had gone in laparoscopically. Still, Bobby lifted his shirt, revealing the softened planes of his stomach, the evidence of weight lost.

Harry lifted his own shirt, showing the deep scar along his back.

They had saved each other's lives, both men knew, without saying it.

Bobby wondered what Alfonso might be thinking, because sometimes he could still hear the gentle man's thoughts as he accepted Harry's invitation to touch it.

～

AFTER THE FIRST—AND then second—vomit-bang had been utilized (such quiet retching sounds the vomit-practiced boy could make), and after blaming both incidents on turbulence over the Atlantic, by the time the jet's wheels bumped down—not gently enough—at Charles de Gaulle, Harry bore that particular gray-green color that made Bobby think of old pastrami and John think of first-year law students about to throw up before their first presentation. The landing itself was fine; it was Harry who could not be convinced the plane was no longer moving. He stood up too fast, sat down again, stood halfway, put a hand on John's shoulder as if John were the only stable surface left on earth, and muttered something about needing "air," "God," and "Sprite," in that order.

At passport control, he went quiet in a way that unnerved them all. This was usually the place where Harry flirted with authority—smiling, joking, over-nodding in a way that somehow always worked—but now he just stared at the officer, answered in monosyllables, and walked through the open gate as if being processed into a low-security prison.

By the time they reached the Airbnb—the cute four-bedroom, small-but-chic pad on Rue Vieille-du-Temple—the Chivalrous Chicano, as Andy groused, had grown more than a little dizzy. The elevator was on the fritz. The prospect of getting Harry up four flights of stairs, and also Jim, sank Andy's spirits.

Andy felt swamped by guilt. Did they really need to go to Paris? Yes, it had been Bobby's idea—but it was also Bobby's way of honoring Andy's journey, and Andy had left Paris, in his work with Dr. Glitter, as a past he'd rather forget than a future that might change him beyond his wildest dreams.

So, to be a "team player," he'd thrown his hat in the ring. He'd lobbied for Rue des Rosiers, insisting that if they were going to stay in the Marais—everyone's preference—they should stay somewhere properly queer and historical, preferably above a falafel joint or a bar with a backroom known for piss and vigor, emphasis on the piss. Bobby and John, meanwhile, had pleaded for Rue Charlot's quiet dignity, while Andy also advocated for Rue des Blancs-Manteaux, where he swore Colette's ghost still lingered with a cigarette holder, murmuring, *What a wonderful life I've had! I only wish I'd realized it sooner.*

In the end, they compromised on Vieille-du-Temple—which offered Andy the gay pulse he wanted and Bobby the aesthetic harmony he needed.

Harry had no capacity to participate in the discussion. He didn't "give a fuck about whether the crib sucked ass or was near the Anne Frank park or not type shit," and could they please "change the subject to what we were gunna film," already drafting scripts for TikTok for the good of the GQ MAP—or was it the GQ Shift, could Andy "make up his fuken mind about the mechanics," haha, do the mechanics, that could be a movie—along with references to Bobby's prostate surgery, veiled hints about an elder lover's need for a new knee, unfinished fantasies of executing the homophobic executioners in their own minds, and warnings to watch out for Jobbie John, who was "fuken swear the bro is getting cold feet about proposing to me or not."

Was Harry serious about this marriage thing? Was he an assimilationist? Or just, as Bobby thought, a hopeless romantic—emphasis on the hopeless.

Andy enjoyed watching Harry emerge as both man and child, instead of an adult child. He even had the gall to punctuate his critique of their "bullshit" and "hidden fucked-up psychological violence" by demonstrating his "facility" with the gutter French he'd learned from Wes's French—after Wes dumped him—sounding like a wise guy from Pico Rivera reciting Rimbaud (*Je est un autre*) or Artaud (*Il faut en finir avec les chefs-d'œuvre*).

Andy translated—patient, professorial, just a touch smug

—for a bemused Bobby and a distinctly unamused John: the Rimbaud as "I is another," the Artaud as "We must do away with masterpieces."

"You is another, indeed," John muttered, scribbling a note to Bobby on a Post-it about Harry's marriage fantasy and Señor Queer Theory's vanishing scruples.

"I think you think you want marriage," Andy said, "but all of us are in some stage of the marriage process—and we're all here without our partners. Ever think about that?"

Then Andy switched languages—because if you wanted a truth to land on Harry, you didn't say it in English. You said it in the tongue of mothers, cousins, threats, and the first boy he ever loved.

"*Creo que piensas que quieres matrimonio,*" Andy said, voice low and cutting, "*pero todos nosotros estamos casados—y míranos: aquí estamos, sin nuestras parejas. ¿Alguna vez pensaste en eso?*"

He repeated it in English, quieter this time.

Harry sparked his backwood and blew smoke indecorously into the face of a man everyone knew worked his sobriety steps the way Harry worked his ever-refining abs—talk about not doing away with masterpieces—and simply said, "Touché."

But not before retracting the middle finger he'd been brandishing, revealing an unmistakably empty ring finger.

That's when Andy touched his engagement ring—an unconscious gesture—and a rapid series of thoughts flared through him: the fantasy of making Jim wear the Puppy Mask full-time so Andy could chase his dreams without the Irish man's relentless barking about deadlines; the quieter, shame-drenched idea of postponing the wedding until psychology school; and then, unbidden, the counter-thought he imagined Dr. Glitter might name if he were standing beside him—that maybe the life he had was already the one worth choosing.

You chose a man who would love you imperfectly over men who would never love you perfectly.

The line landed in him like a bell—true, inconvenient, and echoing.

WHEN THEY FINALLY STEPPED INTO customs, Harry—green, in more ways than one—was stopped for being drunk and surly, and Bobby waved his blue leather V wallet in the air like a woman who had merged the Two Blanches (*Streetcar* and *Golden Girls*) to coax the driver into helping with the bags. The car sped them onto Rue Vieille-du-Temple, the street itself seeming to take sides in their earlier argument.

Just before the driver got out, the Paris light caught the wallet's blue leather just right, and Bobby felt Ezra's voice flicker through him like an unwelcome prayer.

They hadn't met in some baroque Parisian fantasy of Ezra dragging Bobby into an LGBTQ-friendly synagogue in the Marais—where, according to Ezra's ever-expanding mythology, the Southern Belle fell in love not just with the Hebrew melodies but with the way Ezra cried when he sang them— but in the fluorescent humility of Overeaters Anonymous at the LGBTQ Center. Bobby had briefly, disastrously considered being Ezra's sponsor. Ezra waved the idea away with a Yiddish *feh*, declaring he preferred Weight Watchers anyway, that his mother would always complain he was a tad chubby but "the Bears love me," and—more importantly—that Bobby was "too funny to play priest."

Even when Bobby spoke about helping his ex-Alfonso die from AIDS, about taking over the organization for a while before returning to Hollywood, Ezra had simply said they should date instead—casually, as if ordering challah at

Cantor's or checking the bolognese for pork. Absurd, mortifying, strangely holy: their origin story in a nutshell.

As Bobby watched John haul Harry out of the cab—grumbling that it was Harry's job to do the heavy lifting—Ezra's more polished version of the tale returned to him.

> It was our first date—the real first one, when you wore that scarf you wear when you're nervous—and I remember thinking, *My God, this man has survived so much and still walks like he's carrying light.* You don't let a man like that pay for his own wallet.
>
> We walked past Valextra—the blue one, glowing like a sign—and you looked at that wallet the way some people look at stained glass. So I told the saleslady, "He'll have that one." A man like Bobby deserves something elegant. Something with a V—V for Victory.

The ring he'd taken off before the operation. The wallet he'd kept.

Once the driver arrived at Rue Vieille-du-Temple, Andy became French. He hailed a young French African bro with his pals, *un mec et ses potes*, to help with the bags as the cab driver proved too gruff, and to steady Harry at the curb while he barfed and the squad had a smoke and a chuckle. For some reason they treated Andy like a hero; the guys had not seen him so popular as he shoved some euros into their tight jeans.

The crew climbed the third-floor walk-up—smelling of yesterday's croissants, cigarettes, and café steam—past a narrow balcony opening onto a sliver of Marais slate roofs and crooked chimney pots.

They arrived just in time for Harry to collapse into the bed nearest the window, the very one he had sworn he wouldn't take because he "didn't want to be anywhere he couldn't see or touch John," before pulling the covers over his head with such adolescent finality that Bobby and John exchanged the look of co-parents realizing the toddler had, in fact, come along—and that they had neglected to pack age-appropriate toys.

"I guess I should take small comfort," John whispered to Bobby, "knowing Wes and Guillermo never saw Harry like this."

Andy found the kettle, started tea and coffee, then ran down to the boulangerie so the men could decompress.

Within an hour, the panicking began. Harry surfaced long enough to say his head was "full of bees" and the room was "crooked," then fell back into a sleep so heavy that even Bobby's loudest stage whisper didn't move him. John hovered, taking Harry's temperature with the back of his hand like a grandmother from a black-and-white movie.

"Should we call someone?" John said. "A doctor? An ambulance? Guillermo via active imagination?"

"May he rest in a very long peace," Bobby said, "for almost taking our boy with him."

Andy, without looking up from his phone, said, "I know someone. A doctor. From my Wolof group. He does… situations like this."

"Situations?" John asked.

"Jet lag, emotional dysregulation, substances, Catholic guilt," Andy said. "He's basically a specialist."

Twenty minutes later, the doctor—a grey-haired Afro-Français man in a white suit of no small elegance—arrived carrying a small black case, calm in a way that suggested many former emergencies had survived.

The doctor took one look at Harry, rolled him halfway

onto his stomach, one leg dangling off the bed like a discarded doll, and nodded as if to say, Ah yes. This model.

Bobby hovered, clutching his blue V wallet the way he had once clutched Ezra's good intentions—tight enough to steady himself, loose enough not to admit he needed it.

"What did he take?" the doctor asked.

"Airplane chardonnay," Bobby said. "And life."

"*Bah*," the Wolof said—not to life but to Air Canada chardonnay.

"A French African Nurse Jackie," Bobby said to John.

"Okay," John said softly, channeling his inner Edie Falco, "everyone breathe—this is the part where nobody dies, but we all learn something."

There were questions, pulses taken, a small flashlight swept through Harry's sunken brown eyes; a B12 shot administered without ceremony; drops of bitter balm under the tongue, chased with medieval honey. The doctor paused only long enough to mutter, "Too much wine. Too little water," then launched into a mumbled French lecture on hydration that left everyone vaguely sinful for having ever been thirsty incorrectly.

When he briskly left—having pronounced that Harry would "wake up, probably alive," as if that settled it—Bobby slipped him extra euros and whispered, *Béni soyez-vous, Docteur Wolof*, in Google Translate French: twenty-five percent Colette's gossiping auntie, twenty-five percent Queen Latifah, twenty-five percent Ezra, twenty-five percent the new Bobby. Aristophanes should be so lucky.

Planting a brief kiss on the suffering CC's forehead, Bobby said quietly, "Be bold. Be brave. Be yourself, you ridiculous, beautiful, fallen gay boy—who I once, wrongly, feared. Paris demands a resurrection. I've already had mine."

~

Harry's shame woke him around 5:30 a.m., while the others slept (and snored) in their proper beds. He berated himself—what a drunk. The self-proclaimed Sex Magick Guru, who knew when to use party favors and when not to, had utterly embarrassed himself, and in front of the very man he wanted so badly to impress.

Then he remembered his work with Dr. Glitter and got a handle on the internal Inquisition, steadied himself—or rather, steadied his gay child self—invoking the ghost of Guillermo, Mother Mary (her queer version), and the therapist's litany: GET GROUNDED. DRINK WATER. MEDITATE. And then an idea occurred to him. *Fucking voilà.*

In the mirror—bare feet slapping parquet, hair shooting in contradictory directions, eyes bright with childlike resolve—he winked at himself, *Good boy*, and grabbed his phone to check the joint account he shared with Mr. González, which he had sworn, the last time he saw his old man, he'd never touch.

True to form, the man had stuffed it with more crack—which is to say, bands—than a recovering "spoiled brat" (as his sisters called him behind his back) should ever encounter.

Harry wasn't well traveled, but between the twinks, daddies, and riffraff he'd fucked with, there had to be a plug in Paris—someone who could get him a car that would wow the guys and help him reclaim Gaul as his own. *Órale.*

As he started hitting people up on Snap and hearing the replies—*I'll get you a car, bro, but my buddy finna want some ass*—he found himself humming *Marvin's Room.*

I'm just sayin', you could do better…

Last thing he needed, on a trip he'd agreed to only to win over John, was to defile a French fry on night one. But like St. Augustine, he prayed for redemption—but let me have one last shawty?

"Okay," he texted an Inglewood bro. "Tell your French plug to call me—but *ahorita*, not tomorrow—if he wants my money and my cock. Get me the Porsche Cabriolet. And don't fuck with me."

The call came a minute later.

"The code to tell the Car Guy you're my boy," the voice said, casual but firm, "is *Clovis I.* It's a favor, and it's not even five a.m. in Paris. What you on right now?"

"Clovis who?" Harry asked.

"The first French king."

Harry repeated it under his breath like a spell, dying for a clove cigarette.

The rental guy kept repeating *cinq cent vingt euros par jour*, but Harry insisted on converting it into francs—3,411 of them —because if his father saw a four-digit AmEx charge starting with a three, the man would rappel into Paris like the GI Joe his father's father had been.

Then he remembered Gloria.

Gloria, patron saint of math and trans Latina judgment.

He texted her.

She replied with a forty-seven-second voice note.

"HARR-RRR-Y, mi amor… France hasn't used francs since two-thousand-and-freakin'-TWO. And stop renting cars from boys who send you to live in hell with Guillermo."

She followed with the euro conversion.

Real numbers brought calm.

Harry knocked out a hundred push-ups, pulled on his tough-guy leather jacket, sparked a Gauloise, and rehearsed a bro persona tight enough to hold back the part of him that wanted to breakdance when the car arrived.

And then he saw his new baby.

A 2025 Porsche 911 Turbo S Cabriolet—top down, engine snarling his name.

When the French guy finally stepped out—thinner, sharper, an angrier version of Harry in the face—he said something that sounded like, "Ah, so you are the famous dirty *mec*," which Harry, already keyed up, heard as a slur.

"What you call me?" Harry said.

"The code?" the guy asked.

"Charlemagne," Harry said—too fast, the first big French king that came to mind.

"Wrong code."

"Fuck the code," Harry snapped. "I got two other guys circling—one with a Lamborghini Huracán, one with a Mercedes-AMG. I don't need your fucking Kings."

The engine revved.

"Yo," Harry added, jaw tight, "*y además*—no. You can't suck my dick. *Vas a choke, cabrón.* Forget who the fuck is king— or queen, *salope.*"

Later, when Harry texted Gloria a photo of the euros he'd saved, she replied:

"Jarry… did he swallow or not?"

Then, softening—because she already knew—

"*Te mando un beso, mi niño.*"

A kiss blown from East Los.

IN DEBRIEFING with Dr. Glitter later that week, Harry realized how thin the line had been between getting the car and getting sent home alone.

Clovis, my ass.

WHEN HARRY RETURNED to the apartment—spent but restored—he ran from room to room, waking each man with kisses and hugs.

"You will not believe, fools, what Prince Harry has fucken done!"

Andy, always a light sleeper, kissed him back, relieved to see that Dr. Wolof had saved the day again and that his best friend was back to his normal, goofy self.

"Why the hell," John asked, groggy, irritated, and secretly joyous, "do you seem more awake than me? I feel like I got hit by a Mack truck."

"That's 'cause you fucken with the Ambien," Harry said. "Be careful what you're off of."

He dug through the cupboards for turmeric, ginger, garlic tincture, vinegar—anything.

"You gotta infuse to diffuse. Don't let that go over your head."

He started making an infusion to wake everyone up.

Bobby squinted. "You've been up to trouble?"

"Trouble?" Harry said, almost glowing. "I figured out a problem concerning our trip."

John—his mug of mint tea rising and falling like a barometer of dread—asked which problem he meant. There were always so many.

Harry didn't answer.

"Come see."

They followed him downstairs—John anxious, Bobby bracing, Andy half amused, half afraid—until Harry stopped at the curb and pointed to the sleek black Porsche sitting under the morning light like a hired extra from a movie none of them had auditioned for.

"You stole a car," Bobby said.

"Microaggression," Andy said.

"I rented it," Harry replied. "With a discount."

"With what?" John asked.

"My smile," Harry said, holding out his wallet like Bobby with his Valextra. "And my California license. And my tragic backstory about my boyfriend still pining after his ex, and my other homie having some prostate cancer bullshit, and my other homie who still isn't telling us his dark past—Master A, fucken A. You're welcome."

"I'm texting Glitter," John said.

"I sent him a picture of the car, and he told me it was okay."

"Liar," Bobby said, reaching for the phone—but Harry knew how not to let go.

THE FIRST DRIVE was meant as an icebreaker—a quick loop, maybe the Seine—but within minutes they were lost. Harry laughed too hard at the wheel, Andy half-read the map while free-associating history, and John and Bobby clung together in the backseat, laughing with the brittle glee of men who knew they were no longer in charge.

"This is not the Seine," John said.

"I swear to God, if we die in a car you flirted into existence—" Bobby began, just as Harry accelerated.

The car tilted. Bobby yelped. John braced his knee against the door, pain flaring sharper than the turn itself.

Then Harry slowed, distracted by messages from a local contact pointing him toward Saint-Denis—Paris's answer to Inglewood, where engines were judged like bloodlines. He pulled in just long enough to show off the Porsche, spin a few reckless donuts, collect Instagram handles, and feel briefly, intoxicatingly seen—before tearing off again.

THEY ATE beneath the Pont de la Tournelle at a tiny place Bloch had recommended, the owner calling them *les amoureux*

without specifying which pair he meant. Harry devoured an alarming amount of ham, while Bobby and John shared salad and bread and Andy ordered cheese and wine. Later, along the Quai de Conti, the city opened into something so crooked and luminous that even John forgot his color-coded itinerary.

"Let's get out and take some pictures," Bobby said, relieved they had survived.

That's when John's knee betrayed him.

He stepped from the car too fast, his mind already composing a message to Carter, and the pain hit sharp and white. Bobby grabbed him. Harry froze, keys in hand, suddenly thirteen again.

"It's fine," John said—which everyone now knew meant it wasn't.

Within the hour they were in a Paris emergency room, Harry pushing the wheelchair with the anxious devotion of someone auditioning for the role of wife, Andy handling the forms, Bobby handling the drama, and John handling the familiar shame of becoming—once again—the patient.

HARRY TRIED to fix the downer situation with a camera. John lay propped on the hospital bed, knee wrapped, the room washed in fluorescent calm while they waited on X-rays delivered in accents charming enough to dull the edge.

Harry started to film—not with his usual *look at me*, but with the focused attention of someone who had wandered, accidentally, into the gravity well of another person.

"So, baby," he said, angling the lens as the light caught the silver at John's temples. "How does it feel to get older?"

"Turn that shit off," John said.

"When did you first notice your knee was like this?" Harry asked, softer now.

"About a year ago," John said. "Tennis court."

"And you didn't tell me."

"No."

Harry held the camera anyway.

John exhaled. "I called my surgeon. I'm getting a steroid shot. I'll live. But sightseeing's over—for me." He paused. "You want to keep that camera rolling? I've got a friend with a studio in the Sixth. Sitting, talking—I can do that."

That's when Bobby and Andy came back from their own consultations, just in time to catch John being prepped for the shot—and the trip quietly changing shape.

THEY ARRIVED at the studio just after dusk, a Left Bank space that smelled faintly of hot cables and old coffee, brick walls sweating history under track lights that never quite forgave anyone. A red bulb blinked above the door: LIVE.

Harry checked the camera with a practiced flick—levels, frame, thumbs-up—while John adjusted his chair, the cane set deliberately beside him, visible but unremarked. Around the table, Andy and Bobby took their seats like witnesses who knew the trial was already underway.

Each of them clipped on a mic. Paper and pens were passed—real paper, the scratch of it grounding. Phones went face down. Comments stacked silently on a side monitor, the world leaning in.

Andy glanced at the blinking light and murmured, half to himself, half to the gods, "Well. *Antigone* would approve."

Bobby smiled once, sharp and fond. "Let the *polis* listen."

Harry leaned toward the lens. John met his eye.

And then they went live.

HARRY

So—you been holding out on me. You really got a stick up yo ass about the marriage thing. You know I need this from you, and we're like karmic bros, so what's the dealie—is it like John the Baptist so fuckin holy he can't break bread with the ghetto lepers type shit?

ANDY

Did Harry just call himself a leper?

BOBBY

Did Harry just refer to John as John the Baptist?

JOHN

You think these feelings are going to last forever. But they won't. They can't. They are not supposed to.

ANDY (chorus)

Not as they are.

BOBBY (chorus)

Forever is cute. Ask the body how that's going.

HARRY

But yo—you see how much I've changed. I'm a fucking poster boy for molting, no cap. On this one thing, though, I have not altered—not one goddamn iota, you stubborn POS. Yeah, I fucked with Wes, but you never gonna understand me—low-key bullshit—it was 'cause I was lost till I found your ugly ass.

JOHN

You have changed so much in the last two years that you

are not recognizable. You've become a true Harry—which is complex, childlike, silly, stupid, and magical.

BOBBY

A real Hairy.

ANDY

Not an idea. A creature. Caliban.

BOBBY

A virtual Golem.

HARRY

And you? You stayed pretty constant. Ever since I dabbed you in the Doctor's Overture, I knew you was into your *si si*.

JOHN

And I am not the same person you met. I am darker, more serious, more skeptical—and you are right, I have never been so taken with life, or with another man, as I am with you. That has stayed consistent.

BOBBY

I have been a witness.

ANDY

An enlightened one.

HARRY

So what the hell—if you're taking the anti-assimilationist position, why are you fucking with me in the first place? Best not be to waste my time. I'm getting on in years.

JOHN

I fuck with you because you are old in your youngness. Broken in your flexibility.

HARRY

Old? Broken?

JOHN

Not like how Bobby, Andy, and I are barely alive. You're depressed too—but you also spring alive.

BOBBY

Yes. We are the walking dead.

ANDY

Reassembled.

JOHN

So you're like this Frankenstein monster—partly grotesque like us three, and partly still young and fresh and full of life.

HARRY

So you're afraid.

JOHN

Yes—but not of anything that could happen to me. I'm afraid of buying into a lie that will fuck with you.

HARRY

Then why not just… choose me? Simple, soldier.

JOHN

You will tire of me, especially as I grow old. I'm okay

with that. But if we are married, it makes the process of moving beyond the other person so complex.

HARRY

But what if I want it written down legally that I will not move beyond you. It's a pledge—a pledge to God.

JOHN

You need a marriage contract to pledge your love to God?

BOBBY

God only loves those who marry legally.

ANDY

God is dead.

HARRY

So what do you want us to be?

JOHN

Constantly changed. Questioning. Developing a new idea of being gay—one that breaks down what has been received.

BOBBY

Teachers.

ANDY

Not owners.

HARRY

And marriage—gay marriage—is not a fuckin teaching?

JOHN

To marry you would possibly send the wrong message—
not to anyone else, but to you.

HARRY

What message?

BOBBY

Truth spoken late is cruelty.

ANDY

Truth spoken now is mercy.

HARRY

You think this is about my father who never was.

JOHN

I can't help but feel you're reaching for the father you
never had—that you could get with Guillermo, or your own
father, or with Glitter—but that you get with me because
you're so goddamn needy.

HARRY

And you?

JOHN

And I'm addicted to your smell, your touch—even when
you smell rank from the gym or your motorcycle or your
wake-and-bake, which I deplore—but your smell mesmerizes
me. Hunger for a body does not equal marriage for a
lifetime.

BOBBY

Desire is not consent.

ANDY

Attraction is not architecture.

JOHN

So I, being a cold Capricorn, can't say no to your touch
—but that only fuels your addiction to the idea of marriage,
not to what we should be working on.

HARRY

Which is?

JOHN

Laser focus on the merger of two selves into one
tendency when it drags us down into endless nights of
Netflix.

BOBBY

The quiet seduction.

ANDY

The fatal anesthesia.

JOHN

You know how many years I wasted with Carter? After
long days—no talking, making dinner, sitting like mom and
pop middle America watching *The Crown, Stranger Things,
House of Cards*—

BOBBY

The Lost Years.

ANDY

Drinking matcha.

JOHN

It was comforting. It was what we needed. And it held us back—like any addiction. I didn't grow. Didn't do therapy. Didn't write. Didn't meditate. Didn't engage my shadow. Ignored my trans partner. Got me a big fat heart attack.

BOBBY

God's plan.

ANDY

A brutal syllabus.

JOHN

Yes—it got me to Glitter, and to you guys. But I won't sign on to that hill of lies and illusion just to get my dollop of pleasure with you.

HARRY

We will never be that, dawg.

JOHN

Unless we're breaking apart and coming together, we'll bore each other. We'll become lap cats tipping over their Purina.

BOBBY

Domesticated despair.

ANDY

Soul extinction.

JOHN

Until another heart attack comes. Or the felons build concentration camps. Or global warming tears us apart. I'll be dead by the worst of it—but you'll have to contend with the horror my generation ignored.

HARRY

So you can't give me this—so I can be strong when you're gone?

JOHN

How can I grant you the thing you think you want—when it's not going to bring us healing?

HARRY

But what if I'm not asking for fucking healing? What if I'm just asking your lame ass to stay?

ANDY

Ah.

BOBBY

There it is.

ANDY

Need speaks now.

BOBBY

Not philosophy.

HARRY

I know I'm needy. I know I want too much, too fast, too loud. But I'm not lying. This—whatever this is—I don't want to be brave without it.

JOHN

I'm asking you to be brave without a crutch.

HARRY

If marriage is a lie, fine—call that shit something else. Call it some fucked-up science experiment where we both sign the waiver and see who plays Jeff Goldblum the best when the fly's in the ointment.

He swallows.

HARRY

But don't tell me I'm dead-ass wrong for wanting to belong somewhere. Don't tell me I'm broken 'cause I wanna be chosen.

BOBBY

Chosen—for what, though?

ANDY

For what happens anyway.

HARRY

I'm asking you to stand still, bro—just long enough that I don't gotta keep proving I'm real.

JOHN

But how are we not already doing that? How are we both always trying to get each other to stand still so we don't have to keep proving we exist? Do I need to remind you—the chaos is because of you. You almost made us miss the flight. You got so drunk we had to call a witch doctor. You rented the sports car. You drove it like a crazy boy from the hood, shook it so hard I'm sure that's when the knee gave out. How is marriage going to cure you of you? That's not what I'm asking for in being your friend.

HARRY

Then what is it, JJ? If it's not marriage, if it's not the ring, if it's not the rules—what is the thing you're actually asking for?

A long pause. John shifts in the chair, the cane visible now, the camera still rolling, the world stacked in the comments.

JOHN

It's not the ring. It's not what you think.

ANDY

Listen.

BOBBY

This is the thesis, honey.

OFF TO THE SIDE, Andy wandered to the bank of windows that had called to him, where lush plants sat in wooden boxes along the sill like something carefully kept alive indoors. He looked out at the rue: rain pattering, people rushing toward their lives, thinking in French—or Arabic, or Spanish, or Cantonese—more than they realized, moving with the disciplined urgency of bodies that had learned, over generations, how quickly one must walk to avoid punishment. Andy felt suddenly aware of how much blood had been spilled just to allow a street like this to exist, how many backs had learned to bend, how many necks had learned not to rise too high—and now, absurdly and unforgivably, he felt punished by his friends' joy.

He could not bear to fix his gaze on the love birds—John and Harry—not only because of envy, but because of the violence beneath it, sharp and destabilizing, like what he imagined a heart attack might feel like if it began not in the chest but in the gut. Whatever form their bond would ultimately take—married or not, ring or no ring—they were already entangled in a way that was unmistakable, feeding each other's hunger and certainty in real time, and Andy knew with a quiet, corrosive grief that this was a form of emotional marriage he might never fully be allowed to inhabit.

He had asked Dr. Glitter about it once, circling carefully around the ethics of a group in which two men's feelings for one another might eclipse what they felt for their therapist, and whether that imbalance might poison the work. But Glitter had refused the abstraction and returned Andy instead to the familiar wound of being on the outside looking in—to the old ache of the child who learned early that wanting too much was dangerous, and that love, if it came at all, would arrive conditionally and late.

Together, Andy and his therapist had begun knocking on the door of the dungeon his psyche had built, the place where Little Andy had been sealed away because the adult feared he would not survive the flood of sadness, anger, guilt, and murderous resentment that child carried from growing up in a family that appeared "perfect" from the outside. He had been the star child, the gifted one, the useful one—which was another way of saying the child who learned that performance was safer than truth.

And envy—real envy, not polite jealousy dressed up as sophistication—had been the key. Not envy of John and Harry as men exactly, but envy of the child who had been allowed to want without apology, envy of the child who had been held while wanting, envy of the obscene and radical right to be messy, loud, dependent, and still beloved. The adult Andy could discipline this into ethics and theory, but the child Andy wanted to tear the curtains down, to expose romance as a lie before anyone could notice how much he hated them for having what he had been trained to renounce.

But something else happened—something he had not anticipated—because the envy did not collapse inward or harden into contempt. Instead, it cracked open and became a river, violent and uncontrollable, pulling with it everything he had buried in order to survive.

Andy saw—without flinching now—how early he had learned to sacrifice that child, how he had exploited his own brilliance, his precocity, in order to be useful, to justify his place, to prop up structures that rewarded obedience and punished need. Frankenstein, he realized, was a comforting lie; the real monsters were not stitched together in laboratories, but produced slowly and lovingly inside families, schools, and nations that demanded adaptation at the cost of the soul.

He understood now—without romance—that yes, he was a surviving homosexual, yes, he had needs, and yes, those needs had been warped by danger. He had fallen in love the way he knew how—through darkness, ritual, control, and the careful dismantling of another man's defenses—and how bitterly ironic it was that, in pursuing self-knowledge through psychoanalysis, he had bound himself to a man with no interest in understanding the psychic machinery that made intimacy in daylight feel like exposure rather than relief.

Andy loved Jim deeply, with a loyalty that felt both noble and masochistic. They could talk for hours—work, poetry, history, languages—but Jim could not meet him in the place Andy most needed to be met, and Andy could not tolerate the image of Jim alone, aging inside his armor, because Andy knew, with terrible tenderness, that he might be Jim's final experiment with love.

The grief arrived then—unmanageable and bodily, not refined or instructive, but feral and humiliating, the kind that makes a person want to tear something down just to prove they are still alive.

Andy thought of texting Dr. Glitter, but instead let Glitter enter his mind, practicing the very thing he had once dismissed as indulgent nonsense. Active imagination worked not because it was clever, but because it was violent enough to interrupt the free fall, slowing the descent until the feelings could be felt rather than acted out.

And then the insight landed—not as theory, not as redemption, but as relief—because this was no longer envy, but the beginning of the healing of envy: the moment when the child who had never been allowed to want was finally being seen without being forced to earn that visibility through sacrifice.

The relief arrived as heat, as pressure behind the sternum, as a sensation so expansive it bordered on panic—as if the heart, long trained to contract, had forgotten its own limits. He felt too alive, flooded with a pleasure that did not cancel the grief but rode directly on top of it, the way orgasm rides the edge of fear. This was not happiness; it was the dangerous joy that comes when something frozen finally thaws and the blood remembers how to move.

Andy's heart broke open—not only for himself, but for all the children beaten, shamed, corrected, trained to distrust their inner lives, taught to survive by shrinking their expectations and anesthetizing their rage. He understood now what Glitter had always meant: that love is not possible without loving what was first hated, and that hatred must be metabolized rather than denied.

When he looked back at the room, he saw Bobby—once outrageous, now deliberate—moving into a circle dance with a grace earned through loss.

And inside that tangle of sadness, rage, envy, and emerging self-love, Andy knew what he had to do. He would return to Ohio and confront his father while the man was still alive and capable of hearing what he had done.

For now, an inner voice—perhaps Glitter's, perhaps his own—told him this was enough for today, that he was allowed to re-enter the room without resolution.

Andy let the meditation go. After drinking water and steadying his breath, he now felt ready to join his friends in the circle dance.

Bobby caught his eye and didn't ask questions. He just reached out a hand.

Someone put music on—Bread, *Make It With You*—the kind of song people used to sing when they didn't know if they'd survive the political crises of their time but still believed love might be a shelter. Bobby led them into motion, not quite a dance yet, more an agreement to stay upright together.

They didn't remember all the lyrics. That helped.

Bobby began, calling them his lovelies, asking whether they had ever tried.

Harry followed, singing about reaching for the dark, but also the love side.

John added that he might be climbing a Socratic ladder.

Andy sang something about somewhere over the rainbow.

All together—a mix of a hora and a minuet—they sang what they could remember and made up the rest as they went: okay, baby bros, here goes—dreams are for us to keep, so we can heal our shit and dance this stupid dance, and not feel stupid, but gay.

EPILOGUE

They decided not to linger in Paris or extend the trip but, exhausted, agreed they needed to return home *toute de suite*.

They repaired to have a meal, indulged in a toast that went on a beat too long, and felt the soft, anticlimactic relief of having survived, as Harry put it, "another day, another dollar," although, by waving his ring finger, he showed it was hardly just another day.

Then there were airports, Ubers, car keys, familiar rooms —the quiet re-entry into lives that received them as if they were all personifications of Bobby's three tabbies and his two pit-and-lab mutts.

This time, there were no vomit bags.

My own trip to queer and biological family was also coming to an end.

I would land back in Hollywood just in time to resume individual sessions with them in person and check in for a Group Consultation to talk about the future plans—and projects—yet to come.

Each had resumed individual sessions in my Hollywood office, and it would be something else to see their tired faces—and their more enriched souls—in person again.

CODA: JOIN THE G+Q
MAP COMMUNITY

This work of psychological narrative fiction has been an experiment in what happens when therapy becomes theatre, myth becomes memory, and gay life becomes a site of healing rather than a singular mythos of capitalism and assimilation.

But the work is not over.

A companion volume—the GQH/MAP Workbook (Gay/Queer/Human – Meaning/Memory/Mythic, Action/Assessment, Plan/Psychology)—as well as a book for instructors, therapists, and students, Queer Pedagogy, are forthcoming. The latter will include analytic asides for each Canto, a list of ancestors, and a guide for teaching workshops and running classes.

To stay in touch, ask me and the guys questions, and learn about events and publication news, please visit:

www.psychologyforthepeople.org

And also:

Douglas Sadownick's Substack

ABOUT THE AUTHOR

Douglas Sadownick, Ph.D., is a psychotherapist, educator, and author devoted to LGBTQ+ healing and multicultural clinical practice. He founded the LGBT Specialization in Clinical Psychology at Antioch University Los Angeles (2006) and co-founded COLORS LGBTQ Youth Counseling Services (2011). A former award-winning journalist for the *Los Angeles Times* and *LA Weekly*, he has spent three decades weaving scholarship, community work, and storytelling.

His novel *Sacred Lips of the Bronx* returns in a new edition from Rebel Satori Press. He teaches at The Chicago School of Professional Psychology – Los Angeles, maintains a private practice, and shares essays and talks on YouTube and Substack under the "Psychology for the People" mission.

Forthcoming titles include Healing Gay Sex and Love: A Group Experience (Fall 2025) and the companion GQMAP (Gay/Queer Mythic Assessment & Plan) Workbook.

He can be reached at www.psychologyforthepeople.org.

ACKNOWLEDGMENTS

The voices of thousands of students and clients advancing the LGBTQ movement into a psychological stage of action led to the writing of this book. During a twenty-year tenure at Antioch University, forming the LGBT Specialization in Clinical Psychology and the COLORS LGBTQ Youth Services Center, the work of establishing a program with no precedent taught me how to bring healing technology into real-world program development and management.

I owe special gratitude to Dr. Joy Turek, whose original inspiration launched the LGBT Specialization, and to the team who helped it flourish—Thomas Mondragon, Dr. Lauren Costine, and Dr. Cadyn Cathers. I thank Antioch's leaders, Tex Boggs and Mark Hower, whose faith made COLORS possible, and our donors—Doug Moreland, James Front, Tom Saffron, and Lily Dulan, dedicated to the health of our queer youth.

The gay men in my current therapy groups continue to provide inspiration, vision and learning.

For four decades, the late editor, writer, and publisher Felice Picano was my mentor and guide. This book is dedicated to his role in midwifing my work into published form.

I am grateful to editor and poet David Groff, whose counsel spans decades; to the late scion of gay publishing Michael Denneny, and to editor Patrick Merla, who first believed in my work; agent Charlotte Sheedy, to Kit Rachlis;

and to writers lost to AIDS—Michael Callen, Steven Corbin, Barry Laine, Essex Hemphill, Marlon Riggs, Asotto Saint and Arnie Kantrowitz. I also thank artist-writer-activists Sarah Schulman, Rabbi Robin Podolsky, and Joan Lipkin, as well as Charles Rice-González, Tom Cardamone, Tim Riara, and Tim Miller.

I acknowledge colleagues who endured rigorous training over decades and emerged as close friends: Thomas Mondragon, Bryce Way, Kellum Lewis, Enrique Lopez, Roger Kaufman, and Dustine Kerrone.

Psychologist and author Mitch Walker pioneered integrating Gay Liberation through a depth psychological lens.

The late Sandra Golvin, lesbian artist and psychotherapist, remains a constant companion.

Maziah Brown, Bhaavika Gaddam, Samantha Danielle Cabarles, Ethan Cvitanic, comedian Ally Noel, and writer-performer Beth Lapides formed a circle of helpers.

Friends advancing Latino Gay Liberation—Dr. Enrique Lopez, Roland Palencia, and filmmaker Dante Alencastre—have supported this work over many years.

Dr. Cheryl Aruitt and Dr. George Bermudez provided clinical oversight. Amita offered mentorship in Tarot and astrology.

Thanks to the circle of support: Alex Poon, David Strah, Donovan Smith, Dustin Burns, Corey Raskin, John Duran, Dianne Abbitt, Teddy, Matt Gideon, Denise Flachbart, Leo Garcia, Teddy Schulman, Avigail Sperber, Jonathan Ortiz, Juan Luis, Steven Reigns, Dave Ankers, Dolita Cathcart .Payton Young offered steady support, as did my family—Daniel, Leslie, Hannah, and Penny Sadownick; Lynn Danielle Braunstein; and friends in the Recovery Movement.

Thank you to those who look to the psyche as a frontier of lasting change and freedom.